T0356521

EVERY
BORROWED
BEAT

ALSO BY ERIN STEWART

Scars Like Wings

The Words We Keep

ERIN STEWART

EVERY BORROWED BEAT

DELACORTE PRESS

Text copyright © 2025 by Erin Stewart
Jacket art copyright © 2025 by Beatriz Ramo

GetUnderlined.com

Educators and librarians, for a variety of teaching tools, visit us at
RHTeachersLibrarians.com

Library of Congress Cataloging-in-Publication Data is available upon request.
ISBN 978-0-593-71066-1 (trade) — ISBN 979-8-217-02778-1 (int'l ed.) —
ISBN 978-0-593-71068-5 (ebook)

The text of this book is set in 11-point Warnock Pro Light.

Editor: Wendy Loggia
Cover Designer: Casey Moses
Interior Designer: Cathy Bobak
Production Editor: Colleen Fellingham
Managing Editor: Tamar Schwartz
Production Manager: Shameiza Ally

Printed in the United States of America
10 9 8 7 6 5 4 3 2 1
First Edition

Random House Children's Books supports the First Amendment
and celebrates the right to read.

to ellie
i carry you in my heart

CHAPTER ONE

"I SHOULD HAVE DIED.

I was supposed to die.

Except I didn't—someone else did.

And now I'm living on borrowed time with a borrowed heart just thump-thump-thumping away.

The problem with all this borrowing?

You begin to forget what part of you is actually, well, you."

The video freezes on a particularly unattractive expression where I look like I'm about to sneeze or fart or, horror of horrors, simultaneously do both. If I were going to post this, I'd definitely need to pick a less humiliating final frame.

But I'm *not* going to post this video. I knew that before I even hit record.

An incoming call lights up my phone. Before I answer, I save the video to my drafts folder with all my other unposted clips, sixteen weeks' worth of me rambling about my new so-called life.

When I hit accept, Chloe's face fills the screen.

"You do it, yet?" She jumps right in like we were already mid-conversation. Chloe's never beaten around a bush in her life. I guess that's one of the first things to go when you're slapped with an expiration date. No time for formalities.

I shake my head. Chloe groans, her voice filling my room even though she's six hundred miles away on the California coast, sucking up that salty sea-level air, trying to eke out a little more life.

"Sydney Wells, don't make me crawl through this phone and post that video for you." The oxygen cannula stuck up her nose tells me it's been a bad night. I know Chloe better than to ask about it. "We're supposed to be running this account *together*. I need you."

That's a stretch. Chloe's the force behind TheWaitingList, our YouTube channel, where she posts videos of what it's like to live on a transplant list with a crappy heart. She's honest about it—raw—and also hilarious, which is why we have almost twenty thousand subscribers. She's pretty much a celebrity in the transplant world.

I used to post, too. But now it feels, I don't know, weird. But then again, what doesn't these days?

"It's called The*Waiting*List, Chlo. And maybe you didn't hear but"—I tug my shirt collar down below my clavicle, barely enough to reveal the top of my scar. It's *healing beautifully,*

Dr. Russell says, but it's still purply red enough to have some serious shock factor—"I'm not waiting anymore."

I feel Chloe's eye roll all the way from Cali.

"Hello? That's kind of the whole point," she says. "You're the success story people need to hear."

Chloe leans in close to the camera. Her lips are blue tinged and her eyes have a purple cast beneath them, little semicircles of sleep she didn't get. She definitely pulled an all-nighter.

The guilt sets in quick. Here I am complaining about post-transplant life, and she's sucking oxygen through the equivalent of a crimped straw. This is why I can't post *any* of my videos: I'm the one who lived.

I have no right to grief.

"Our fans are starting to wonder," she whispers.

"Wonder what?"

"If you died."

"Well, as you can see, I didn't."

She leans even closer so she's one big old eyeball.

"Debatable."

In the bottom of the screen, a face I don't recognize looks back at me. Our viewers probably wouldn't recognize me, either. Before the transplant, my face was thin, no, *gaunt.* My lips had the same perma-blue hue Chloe's do now. Near the end, I couldn't go more than ten minutes without my oxygen. Now I'm *pleasantly plump*, as Mom would say. Dr. Russell calls it moon-face, a way-too-cutesy term for how the prednisone makes my face an overstuffed balloon.

"What am I even supposed to post about?" I say. "I'm hardly

inspirational. I'm seventeen and have zero idea what I'm doing with my life, and zero friends unless you include my parents. And you barely count."

"Rude," Chloe says.

"You know what I mean. It's not like we can just get together and hang out at the . . . wherever normal people hang out."

"*Normal* people?" she echoes, but her grin tells me she's messing with me.

"I'm just saying, I have no life worth posting about. At the moment, I have exactly two hobbies." I hold my fingers up to count dramatically in the screen. "One: very slow, old-lady walks around the cul-de-sac with my aforementioned best friends slash parents—"

"Which sounds pretty great," she mutters, and a stab of guilt goes through me.

"And two," I continue, "reading local obituaries."

Chloe frowns. "You're still doing that?"

"Maybe."

"I thought you found her? The girl from that small town?"

I nod. "I'm like ninety-nine percent sure. But it doesn't hurt to keep checking."

Chloe sighs out long and low.

"You need to come back to Broken Hearts Club," she finally says, matter-of-factly. "Oh my gosh, last week, Josh, you know, the liver kid? He was going on and on about how he's going to die without having sex, and I swear I almost banged the kid just to shut—"

A coughing attack hits Chloe before she can finish. She gives me a thumbs-up but then moves the screen away from her face. I can hear her hacking off camera. Her heart may be failing, but it's her lungs that feel it. And her fits are getting worse. They've *been* getting worse since I met her two years ago in the online transplant support group.

Our moms both enrolled us after they got worried we were becoming miserable teenage hermits. It's all very *Fault in Our Stars*, except there are no hot boys with an affinity for metaphor. Oh, and also, those cancer kids weren't sitting around waiting for the phone to ring because huzzah! Someone has died! You get to live!

We talk about waiting (which is every bit as tedious as it sounds), and we talk numbers: oxygen saturations and liver stats and how many people have to die before we get to the top of the list. And will they die in the appropriate mile radius in the right way with the right blood type and perfectly sized organ? Will someone else's tragedy be my salvation?

It's a bit morbid, if you ask me (which my mom did *not* before signing me up). But I did meet Chloe, so there's that. She nicknamed the whole thing Broken Hearts (and Spare Parts) Club and made it almost bearable each week: Watching people get better, watching them get worse. Watching everyone move up and down the waiting list like a macabre game of musical chairs.

Because that's what it is, isn't it? A sick game of chance where winning means someone else loses. Big-time.

I haven't been back to group since my surgery. I highly doubt anyone wants me there, lording my brand-spanking-new heart over their failing organs.

Chloe's face reappears, flushed and sweaty. She takes a swig from the water bottle next to her. It's the behemoth kind with a ribbed straw they give you in the hospital. I guess that's another essential of life on the list: an impressive collection of hospital souvenirs.

"All I'm saying is, you did it, Syd. You're here. That's a *good* thing. Celebrate it." A wide smile spreads across her face. "Speaking of which, I got an email from your mother. Something about a *big day.*"

She says *big day* with ample sarcasm. It's my mom's term, and the definition has grown egregiously generous in the last few years. First poop post-surgery? Big day! First walk around the cul-de-sac? Get some balloons! First clean heart biopsy? Let's make a Chatbook!

And today?

Today, I'm leaving the house. Dr. Russell cleared me to drive a full month ago, but I've waited until I actually have somewhere to go. Somewhere important.

"So, whaddya gonna do?" Chloe asks.

I give Chloe a look, because she knows good and well what I'm going to do. I told her all about my *big driving day* plans last week. She shakes her head.

"No."

"Yes."

"Sydney. That's a *bad* idea." Her face is suddenly somber, a look she reserves for only her most serious disapproval.

And she's right. I know she's right. But for the past two years, I've lived with one thought: if someone doesn't die soon, then I will. That messes with a person. Makes you think about what your life is worth—and who should die instead.

And then, someone does.

"Why can't you just stalk her on social like, as you would say, a *normal* person does," Chloe adds.

"I've looked. Nothing," I say. "Hey, aren't *you* the one who just said I need to get a life?"

"Yeah. Your *own* life."

"Well, consider this my first step." I return Chloe's intense stare. "Who knows, maybe I'll be *so* inspired that I'll film an extensive and utterly compelling video telling all our followers about my *big day* out."

Chloe's lips form a tight line.

"I won't hold my breath." A little smirk plays at the corner of her mouth. "Even if I could."

I laugh, and so does she. This is why we have so many followers—Chloe literally laughs in the face of death.

Before she hangs up, Chloe leans in one more time, until all I can see is her enormous eye.

"For real, though, Syd. The obits thing is weird enough, but this"—she pauses, to let the oxygen catch up to her or because she's trying to find the right words—"just don't get too close."

"Cross my recycled heart and hope to die," I say right before I hang up.

The screen goes blank. My room goes quiet.

Well, except for the thumping in my chest, in my ears, in every piece of me, my new heart just pumping away, steady and even and perfect like it always does.

One hundred thousand beats per day. In sixteen weeks, that's 11.2 million beats.

Beats that should have been hers.

At least, I'm 99 percent sure it's a *her.* And for the past four months, all I've had are questions. What kind of life did she have? What plans did she have for all the years I stole?

The questions rattle around in my brain pretty much constantly. First thing in the morning, last thing at night. With every borrowed beat.

Which is why Mom's right, today *is* a big day. Not because I'm leaving the house for something other than a doctor's appointment or a geriatric walkabout.

But because today, I finally get my answers.

CHAPTER TWO

MOM'S USING THE GOOD DISHES. THE BONE CHINA WITH the platinum band around the edge.

It's part of her cherish-the-little-things plan. Celebrate every day. Use the fancy towels. Light the special candles. Pile the wedding china high with pancakes on a Tuesday.

"What am I saving these for?" Mom said the first time she brought the dishes down from the attic. It was a year ago, after Dr. Russell told me I was in a particularly craptacular spot on the waiting list—not sick enough to be a transplant priority, not healthy enough to make it past my teens.

"*Today* is the occasion," Mom had announced that afternoon. "I'm tired of waiting."

Life on the list can do that to a person.

I stand at the kitchen doorway for a second before entering. Dad's reading a book of poetry while eating breakfast because of course he is. He lives and breathes all those dead poets, and he expects his students at the community college to do the same. If today weren't a *big day*, I'd be sitting next to him with one of my heart books. That's what Dad calls the stack by my bed, a strange mix of medical texts about the human heart and rom-coms about teenagers, aka stories about all the stuff I've missed. I can't get enough of all the tropes—fake dating and enemies to lovers and *oh my gosh, there's two of us and only one bed!* I love it all. Chloe says my kissy-kissy books are boring. She likes dragons and sword fights and far-off made-up lands. I want real life—crushes and kisses and parties and, well, being a normal seventeen-year-old. That's *my* fantasy.

I have my latest read, *Love at First Bite*—which promises ample will-they-won't-they tension in some sort of bakery—tucked under my arm, trying to look as unsuspicious as possible. And I *always* have a book in case there's a long wait at the doctor or Mom has to run into a store that's too peopley for me.

I clutch *First Bite* while Mom lays out my morning pill parade next to my fancy plate. It's quite the cocktail of antirejection drugs, steroids, antibiotics and vitamins, all designed to help my body play nice with my new heart.

I'm not out of the woods yet (as Mom and Dr. Russell *love* to remind me).

Dad reads some poem out loud to Mom while she counts pills, and seeing them there, a halo of morning sunlight encircling them, I seriously reconsider going out today. This house, my parents, they've been my whole world since eighth grade. That's three years of just the three of us. And yes, I'm one part pathetic, two parts loser that my idea of a fun Friday night is a fiction read-a-thon or one of Mom's black-and-white movies, but it's nice. Safe. Familiar.

Dad glances up and sees me, teetering in the doorway. He raises his wineglass of orange juice in my direction.

"Big day," he says with a wink.

"There she is!" Mom claps. "Hold it right there."

She scurries into the kitchen and returns with the car keys and her phone. I pose for the shot with the key ring dangling off my finger, my book under my arm and my hobo bag slung over my shoulder. It contains the most important ingredient for today's outing: my notebook.

It's all a bit silly, really. You'd think it was my first time behind the wheel ever, not just since the transplant. Mom's looking down at her photos. Already reliving this *big day*.

Satisfied, Mom motions for me to sit and stacks my plate with pancakes, if that's what you can legally call these fiber-fortified whole-grain heart-healthy abominations. While I eat, my parents do that thing where they're talking to me, but actually over me and each other.

Mom: So, what are your plans for today?

Dad: Car's all gassed up.

Mom: You know who I ran into yesterday? Bree Bennet's mom. Remember Bree? You used to be such good friends. Maybe you could go see her?

Dad: Checked the tires, too.

Mom: She was a nice girl. Maybe it's time to reach out to your old friends, now that you . . . that things are looking up?

Dad: You got your license? And money, do you need more money?

Mom: Oh, I put hand sanitizer and Clorox wipes on the front seat. In case you go in somewhere. Do you think you'll go in somewhere?

Dad: No crowds.

Mom: Or salads. Or sushi. Maybe don't eat until you get home.

Dad: Andrea, the girl can eat.

Mom: (laughing a bit too high-pitched) Of course she can. It's just Dr. Russell said that thing about foodborne infection.

Dad: Oh, please. She didn't come this far to get taken down by a California roll. Right, Syd?

They're both staring at me now. I swallow a bite of imitation pancake.

"I'm just gonna cruise around a bit. You know, take my new ticker for a spin." I hold up my book. "Maybe stop and read somewhere quiet."

It's a lie. A small one. The perfectly harmless, white variety that's a *must* for life on the list.

We've all gotten pretty good at them over the last three years. *What's meant to happen will happen. The doctors know what they're doing. It's all going to be okay.* We slip the little half lies in without even thinking, anything to avoid looking directly at the truth.

Still, I don't love fibbing to my parents. Even if it *is* for their own good. Because they would for sure agree with Chloe—my plans for this morning are *not* a good idea. And I'm not about to ruin this *big day* for them, or me.

"Well, nothing says freedom like a set of car keys and a book," Dad says.

Mom frowns slightly. "Maybe it's too soon, Mike."

"Mom, everything's going to be fine," I say. "I know *all* the rules. No salads or raw fish or handshakes or people in general or exertion or skipping my afternoon pills. I'll very responsibly enjoy my *morsel* of freedom, okay?"

Mom smiles but I can tell she's still nervous. Before the transplant, her full-time job was getting me more years. Now she's on a mission to make this heart last as long as possible. It's a pretty tall order since my steroids make me vulnerable to every germ on the planet.

The longest anyone's lived post-transplant is some dude in Canada who's going on thirty-seven years with his new heart. I'll be lucky if I get more than ten. Between all the possible complications and side effects, I've got a lifetime supply of Things That Could Kill Me.

"How about I take a mask?" I say, pulling one out of my bag even though Dr. Russell says I don't need one anymore. It's been years since I've been anywhere without one. Even before the transplant, I had to be careful—even the slightest sickness can get you suspended from the list. And what if *the perfect heart* comes up while you're nursing a head cold? Not worth the risk.

Mom smiles, and her shoulders relax.

"A mask would help," she says. "Got any bubble wrap in there?"

I pretend to be searching my bag.

"Nope. Just illicit drugs and condoms."

"Not funny." Mom throws her napkin at me and laughs.

"A *little* funny," Dad says with a wink.

After breakfast, they follow me to the door. I get the don't-want-to-go feeling again, and before it can take over, I give them both a quick hug.

"You guys," I say. "I'm going for a drive. Not shipping off to war here."

Mom hugs me a little too tight.

"I know, I know, it's just . . ." Mom dabs at her eyes. "Well, it's a big day, that's all."

Dad reaches out, grabs my hand, and gives it a tight squeeze.

"'I carry your heart with me,'" he says quietly.

"'I carry it in my heart.'"

I finish the line to the E. E. Cummings poem Dad has turned into our own little thing.

And then, I'm off.

CHAPTER THREE

DRIVING FEELS LIKE BREATHING.

Not the regular kind. The kind like when my lungs fully inflated after I woke up from surgery and a nurse pried the intubation tube from my throat, and I inhaled—really and truly inhaled—for the first time in years.

Breaths that filled me up so full and so fast, my body couldn't contain all the air.

Air I didn't even know I'd been missing. That's what driving again feels like—inhaling the world after years of holding my breath.

I put the windows down and the radio way up. Dad's classic rock station pumps songs I don't know, but I don't even care—the beat feels strong, and so do I. I stick my hand out the window and let the music and air flow through me.

The town of Cherry Hill flashes by my window. I cruise past

the junior high I used to go to before I collapsed in eighth-grade gym class one day and never went back. Between all the doctor's appointments and "bad days," homeschool made a lot more sense.

I drive past the small-town hospital I used to go to before I got upgraded to Dr. Russell up in Salt Lake City. Past the Main Street ice shack where Dad used to buy me shaved ice as big as my head on hot July days. The community theater where Bree and I used to do the plays in the summer.

This town is full of *used to*s, even though I've been down the street the whole time.

It's not like I *never* go out, but life on the list is a tightrope. Life on one side, death on the other, and you never know what might knock you off-kilter.

I slow down as I pass Randy's Burger Joint. In eighth grade, it was *the* spot. The place you'd beg your parents to drop you off on the weekend *unsupervised,* which made you feel like a borderline badass. Nothing tastes as good as an unchaperoned Randy's strawberry shake on a Friday night.

I wonder if my old friends still go there, or maybe there's some new spot. Just because my world stopped spinning in middle school, doesn't mean theirs did.

I cross Cherry Hill's borders and hop on I-15, the long stretch of highway dividing Utah from top to bottom. It's lined with small towns like mine, little rural map dots. At least Cherry Hill has the community college, but as I pull off onto an exit, I enter a town that's little more than a roadway stop for gas and beef jerky on the way to somewhere else.

Rawlins Ridge.

Out my window, fields of cows roll by with the occasional house or mobile home between them. I pull over next to a barbed wire fence and get out my trusty notebook from my bag. On the last page, I've scribbled a note.

1036 W. Clawson St.

Rawlins Ridge

June 6

10 a.m.

I type the address into my GPS, and the computer-generated voice guides me turn by turn.

Turn right at the light.

Left past the railroad tracks.

Continue past the three-legged dog and the run-down build-ing that maybe used to be a Denny's.

After more than ten minutes driving down winding roads, I've passed only one other car and an old man sitting on his front porch, who waved as I went by.

But when I hit a string of cars parked just off the road, I slow way down. I turn off the radio and roll up my windows. Through the glass, I see a group of people huddled together beneath a tree. On either side of them, headstones pepper the green grass all the way back to the dusty brown foothills in the distance.

I squint a little in the sun to see if I can make out faces. Not that I'd know them anyway. But I do see a man and a woman who look kind of familiar. I open my notebook again and turn to a page where I've glued a newspaper clipping—a family photo of a girl with a boy and their parents standing behind, the same two people who are standing near the headstones now, the man's arm slung loosely around the woman's shoulders. She's dabbing at her eyes. He looks like he wishes he were somewhere else.

And honestly, now that I'm here, so do I.

CHAPTER FOUR

I SHOULDN'T BE HERE.

I know this as surely as I feel my recycled heartbeat pounding in my ears.

I'm not supposed to be here.

And I mean that both in the existential sense and the right here, right now, at this cemetery with a huge poster of a girl who has long blond hair with thick purple streaks and green eyes staring at me next to the words *HAPPY BIRTHDAY, MIA!* I should not be walking toward this crowd of people who all loved the green-eyed girl. I should not be letting some random girl hug me and say, "Thank you for coming. It would mean so much to Mia."

She nods at me solemnly, letting our shared grief do the talking for us. She has no idea that everything I know about Mia fits in my chest and the pages of my notebook—all the clues that led me here.

The girl gives me another sad smile. I wonder if she was friends with Mia. Maybe *good* friends. The kind who buy half-heart necklaces and spend Friday nights guzzling strawberry shakes? At least until four months ago.

My stomach feels sick.

I didn't really think this part through, what it would feel like to meet her friends . . . her family. Plus I'm breaking about a million confidentiality rules being here. My transplant coordinator would have a *fit*.

Technically, I shouldn't know anything about my donor except the basics: blood type, size, tissue match. But thanks to a nurse in my post-op room who thought I wasn't awake yet, I also know that I'm, and I quote, "the luckiest girl in the world. Getting a heart from one town over? That's like hitting the transplant lottery."

After I got home from the hospital, I pretty much went full-on donor detective on this sucker. I read all the obituaries from the only two neighboring towns from two days before and after my transplant.

I had some other clues, too, because here's the ugly truth: you have to die in the *right* way to be a donor. Your body has to keep going even if your brain doesn't. And you have to die at the right time—preferably in the hospital, where the docs can get the organs into their new home before they go bad. Kidneys get thirty-six hours, those lucky bastards. A heart gets six, max.

All the clues led me to Mia. Died at the right time, in the right way, with the right heart, literally one town over? Chatty nurse was right: I got all the luck. I should invest in scratch-off tickets.

The girl who hugged me is embracing another girl now. They're both crying. Big old boo-hoos that hang in the air. And the woman from the picture in the newspaper is crying, too, and I can see now that she's standing in front of a small rock garden with a silver urn on a pedestal, waiting to be buried.

A little chill goes through me. *Mia.*

Yeah. Chloe was right, I should *not* have come. What did I think? I could quiz people about their dead friend AT HER POSTMORTEM BIRTHDAY PARTY?

At least I left my mask in the car (forgive me, Mom and immune system), so I don't look *totally* out of place. Still, this was a bad idea. But before I can run back to my car, an older man gets up at a microphone and everyone is quieting down and I can't leave without being *super* obvious. I decide to hang back. I'll just observe—not get too close, like Chloe said.

No one has to know who I am.

The man at the mic says he was Mia's history teacher. He talks about how she was a great—though unpredictable— student. How she thought deeply about the world. *Maybe too deeply,* he says, and everyone laughs.

One by one, more people go up to speak. It's your usual memorial stuff: People cry, they recount moments with Mia, how she loved bubble gum ice cream and *always* had an opinion. How she could rock a ukulele.

I know some of this already from the newspaper articles I've read: *Flash flood death of local 16-year-old shocks Utah town.* But I make mental notes of every new morsel of information.

I can do this. I can totally do this. Get the info, get out, get on with my new life.

The boy from the family photo in my newspaper clipping takes the mic next. He looks a few years younger than the girl in the poster. Same blond hair (just shorter) and green eyes, except his are tinged pink around the edges.

"Today would have been my sister's seventeenth birthday. . . ."

My chest tightens as he talks about how Mia was a gift to the world—to him. How her last gift was her own body.

"The doctors tell us six of her organs saved other people's lives."

My stolen heart skips a beat.

The thump-thump-thump inside me is deafening. I mean, I'm always aware of this foreign heart, but right now it's *everywhere*. In my ears. In my throat. Throbbing through me with a force that leaves me with that familiar gasping-for-air feeling. What if everyone else can hear it, too? Or see the truth of who I am, why I'm here, written all over my face?

It's one thing to talk about the pieces this girl left behind; it's another to see the person who inherited them, in the flesh, just walking around living and breathing and waltzing into memorial services uninvited.

I inch back from the crowd, farther and farther until I'm outside the huddled circle. I consider making a mad dash back to my car, but it's way too far.

That's when I see it. A small doorway on my left. Without thinking, I duck into it and close the door behind me. I stand, eyes closed for a few seconds, trying to calm the heartbeat pulsing through me.

When I finally open my eyes, it's dark.

And musty.

My eyes adjust slowly until I can see ROSE FAMILY MAUSO-LEUM engraved on the stone wall.

Holy hell.

I'm in a freaking crypt. I have literally trespassed into someone's final resting place.

I am on some sort of creeptastic roll today.

I turn and start feeling my way back to the door when a rustle behind me stops me cold. A voice from the shadows ricochets off the stone walls.

"So. You come here often?"

CHAPTER FIVE

THE VOICE MAKES ME JUMP. LITERALLY. MY HEAD SMACKS the low ceiling of the Rose family's tomb.

"So tell me," the voice continues. It's deep, but in the dim light, I can only make out a shape in the far back of the house-like tomb, sitting on what looks like a stone bench. "Do you often find yourself hiding in graves?"

I half whisper to the shadows, "I'm not hiding."

Another rustling sound is followed by footsteps. A boy a full head taller than me steps into the light spilling through a small window cut into the stone. His eyes are half-hidden by a camo baseball cap that can barely contain the dark hair spilling out from under it, and his hands are stuffed way down deep in his jean pockets. His boots, caked in mud, kick up all sorts of dust in this tiny space, making it hard to breathe again.

Or maybe it's the way he's looking at me, with a half smirk, like we're in on a secret together.

"Okay, then tell me this," he says. "Are *you* not hiding from the same thing *I'm* not hiding from?"

"Which is . . ."

"Them." He tilts his head toward the window. Outside, still memorializing away, a girl is talking into the mic, well, sobbing, really. Her words are indiscernible.

"Hilarious." He shakes his head and smiles, but it's not a *real* smile. It's the kind mom gives when Dr. Russell says my new heart might only buy me ten more years. Like the universe is making a sick joke. "They didn't even *know* her."

He turns his eyes on me.

"Did *you*?"

It's part question, but mostly accusation.

"I . . . I'm . . ." I pause, trying to figure out how to explain exactly *what* I am. My mind spins through all the things I know about Mia from the obits and the news articles. Sixteen. One brother. Flash flood in a slot canyon the day before my transplant. Died the day *of* my transplant, no more than six hours before, to be precise. Didn't someone mention a ukulele?

It's better than the truth.

"We met in a group," I say. "Online. For ukuleles."

"Ukuleles?"

"Ukulele enthusiasts."

The boy squints, inspecting me. I stand up straighter, adjusting my shirt to make sure my scar is covered and trying to seem as legit as possible, and also maybe like someone who plays the ukulele, whatever that looks like.

"I'm Clayton," he says, still eyeing me.

And then, he *holds out his hand.* It hangs there a second

between us while Mom's voice in my head reminds me not to touch people. But I can't *not* shake it, right? Not if I'm going to pull off this whole not-a-total-stalker/cemetery-trespasser vibe.

I shake his hand quick and commit to bathing myself in hand sanitizer later.

"Oh, yeah, um, Mia mentioned you."

I don't know why I say that.

"Well, Grave Girl, she most definitely did *not* mention you." He loosens the tie around his neck. His shirt still has the crisp folding lines running longways down the fabric, and by the way he's yanking at his tie, it's clear he's about as uncomfortable in his getup as I am at this morbid birthday party. "Where'd you say you were from again?"

"I didn't," I say. "But I live in Cherry Hill."

He eyes me again.

"So tell me this. How is it that you've heard of me but I've never heard of you or this dubious online ukulele group—which, pardon my French—seems like a load of crap?"

I should probably cut my losses and run like hell. But I'm *not* going home empty-handed just because a boy with impeccable bone structure is making me jittery. Not before I find my answers.

"Well, do *you* play the ukulele?" I ask.

He's staring at me like he has me, and my secret, all figured out. "No."

"Well, there you go. It's a pretty exclusive club." I say this more confidently than I feel.

He scrutinizes me again. After a second studying my big-fat-liar moonface, his face softens a bit. There's something else, too—a look, full of a kind of distant nostalgia.

"Well, Mia and I were best friends since third grade. *Also* an extremely exclusive club." He turns back to the window, blinking so hard he blinks away the momentary softness, too. His jaw tightens as the crying girl with the mic outside passes it off to someone else. "And it most definitely did not include these phonies."

Her best friend.

Suddenly this tiny tomb feels *impossibly* small. And the heartbeat in my ears feels louder. Crap. I'm about to go all "Tell-Tale Heart" in here.

"You've *got* to be kidding me." Clayton's leaning toward the window, his mouth hanging open. A group of kids is standing by the urn now, singing an a cappella version of "Stand By Me." This latest turn of memorial events is the last straw for Clayton's already-strained relationship with his necktie. He rips it off in one angry motion.

"Oh, *now* they love her?" He flaps his tie toward the singers. "But when Mia auditioned last year, did they give her the time of day? And just look at *him.*"

He points to the man from the family photo. He's dabbing at the corner of his eyes now, his arm still around the woman's shoulders.

"Her dad?" I ask, kind of proud that I knew that one.

"Talk about hypocrites. Acting like father of the year?" His voice is getting louder, angrier. "All because she's dead?"

He kind of yells this last word. It bounces off the walls of the mausoleum like a rubber ball, the final *d* ricocheting off the tiny plaques with the names of the deceased Roses.

He takes off his hat and rakes his fingers through his hair.

"Sorry, I—"

"No, no, it's okay," I say, and I'm about to add something empty and clichéd like you're supposed to say at memorials of dead best friends, but I stop. He clearly thinks this whole birthday memorial is a joke. So, I do what Chloe would do—I laugh in the face of death. "It's normal to be emotional. We're in a very grave situation here."

Clayton looks at me, wide-eyed.

"Did you just make a death joke?" he asks. "At my dead best friend's birthday party?"

"Maybe?"

He takes a step back from me and scans me, top to bottom. I'm suddenly very aware that I'm wearing a skirt that probably went out of style when I said sayonara to life in eighth grade. And did I even brush my hair this morning?

I smooth down my hair as he stares at me.

"That is *wildly* inappropriate." His eyes shift straight to mine, and his half smirk threatens to become a whole smile. "I can see why Mia liked you."

The anger in his voice is gone now, replaced by something else. Something vaguely . . . flirty? So, okay, I'll be the first one to admit that my flirt-o-meter needs some serious recalibration. Heart failure doesn't leave a lot of time for breathless romance, so my experience on the matter comes exclusively from books like *Love at First Bite*. So, yeah, it's probably in my head, but this Clayton kid is still looking at me with that jawline just casually being all chiseled from stone in a way that makes my stolen heart feel kind of, I don't know, fluttery.

"I don't remember you from the funeral," he says.

"Wasn't there." I leave out the part about how it was because I was lying in a hospital bed after having my rib cage cracked open to remove my dying heart.

"Consider yourself lucky. Nothing but trauma groupies." He hangs the tie limp around his neck and unbuttons the top button of his shirt. "To them, she was just a headline—a nobody girl from a nowhere town."

I lean my arm against the cool stone. "She was *somebody* to me."

It's the truest thing I've uttered since I walked into this tomb. Clayton's face softens slightly.

"So how come I never met you before?"

"Oh, uh, Mia and I never met in person. We always meant to. Just, I don't know, ran out of time."

He meets my eyes for a moment, and something passes between us, something real, as real as the heart beating like mad inside me.

He pulls a phone from his back pocket. "What's the best way to reach you?"

The heart flutters go berserk.

"You're asking for my number? Here?" I gesture to the stone walls around us. "*Wildly* inappropriate."

He holds up his hands in defense.

"Whoa whoa whoa. Not sure what Mia told you about me, but I'm not some creeper who picks up girls at cemeteries."

"*Exactly* what a creeper would say," I reply, and if I'm being honest, *my* voice is vaguely flirty now, too. At least I think it is.

"Touché, Grave Girl. Touché." He takes a step toward me. I

have to lean my head back to look at him. From this close, I can see the freckles lining the bridge of his nose below his hazel eyes. "I'm asking for your number because if you were friends with Mia—"

"Which I was."

"Right—*since* you were friends with Mia"—he raises his eyebrows at me for approval—"then you might be interested in something I'm working on. For her."

Chloe's warnings ring in my head: *Be careful. Don't get too close.* I'm like 105 percent sure that giving my phone number to Mia's best friend counts as *way too freaking close.*

But the heart inside me is skipping about in a way that's new and weird and kind of amazing.

"Well, if it's for Mia . . ." I type my number into his phone under the contact he's started—*Grave Girl*. I hand it back. "It's Sydney, actually."

He looks down at me through the dark hair that's fallen in front of his eyes. "Well, Sydney, you know what Mia would say about us hiding in here, right?"

I shake my head.

"That we're chickenshit," he says.

I fake a little laugh. "Classic Mia."

I loathe myself.

"She'd say I ought to get out there and join the mob," he says. "Show my support."

"Yeah."

"Soooo . . ." He draws out the word like he's waiting for me to stop him. "I guess it's time to return to the land of the living?"

"Guess so."

He stops at the entrance to the tomb, the afternoon sun silhouetting him.

"Of all the graves in all the towns in all the world—"

"She walks into mine." I finish the famous line from one of Mom's favorite movies without even thinking. Clayton looks surprised.

"You know *Casablanca*?"

I shrug. "It's a classic."

"That's what Mia says." He pauses and his jaw clenches tight again. "Said. That's what Mia *said.*" He shakes his head like he's shaking off the past. "I didn't think anybody else our age knew that old stuff."

"Well, maybe I'm not just anybody."

He touches the tip of his baseball cap in a mini salute and gives me an almost-grin that's still tight, forced on his face. But his eyes seem like they mean it.

"No, Grave Girl, I don't think you are."

I linger inside the tomb, watching him rejoin the group. He hangs on the fringes, the brim of his hat pulled low, hands shoved back down into his pockets. All traces of even the most reticent smile vanished. I wonder why. What is *he* hiding from?

But mostly I wonder at what point my little white lies became *actual* lies. Like gigantic, shameless works of fiction.

Because I *wasn't* friends with Mia.

I've never touched a ukulele in my life.

And also . . .

Clayton catches me staring and gives a little eyebrow raise

in my direction. I sink back against the stone wall, my breath catching in my lungs.

And also, I'm only alive because that boy's best friend is not.

Chloe was wrong—this isn't just a bad idea.

It's the worst one I've ever had.

CHAPTER SIX

THE FIRST TEXT COMES THE NEXT DAY.

I'm FaceTiming with Chloe when my phone dings, which is a little alarming since Mom and Dad are home, and Chloe is staring at me through the screen, and that's pretty much my entire social circle.

But there it is, a text.

Infiltrated any burial grounds today?

This heart inside me does the same stupid little fluttery thing again as I swipe away the text from an unknown number. Now that I've had a moment to think, I've realized that I have zero business talking to this particular unknown.

"Who was that?" Chloe asks.

"No one."

"You got a text from no one?" Chloe *never* lets me get away with little white lies.

"It was just this boy," I say. "From yesterday."

"A boy?" Chloe's face is up tight to the screen in one second flat. "You told me about the crying girls and the brother's transplant guilt trip and the pastures full of cows, but a *boy*? You did not mention *that*."

I shrug. "It was nothing."

"Sydney Abigail Wells. You. Spill. Now."

I sigh, but saying no to Chloe is a losing battle. So I tell her about the whole embarrassing thing. How we met in the mausoleum. How he may or may not have been flirting. I try to imitate how he said I was *wildly inappropriate*.

"Definitely flirty," Chloe decides. She's smiling so huge I'm afraid she's going to pop her cheeks. She gets her grin under control and feigns seriousness. "Now, I've heard rumors about these country boys, so I need you to answer this question with total honesty." She pauses dramatically for a big sigh. "How tight were the jeans? Like spray-on, I-can-see-the-whole-enchilada tight or just snug enough that you get a solid mental picture of what they're working with?"

"You have serious problems."

"What? You *know* I have a thing for cowboys."

"And surfers. And ski bums. And nerds with a hidden wild streak that only you bring out."

"What can I say? I'm equal opportunity." Her grin is back. Even with her oxygen tank and failing heart, she's been on a bit of a boy bender this year. But me? I've never had a boyfriend or even a first kiss. I guess that's how Chloe and I are different—she wants to go out with a bang; I started fading before time of death.

Chloe points at me again through the screen. "Now, next time you see this boy, FaceTime me in. I'll assess the Levi's situation myself."

I shake my head. "Not gonna be a next time."

"Sydney. He sent a text *the next day*. That means one thing: he is *wooing* you. Have you learned nothing from all those books of yours?"

I roll my eyes.

"First of all, we're not in a rom-com. Nobody is *wooing* anybody." I allow myself one more peek at the text from the unknown number. "Second, it's complicated."

"*Life's* complicated, Syd."

"No, you don't—" I pause. "You don't understand."

"I understand that you came up with this whole seriously absurd scheme. I said you were being a major creeper, but you did it anyway, and now the situation has changed."

"What situation?"

"Mr. Levi's! As your best friend in this fragile, fleeting life, I'm telling you, you need to ride that horse as far as it will go."

"Chloe!"

"Metaphorically, of course."

"And I'm telling *you*. It's not gonna happen."

"Why?"

"Because." I have to steel myself to say it. "Because he was her best friend."

"Whose best friend?"

"Mia's. The girl. The"—I swallow hard and whisper into the phone—"the donor."

"Oh." Chloe leans back in her chair like I've punched her in the gut. I watch it settle into her brain. "Oh no. No no no no."

"Yes."

Chloe shakes her head. "Well, what if you're wrong about her?"

"I'm not wrong."

"You said it could also have been that boy, right? From the highway crash?" Chloe says. "Maybe *he's* the donor."

Her mom has come in now with her meds, so I wait to answer. I don't need her mom chatting it up with my mom about all this on their occasional mother-of-a-transplant-kid check-ins. When Mom found my research notebook a few weeks ago with all the obits and articles and clues about my donor, she was *not* happy.

We had a whole thing about it. She said it wasn't healthy. I agreed. Told her I would stop.

And then I hid my notebook better.

"Hi, sweetie," Chloe's mom says, waving at the screen.

"Hi, Mrs. Munoz."

"How's that new ticker?"

"Ticking."

She smiles and rubs Chloe's back.

"Well, pass some of your good luck over here, will ya?"

"Will do," I say.

After she leaves, I whisper just in case.

"It's *not* the highway boy. Trust me. I *know*."

Chloe pauses, her hand in the air as it drops a pill into her mouth. She closes her eyes. "Ay-yi-yi. *What* did you do now?"

I shrug. "I may or may not have called his family and impersonated hospital personnel to verify his blood type."

"Syd!"

"I know, I know! But I *had* to find out."

"And?"

"He was A negative. So it's Mia. It *has* to be."

Chloe swallows her last pill. "Okay, so it's her. Mystery solved. Move on."

Chloe still doesn't get it. Ever since I first blinked awake and felt *her* heart beating in *my* chest, all I could think was: *My heart is gone. I have someone else's—a stranger's heart.*

And I guess that's when it started—in that very moment, with Mom crying over me and Dad trying not to cry and the nurses saying, "You did so great, honey." That's when I first started thinking about the *someone*. What were they going to do with the life that now beats in me?

"I don't just need to know her name," I explain. "I need to know who she was. What her heart wants."

Chloe rolls her eyes. "Not this malarkey again."

"It could be true," I say. Our argument about this started when I read an article about how the heart never forgets, that it always contains some cellular pieces of its original owner. Like a lifelong vegetarian will wake up from a transplant craving meat for the first time ever. Or they'll recognize someone they've never met.

Chloe thinks it's nonsense. But what if it's not?

Chloe sighs. "It's *your* heart now, Syd. Which means you're right: this boy is a no-go. Even if he *is* into you."

"He's into *her*. You should have seen him, Chloe, when he talked about Mia. If he knew I had her heart, he definitely wouldn't be flirting." An image of Clayton's angry face, watching all the phonies at the funeral, pops into my head. "He'd hate me."

I knew all this from the moment he told me who he was, but somehow, saying it out loud gives me a little ache in my chest. Not a full-blown, gotta-go-see-my-cardiologist pain, just a subtle twinge of loss.

Except I'm not really losing anything. I shouldn't have been in that cemetery in the first place. I should never have met Clayton. And it's not like we had some torrid love affair in that tomb. We met, we flirted, end of story.

Because that's as far as *this* story can go.

"You were right," I say. "It was a mistake. The whole thing. Which is why I'm definitely not texting him back. So can we *please* talk about something else? Like what's going on with you? You look like hell."

Chloe lifts her hands in the air like *whaddya gonna do?*

"For real, Chloe, talk to me. What's up?" I push.

"My fluid retention." She does a ba-dum-ching motion on invisible drums.

"Not funny," I say.

"You know me, I can't help but *be* positive," she says with a weak laugh. It's her favorite pun about our shared blood type.

Technically, that means Mia's heart could have saved Chloe, too. Same blood type, same transplant region, same craptastic prognosis. But I got it, and now Chloe is the one stuck waiting and Mia's in an urn beneath a rock in a Podunk cemetery and I'm out here pretending like I'm a normal girl who can flirt with boys.

It's a wonder Chloe doesn't hate me, too. Sometimes, I think she should.

"Your heart's coming, Chlo. I know it," I say.

"Don't do that," she says.

"What?"

"You *know* what." She closes her eyes for a second like she's gathering herself. She opens them again and smiles. "Now, where did we land on the whole tight-jeans situation?"

She blinks a tear back so fast that I almost don't see it.

But I do.

CHAPTER SEVEN

TWO DAYS PASS BEFORE I GET ANOTHER TEXT.

Mom's driving me to my weekly checkup at the hospital in Salt Lake when my phone buzzes.

> This *is* Sydney isn't it? Ukulele enthusiast with a deadly sense of humor?

Mom looks at me out of the corner of her eye while dodging diesels on the highway. We've taken this trip so many times she could probably do it blindfolded.

"Chloe?" Mom asks.

"Yeah."

Mom keeps her eyes on me a second longer than feels totally necessary.

"Stats are down," I add for good measure.

"Poor girl," Mom says. "I need to touch base with her mother."

I think Mom feels just as guilty as I do about me getting a heart before Chloe. Technically, Chloe was on the list first, but getting a transplant isn't like taking a number at the deli counter. It's more like a pool, a bunch of hopeful candidates in geographic regions who get reranked constantly based on how sick they are when the organ comes in. So if my heart hadn't taken a massive nosedive just a few weeks before, Chloe might be the one heading to this post-transplant appointment, and I'd be the one still sucking oxygen from a tank. But my heart *did* start crapping out big-time, and Mom was stroking my hair, and Dad was holding my hand by my hospital bed, and we were all so sure that *this was it.*

But instead of a finale, I got a curtain call—a second chance. My bad luck bumped me to the top of the list. I got the heart— Chloe didn't.

I swipe away Clayton's latest text.

Once we get to the hospital, I try not to think about Clayton or his messages (or his jeans—thanks for that, Chloe). While I'm getting my echocardiogram, I focus on the images on the screen, a pulsing white-and-black ultrasound of this heart.

The tech slides the little lube-covered paddle up and down and around my chest. There's the mitral valve, flicking like a little tongue between the chambers. Now the tech's measuring the ventricles. I can tell how much healthier Mia's heart is than mine. By the time I made it to the transplant table, my lower right chamber had ballooned up with all the blood it couldn't squeeze out fast enough.

The tech turns on the audio, and the beat of Mia's heart fills

the room. Whoosh-whoosh-whoosh. I may not know a lot about
Mia, but I know this—her heart is strong. Each beat pumping in
perfect rhythm.

I can only imagine how Clayton would react if he could see
this, *her* heart just beating away inside me.

"I know what you're thinking," the tech says. She's paused
with the echo wand up in the air.

"You do?" I ask. The heartbeat on the monitor picks up, ticking faster through the darkened room.

She smiles. "You're thinking this is better than a biopsy,
huh?"

I breathe out again.

"Totally."

Okay, so the tech's not a mind reader. Thank goodness—I
don't need anyone finding out that I was in Rawlins Ridge. But
the tech's not totally wrong, either. This echo is *way* easier than
the biopsies where the docs snake a wire through me to take
back a tiny sample of Mia's heart.

Because most of the time, the heart doesn't tell you when
it's in trouble. It's a scrappy little sucker that will burn itself
out before sending up a white flag. So by the time your doctor says, *It might be your heart,* it most definitely *is* your heart
and it's been heading toward complete and utter failure for
months.

Pretty shoddy engineering, if you ask me. But the doctors?
They call it cardiomyopathy, which in Greek means *heart suf-
fering.* Gotta give it to the Greeks—they can make everything
sound beautiful.

"Well, no biopsies today," the tech says as she disconnects the electrodes and hands me a towel for the gel on my chest. "Relax, girlie. You're past the hard part."

When Dr. Russell comes in, she's beaming. To be fair, she's always kind of smiley. That's why last February, when she came in with a frown, I knew I was toast.

She told us a bunch of numbers and statistics, too, but mostly, I remember her face. And Dad's. He's also a silver-lining kind of guy. But that day? It was like he'd finally realized the truth: I was going to die.

He looked so . . . broken. I hated myself for it.

But today, everyone's all smiles.

"Well, Sydney," Dr. Russell says. "This heart loves you."

"And we love it!" Mom says, squeezing my hand.

The doc tells us how "phenomenal" my lab results are. She tells us we can start coming every other week, and soon, only every month. Mom cries a little. Her tear ducts are conditioned to go into overdrive in here.

"Bottom line," Dr. Russell says. "I see no signs of rejection."

Ah, the big, bad beast of post-transplant life. Except, isn't rejection exactly what my body *should* do—push away anything new and scary that could hurt it? The antirejection meds I take like clockwork are basically a way to trick my immune system into *chilling the freak out* and not attacking the one thing that could actually save me.

"Well, you can thank my mom for that," I say. Mom's the one

who counts the pills, sets timers for my meds and stays up late researching heart-healthy meals.

"Well, whatever you're doing, keep it up." Dr. Russell scoots her little rolling chair up to me. "So, things seem *very* good on the physical side, but how are things . . . mentally?"

"Okey-dokey," I say.

Mom and Dr. Russell exchange a glance, one that clearly says there's been a conversation sans yours truly.

"What about friends?" she asks.

"Got 'em."

Mom clears her throat *so* not discreetly. Okay, so maybe I don't have like throngs of BFFs or anything, but who cares? Chloe's all I need.

Bree and my other friends were around for a little bit after I started homeschool, but things were just, I don't know, awkward. There were the rumors, of course: I was missing school because I was pregnant. In drug rehab! Contagious! And also, we had completely different interests: They were planning their futures; I was planning a funeral.

"What about your website?" Dr. Russell continues. "What's it called again?"

"TheWaitingList." I shift my thighs. The paper on the exam table crunches beneath me. "I'm on hiatus."

She makes a note on the computer, but I don't see how my online presence has anything to do with, well, anything.

"Your mother tells me you've shown quite an interest in your donor. That you were doing some"—she pauses, like she's trying to find the right words—"research?"

I look at Mom. I didn't know she'd filled my transplant team in on the notebook situation.

"It's very normal to have questions about your new heart," Dr. Russell says before I can even try to make excuses. "Have you given any more thought about writing a letter to the family? We send them anonymously, and it helps a lot of people feel some closure. Helps them move on."

"Yeah," I say. "Maybe."

I say this as if I don't have a bunch of unfinished versions of that same epistle on my computer next to all my unposted videos. I mean, what do I even say? *Hey, it's me. The person who lived because your daughter/sister/best friend died. Thanks for her heart and stuff. Bye!*

Dr. Russell scoots closer. "Whatever you're feeling, I promise you, it's *normal.* Some people feel depressed or anxious after a transplant. Some feel guilt. Or even shame."

I nod along to the list of things it's okay for me to feel. But I'm having a hard time focusing because my phone is vibrating in my pocket, and I'm wondering what Clayton is saying, and also how Dr. Russell and Mom would react if they knew Mia's best friend was texting me because I WENT TO HER BIRTHDAY MEMORIAL.

"But, Sydney. Getting overly concerned about your donor isn't healthy. And it will only stall your progress, mentally *and* physically."

Dr. Russell swings her computer screen around to face me. My echo is on the screen.

"Every heart has a rhythm—it lets blood in, it pushes blood

out. That's its whole job," she says, pointing to the flashing reds and blues showing the blood flow. "When your heart failed, it couldn't do its job. It was holding on to too much, and it lost its balance, its rhythm."

She pauses to make sure I hear her metaphor, which I do, loud and clear. Then she pulls open a drawer and hands me a notebook.

"For you," she says. I open the flowery cover and thumb through the pages. It's a planner. "Find something else to focus on. A new project—or an old one. As I recall, when we first met, you had just finished a local play?"

"Yeah, my *last* one," I say, emphasizing the word to make it clear that my theater days are behind me.

"Okay, well, what about this summer? Any plans? You're going into your senior year, right? What about beyond high school?"

I flip through the calendars, all the blank pages, all the empty squares. There wasn't supposed to *be* a beyond.

I don't even realize I'm getting emotional until Dr. Russell hands me a tissue. Mom's hovering over me, probably surprised because I'm not a big crier, and to be honest, I'm a little bewildered myself.

"Gotta love those steroid mood swings," I say, wiping my face. They're both just giving me this awful look of pity, so I ask if I can use the restroom.

Alone in a stall, I stare at the calendar again—all the time I never planned on. I slam it shut when I feel the tears brewing again. I blow my nose and then tell my reflection in the mirror to *get it together.* It's a *planner,* for heaven's sake. I splash some cold water on my face before I head back in.

Dr. Russell's waiting outside the restroom.

"Everything okay?" she asks.

I flap the planner between us.

"Just a lot of empty days in here," I say with a weird little laugh.

Dr. Russell hands me a printout of the echo image.

"*More* days. That's a good thing."

"Yeah. Totally. It's just"—my voice catches again, and I don't even really know why—"when you've been the dying girl for so long, it's hard to be anything else."

Dr. Russell puts her hand on my shoulder and flashes her big silver-lining smile.

"Well, *think* about it," she says. "Make some plans. I mean, isn't that what this whole thing is about?"

Mom side-eyes me all the way home, trying *so* hard not to ask me what all that was about. And to be honest, I'm not quite sure I have an answer. All I know is all those little squares—all that time—made me feel a bit . . . untethered.

I read Clayton's latest text while we drive.

> Ah, I see. Playing it cool. I can play hard to get too ya know.

I don't answer. I don't engage with Mom, either, who keeps trying to find out how I'm doing without directly asking. I give her short answers because I *really* don't want to talk about it and also maybe I'm a little pissed at her that she shared my private business with Dr. Russell, who now thinks I'm drowning in a sea of post-transplant trauma or whatever.

"What's this one about?" Mom says, nodding toward the book I've buried my face in as she drives.

"Life," I say.

"You like it?"

I turn toward the window.

"Too soon to tell."

Clayton doesn't text again for more than twenty-four hours. It's not like I'm sitting around waiting or anything, but I do check my phone during the weekly old-movie marathon with my parents, just in case.

Mom raises her eyebrows at me when she sees me on my phone. Movie night is serious business—no phones allowed. But she doesn't say anything, probably because of my planner-induced meltdown yesterday.

I shove my phone between the couch cushions as Mom says, "Okay, so this is the best part. Watch, watch."

She sits on the edge of the couch, her hands clasped together, watching *Casablanca.* (I may have requested it.) Ever since she gave up her undergrad film studies gig for the full-time job that is keeping me alive, she *lives* for classic-movie night.

I've seen this movie at least a half dozen times. That's how I could quote it right back at Clayton. But this time, I'm seeing it through Mia's eyes, looking for clues in every scene. What parts were *her* favorites? What other lines did she know by heart?

My phone dings.

> Fine! I give! I GIVE! I actually really need your help.

"It's Chloe, can I . . ." I gesture to my room, and Mom nods like *go ahead.*

In my room, the texts keep coming.

> Here's the thing. . . . I refuse to be THAT guy. The one you're forced to block because he JUST WON'T TAKE A HINT.

> So if you don't reply, I promise this is the last you'll hear from me. I'll just be a random, devastatingly handsome boy you met in a grave.

Another ding:

> But you and I both know Mia deserved better than that fake-ass memorial. And I have a plan to give it to her.

And if he hadn't used the word *plan,* maybe I would put the phone down right now and never look back. But he did say *plan,* just like Dr. Russell did about a bajillion times yesterday.

> Tell me more about this plan

> She's alive. ALIVE!

> Plan?

> Better if I show you. tomorrow?
> 637 E. Snowsprings Dr. 10 a.m.

For about two seconds, I think about texting back. Telling him who I am and why we can *definitely* not be friends, or whatever it is he wants to be. It's a big fat dead end. Because hanging out with a boy who makes this heart feel funny—funnier than usual—who also happens to be my donor's best friend is definitely not the kind of *plan* Dr. Russell had in mind.

I flip open the new planner while I decide how to respond. Page after empty page lie before me, an entire blank canvas of a life. The echo screenshot falls onto the floor, and I pick it up.

It's just pixelated blobs of white and black. But ask any doctor or poet and they'll tell you, the heart is *everything*—the core.

So how can I make plans for this new life of mine until I know everything about Mia's core?

Because now, it's mine.

> You still there?

Standing there, holding the echo of Mia's heart in one hand, Clayton's text in another, it hits me: this boy can tell me everything I need to know.

He can tell me more than just Mia's favorite ice cream flavor or the instrument she played. He could tell me about her dreams for the future. What plans *she* had for life. If she had a second chance, how would she spend it? How should *I*?

I'm here.

So . . .

10 a.m.?

yep

I'll be there.

I open the notebook to the June calendar and write on to-morrow's square—CLAYTON 10 a.m. The rest of the days before and after are empty.

But tomorrow, I've got plans.

CHAPTER EIGHT

THE SECOND TIME I DRIVE THROUGH RAWLINS RIDGE, I picture a blond girl with purple streaks walking through it. What were her go-to places? Did she stroll these streets on Saturday mornings with her dad? Did she sit in the passenger side of her boyfriend's car while dragging Main?

I told my parents I was going for another drive. I didn't think they'd be super on board with the hanging-out-with-my-heart-donor's-best-friend-so-I-can-find-out-everything-about-her plan.

"All part of my getting-a-life plan," I said, throwing in a little nod to the doc for good measure. Mom agreed this was all very healthy and wise. Dad gave me a sideways glance because, well, he's Dad, and he's got a state-of-the-art bullshit detector.

Still, he let me go. Mom even let me take my evening pills with me in case I wouldn't be home in time, which was *huge* for her. I mean, she did remind me that my tacrolimus doses have to be taken *exactly* twelve hours apart or my immune system will go apeshit on Mia's heart.

On the pill box, Mom's stuck a Post-it with *8:00 p.m.!!!* in Sharpie as if I don't know the big T is the most important part of my day.

But that's this evening's issue. Right now, I'm trying to find 637 East Snowsprings Drive, which is in the exact middle of nowhere. To my left is a small, square brick house with lacy curtains hanging in the tiny front window. The yard is meticulously manicured, a garden oasis in sharp contrast to the wild weeds, dirt and sagebrush around it. If I squint, I can make out one other house way down the road.

I reread the text Clayton sent this morning.

> Come around back when you get here

I walk around the house, careful not to trample the massive geranium bushes that line the crumbling exterior brick walls. The backyard is even more of a Garden of Eden, with a weeping willow tree and brightly colored flowers.

And there, way back in the corner of the lot, where the green of the yard meets the brown of the desert dirt, is an oak tree. And in that oak tree, a dilapidated tree house, with a boy waving at me.

He's got on the same camo hat, his dark hair sticking out from underneath it, but he's not wearing his stiff collared shirt anymore. He's barely wearing a shirt at all, actually. He's got on a white kind of clingy tank top that shows off the muscles in his arms, which are flexed because he's holding a drill.

And since Chloe is the absolute worst, I take a quick glance at his jeans. I jerk my eyes away because this is not about *him*. There will be no *riding this horse as far as it will go.*

Everything Clayton knows about me is one big fat lie, so, really, he could have the body of a Greek god in a Levi's commercial and it wouldn't matter. This is about Mia. About finding out who she is . . . was. Clayton's crooked smile and impeccable jawline have nothing to do with it.

"You gonna stand there staring or come up?" Clayton hollers down at me.

Coming up is harder than it sounds, it turns out. There's not so much a ladder up to the tree house as a few pieces of wood nailed to the tree trunk. And I, stupidly, wore a sundress.

I'm not exactly sure *why* I wore it, but it was hanging in my closet this morning all sad and overlooked. Mom bought it for me after the transplant as part of her getting-back-to-being-a-regular-teenager extravaganza, except I haven't really had anywhere to wear it. It seemed like a perfectly solid choice this morning. Very casual, *hey, let's talk about your dead best friend* chic, plus it has a high neck so it covers my scar.

But as I hoist my leg onto the tree-ladder, trying not to flash Clayton in the process, I quickly realize that a sundress was a totally ridiculous decision and I feel ridiculous in it. Should have stuck with my official uniform of the last three years—joggers and an oversized T-shirt.

Clayton watches me struggle, clearly trying not to laugh. He dips his hand down, and I grab on. He yanks me up hard so that

I pop into the tree house in one movement. He looks at me from beneath his backward baseball hat, and then down at my dress. I smooth out the skirt part and adjust the collar so my scar doesn't sneak out. The last thing I need is for this boy to see all the ways I'm stitched together.

"I didn't know there'd be climbing," I say.

"I should have mentioned it was black-tie optional." He gives me the same wry smirk he did in the mausoleum, and if I'm being honest, it's the smirk I haven't stopped thinking about *since* the mausoleum. A little dimple appears on his cheek, the kind that puckers down by his mouth, and it's like he wants to smile but just . . . can't.

He opens his arms wide, that bicep muscle just bulging away as he gestures to the small, weatherworn tree house.

"Welcome to our sanctuary," he says. He leans his shoulder into a loose board, pushes his drill into it and zzzzzip-zips a screw into place. "It's definitely seen better days, but when we were little, this was *the* spot."

"You and . . . Mia?"

"Yep. Can't count the nights we spent in this baby. When her dad was in one of his moods, she'd hunker down up here, shine a flashlight into my bedroom right"—he puts his hands on my shoulders and turns me around as he points to the tiny window on the back of the house—"there."

He smells like wood shavings. In my rom-coms, boys always have a *scent*, like sandalwood and lavender. And until this very moment, I thought it was made up, something authors add to evoke the senses or whatever.

But Clayton somehow smells exactly like wood chips and masculinity. My stomach does a funky little somersault.

Stop smelling the boy, Sydney. Focus.

"So . . . ," I say, turning to face him and hoping to keep my brain, and this conversation, on track. "What's this plan? It's for Mia?"

He points to the wall behind him, keeping eye contact with me. There, hanging by thumbtacks into the wood, are seven black-and-white photographs, overlapping into a collage.

"Found it after she died," Clayton says as I walk toward the photos. "Came out here to kind of, I don't know, think or whatever, and it was just here. A message from the beyond."

I touch the corner of one of the pictures. It's a close-up of a stack of pancakes. Except the way it's framed—the angle, the textures, the lighting, all of it—makes it feel like way more than a breakfast still life. They're the saddest pancakes I've ever seen.

"Did Mia take all these?"

"Mia and her camera." He holds up two intertwined fingers. "Inseparable. But you know that."

I nod like I do. Like Mia and I had all these late-night heart-to-hearts about the latest portrait she took or the latest book I read that she should totally borrow.

"And she hung these photos here because . . . ," I start.

Clayton's standing next to me now. He leans against the wall with the photos, arms crossed.

"My best guess is it's a vision board. Probably hid it here so her dad wouldn't find it. Bit of a dream destroyer, that guy."

"Like a bucket list?"

"Mia would have said vision board. You know how she is

with all that hippie-dippie crap. All those horoscopes and posi-tive affirmations and manifesting your destiny. But yeah, I think it's stuff she wanted to do."

Next to the melancholy pancakes, there's a cornfield. Then a moonlit lake with a massive NO TRESPASSING sign in the fore-ground. A four-wheeler on a hill at sunset. A close-up of Clay-ton. A hand strumming a ukulele. And finally, a shot of this tree house.

"Do you know what they all mean?" I ask, trying to sound casual. But holy hell. It's like I've hit the Information About Mia Jackpot.

"So, some of them are pretty obvious, right? Like this one"—he points to the lake with the NO TRESPASSING sign—"Mr. Johnson's pond. It's a badge of honor to sneak a swim out there. Definitely something Mia would have wanted to do."

He points to the photo of the cornfield.

"But then this? The only thing that happens in cornfields around here are Friday night keggers, and there's no way Mia wanted to party with all the Rawlins High phonies."

My eyes go to another image, the portrait of him. His signa-ture baseball hat is missing, letting the light spill onto his face, which is caught mid-laugh. I haven't even seen him smile, so see-ing him like that, joy spread across his face, catches me off guard.

"So, why are *you* on here?" I ask.

"An excellent question," he says.

"And what about here?" I point to the big blank space in the middle of all the photos, just big enough for one final shot.

"Now you're catching on."

"Catching on to . . ."

"To why you're here." He points his drill at me. "You're going to help me figure out what these photos mean. Help me finish this vision board for her."

I shake my head, my excitement quickly turning to dread.

"Oh, I don't know. We just knew each other online. I don't—"

"That's more than most," he cuts in.

"I'm sure she has other friends."

Clayton shakes his head.

"Pretty picky in the whole people-I-can-trust department." He pulls his baseball hat down a little bit. "A sentiment we shared."

I can feel Mia's heart picking up speed in my chest. The tree house suddenly feels extra small, like maybe it's getting hard to breathe in here even though that huge hole in the roof is letting in plenty of oxygen. This is *not* what I came here for. When he said a project for Mia, I thought maybe planting flowers around her grave site or something. Not *this*.

I'm here so he can tell *me* about Mia. Not the other way around. It'll take all of two seconds for him to realize I know absolutely nothing about her.

"What about her brother? I saw him at the memorial. Couldn't he help? Or maybe her parents?"

"Right," he scoffs.

"I'm just, I'm not sure I'm the right—"

"Look. Mia believed in all sorts of hocus-pocusy stuff, right? Kismet and karma and signs in the stars."

I smile like I have any idea what Mia believed.

"And I need help to finish this vision board, and you show up out of the blue—a friend I didn't even know she had. Feels like kismet to me."

Or lies.

I crouch down next to the photos, taking a closer look at each one. They *do* sort of feel like destiny. Like I've been handed a CliffsNotes version of Mia, all her hopes and dreams and story lines. Sure, it's written in code, but if we can crack it, I'll learn everything I need to know.

And then, maybe this heart won't feel like such a stranger.

"I barely knew her," I say, the closest thing to truth I can muster. "And you don't know me at all."

Clayton lays his drill on the floor and crouches down next to me.

"You were hiding in a grave. That's all I need to know. You weren't part of the dog and pony grief show. You were there for Mia. You wanted to do something for *her.*" He points to the board. "This is what we can do. This is how we make things right."

The way he says *make things right* guts me. And maybe it's the existential pancakes or the forgotten tree house or the unfinished dreams of my donor staring me in the face, but I can't say no to this boy. This boy whose best friend—what seems like maybe his *only* friend—is the reason I'm alive.

I'll help him with this vision board, learn about Mia, and then we'll both go our separate ways. Everybody wins.

"I'll try?" I say.

"Good enough for me."

He stands, reaching out for my hands to help me up.

"We start here." He points to a photo shot at a sharp angle

from the ground, making the wooden structure seem massive and foreboding—the tree house. "Always said we'd fix this baby up. Just never found the time."

His words twist my gut, but if I'm going to do this, I can't let on. I pick up the drill and press the trigger, giving it a few little buzzes. He puts his hand on top of mine to lower it.

"Easy there, tiger. First, we need paint and—" He stops mid-sentence to look me up and down. I adjust the fabric covering my scar just in case. "Scratch that. First, we need to get you out of that dress."

CHAPTER NINE

THE OVERALLS ARE A CRIME AGAINST FASHION.

And farmers.

Not that I'm in any sort of position to judge when I've been dressing like a feral raccoon for the last few years, but *still*. I snap the overall bib into place and look into the mirror in the guest bathroom of Clayton's house.

The overalls and T-shirt he handed me are at least three sizes too big. They are definitely boy overalls, not the cute kind that Instagram girls can get away with at a fall pumpkin patch paired with boots and a chic hat. These are *working* overalls, i.e., not Insta-worthy.

But the T-shirt covers my scar, so I call it good enough. I lean into the mirror one more time to smooth down my hair, which is a lot more brown than blond these days since I haven't been out in the sun in a while. I probably need it cut, too, now that I'm leaving the house again. I take the hair tie from my wrist and flip my hair up into a messy bun.

When I exit the bathroom, Clayton's sitting on a bench in front of a faded upright piano that takes up almost the entire family room. With his back toward me, Clayton's fingering a quiet melody.

"You play?" I ask.

Clayton spins around.

"A little."

"I thought all you cowboys played guitar."

"*That* is a hurtful stereotype," he says. "But alas, I'm not a cowboy. You'll note the lack of a ten-gallon hat or belt buckles the size of Texas." He stands and grabs on to his very normal-sized belt. "This is way too small for cowboy status."

I look down to hide the smile I can't help.

"N-no, I didn't mean—" He stumbles over his words as red spreads across his cheeks. "I meant my *buckle* was too small. Nothing else. Everything else is perfectly sized. In case you were wondering."

"I wasn't."

"Good."

"Good."

We stare at each other across the room for a few more seconds, until finally, thankfully, Clayton breaks the silence.

"But speaking of cowboy country, you look . . ."

I do a spin with my arms out, showcasing my oversized overalls.

"Am I giving Rawlins Ridge regular?" I ask.

"It's definitely . . . a vibe."

"Well, slap my hide and butter my biscuits, all my dreams are coming true."

And if I didn't think this boy was completely incapable of *actually* smiling, I'd swear he almost does.

"Nobody dreams of *living* in Rawlins," he says. "They dream of leaving."

"What's with the hometown hostility?"

Clayton shrugs. "Around here, I'm what they call a *transplant.* And locals, they like things homegrown."

"Transplanted from . . ."

"Salt Lake," he says. "Mom dropped me here with Nana when I was nine. But I never quite fit."

Through the kitchen window, I can see the tree house, where he and Mia used to meet. I can almost see them there, hiding together.

"What about Mia? Did she fit?" I ask.

"We fit together." He gets this hazy look for a minute, and then it's like he registers me again. "Not together, together. Obviously. I mean, there was that *one* kiss, but it was purely experimental."

"Experimental?" I ask, trying to ignore the weird and totally inappropriate surge of jealousy going through me. *Best friends,* he said. But were they something more? Is *that* why Mia's heart feels like it's reaching out to him? Why it gets all funky when he looks at me? Maybe I inherited it, just like I was telling Chloe.

"In eighth grade," Clayton continues. "Kissed in the tree house. Just to see how it would feel."

"And . . ."

"And it felt like kissing my sister."

Relief washes over me, along with an ample serving of shame for caring about who this boy kisses. Today's mission is about Mia, I remind myself. And *only* Mia.

But still, I want to ask more. Like is there anyone else he's currently *experimenting* with? And also, why did his mom leave him here and does he *really* play the piano and what else does he do when he's not finishing bucket lists for dead best friends?

"So, now what?" I ask instead, doing my level best to stay on task.

He stands up, puts his baseball hat back on and opens the front door for me.

"To the hardware store." He gives one of my overall suspenders a little tug and lets it snap back against me. "You'll fit right in."

I drive since my car is parked behind the carport that contains Clayton's very dusty pickup truck, which, if you ask me, is like the calling card for cowboys, no matter what Clayton says.

Before Clayton gets in, I throw my notebook into the back seat. Nothing says stalker alert faster than page after page of articles and notes about Mia. I toss all my pills back there, too.

Clayton leads me down to Main Street, which cuts through the center of Rawlins Ridge. All the towns around here have a Main Street—some bigger than others. This one is like stepping back in time.

We get out and walk down the row of storefronts made of brick with names plastered above them in old-fashioned block letters. PETERSON'S PHARMACY, GOODWILL, STODDARD HARD-WARE.

The name above us stops me.

"Wait, Stoddard as in *Mia* Stoddard?"

Clayton nods and points to white letters on the double glass door: *Family owned and operated since 1956.*

A cowbell tied to the door jangles as Clayton opens it. He gestures for me to go first. I slink into the store, doing a quick scan for people. I'm not ready to have a meet and greet with Mia's family. An image of the crying woman at the memorial pops into my head.

Yeah. Not sure I'll *ever* be ready for that.

Stoddard Hardware is a mom-and-pop-style store with only one cash register and an eau de fertilizer that smacks me in the face as I inch past the welcome mat. I follow Clayton past all the farming equipment to the paint aisle.

"What color?" I ask.

"Whatever you think," he says, but he's not looking at me. He keeps checking the front of the store like he's waiting to see someone, or hoping someone doesn't see *him.* I know why *I'm* freaked out being in the Stoddard family store, but why is he so nervous? "Something Mia would like."

I study the little bubbles of color on the side of each can, trying to think which one Mia would pick. How in the world would *I* know? This is my first test and I'm already failing. Come on, brain, think of something. Anything.

I picture the huge poster-sized photo of Mia at the birthday memorial, the one showing off the almost-neon-purple stripe in her hair, right by her face. Better than nothing.

"How about this?" I say, holding up the brightest purple I can find.

Clayton nods approvingly. He grabs another purple can off the shelf and gives my shoulder a little shove with his. "See, you're indispensable already."

And I know it was totally lucky BS, but a win's a win, and for a second or two, I think maybe I can do this. I can fake my way into everything I've ever wanted to know about this heart.

I'm feeling pretty confident until Clayton rings the little bell at the checkout. A boy emerges from the back. I recognize him instantly—Mia's brother. When he sees us, he stops. He mutters something that sounds a lot like a swear word.

"What are *you* doing here?" He throws a red STODDARD HARDWARE apron around his neck.

All my muscles tense up. Does he know who I am? That I shouldn't be here? Is he going to out me right here, right now?

But then he looks up, not at me but at Clayton, with the kind of expression reserved for someone you loathe. Clayton straightens up a bit and adjusts his hat.

"Painting."

"The tree house?" Mia's brother asks.

"Maybe."

"I saw you up there this morning."

"So?"

He bangs the paint down on the counter after scanning it and meets Clayton's stare.

"So you need to leave it alone."

"Leave what alone?"

"You *know* what."

"It's a tree house, Tanner. *My* tree house."

The boy shifts his eyes to me.

"And who's this? A replacement?" He shakes his head as he swats at the little electric total-due sign so it swings toward us. "That was fast. Guess you can hustle when you want to, huh?"

Tanner and Clayton have some sort of stare-off that only lasts five seconds but feels like forever. I could cut the tension with a shovel from the clearance rack. Clayton's hand balls into a fist at his side, the muscles tensing all the way up his arm. Finally, Clayton shoves a wadded stack of bills at Mia's brother and yanks the paint cans off the counter by the handles so hard that one of them swings into the shelf of gum/candy/impulse buys behind us. A bunch of Neccos fall to the floor.

Clayton walks off without getting his change. Mia's brother squats down to pick up the scattered candy while I stand there, wondering what just happened.

He talks to me without looking up.

"I don't know who you are or what you're doing with *him*"—the word drips with hate—"but a word of advice: His own mother dropped him here like a bad habit. You'd be wise to do the same."

Tanner tosses the candy back on the shelf, continuing his rant without a pause.

"I know, I know. I've heard the rumors. Mom was strung out. Big, sad sob story. I don't know and I don't care." He points to the parking lot, where Clayton is standing by the car, waiting for me. "He's a menace."

Clayton's kicking up a cloud of dust with the toe of his boot in the gravel lot, mumbling to himself.

"He doesn't seem—"

I stop, mid-thought, when I look back at Tanner. His eyes are narrowed, like he can't quite believe I'm about to challenge his opinion on the matter.

"You're not from around here, huh?"

"No."

"Then let me tell you everything you need to know about Clayton Cooper. That boy right there?" He gives one more hate-filled glance to the parking lot and then meets my eyes, dead-on. "He killed my sister."

CHAPTER TEN

CLAYTON'S QUIET ALL THE WAY BACK TO HIS HOUSE.

I think back to everything I've read about Mia's death. She was caught in a flash flood in a slot canyon on the northern edge of town. She hit her head. She was declared brain-dead at the hospital.

How could Clayton be responsible for *that*?

I think about how we met, hiding in that tomb. About how he stood on the outskirts of the memorial, eyes cast down, brim of his hat pulled low.

What secrets is *he* keeping?

When we get back to the house, Clayton's still quiet, but he helps me up the rickety tree house ladder.

"Sorry," he says at the top. "Kind of let my emotions get the better of me back there. Tanner and I have"—he pauses—"history."

"History?" I ask, trying to sound casual and not like I'm prying because *Oh, BY THE WAY, that guy just told me you're the reason Mia's dead!*

"Yep," Clayton says. "But Nana says the past is the past. That I need to move on."

I grimace. "I hate when people say that."

He gives me a sideways glance.

"What do *you* have to move on from, Grave Girl?"

My throat goes bone-dry. I shouldn't have said that.

"You know, just . . . life."

And even though I want to know why Tanner said what he said, I decide right then and there that this Nana lady is right: the past should stay put.

Clayton's secrets are his. And mine are mine. It's better for everyone.

"We don't have to talk about it, you know," I say. "The past."

Clayton meets my eyes with a slow, thoughtful nod and then dips his roller in the paint. I take my roller and start painting the wooden slats like Clayton shows me and try to forget what Tanner said. This mission isn't about Clayton anyway—it's about Mia.

The tree house is just a small area, no more than twelve by twelve feet, but I can feel the skin around my scar stretch as I reach to get in all the cracks and crevices. I graduated from cardiac rehab weeks ago, but my body's still getting used to, well, living.

I pause to catch my breath.

"So, tell me your theories," I say, hoping Clayton will be so glad for the subject change that he won't notice I'm out of breath from a little painting.

Clayton keeps rolling the walls while he talks.

"Not totally sure but maybe the pancakes are from a restaurant she wanted to try? She was always finding these hole-in-the-wall places no one else had ever heard of. You know Mia—always doing her own thing."

He keeps talking, and he's every bit as excellent a source as I'd hoped. While he paints the tree house, he paints a picture of Mia in my mind: A stubborn girl who never compromised, even when it drove everyone else crazy. A generous soul who literally gave someone else her shoes once and walked home barefoot just because *they needed them more.* A dreamer, the kind of girl who took photos of all the things she wanted to do in her life so she didn't miss a thing.

And I know this was the plan and pretty much *exactly* what I hoped for, but as he talks, a thought pops into my head: she sounds so . . . perfect. And that thought makes a little ache sprout in my stomach.

I look at Mia's vision board. All her plans. All *I* have is a blank calendar at home and no idea what I'm going to do with this second-chance life.

It's not like I gave up on a future all at once. Just like my heart, it failed over time. I stopped doing plays. Then school. My life shrunk down around me. The size of my house. The size of today. Maybe tomorrow, if I was lucky.

But Mia had dreams.

I touch the blank space in the middle of the collage.

She should be the one still here.

I don't know if it's the thought or the fatigue or the paint fumes, but the familiar feeling of not getting enough air hits me all at once. I close my eyes and try to slow my breathing, tell myself this heart is fine—it's good, strong. Like Dr. Russell said, it's *phenomenal.*

Just like Mia.

"You okay?"

Clayton's voice interrupts my spiraling thoughts.

"Just thinking," I say.

"About Mia?"

I nod. It's true. Just not in the way he assumes.

"Earlier, you said you wanted to do this bucket list to *make things right.* What did you mean?"

He's standing next to me now, our rollers dripping little dots of paint onto the wood.

"It just doesn't seem right, you know?" he says. "Mia was like this force—headstrong and chaotic and unstoppable. And now she's just gone. Her death was so . . . so . . . unfair."

My heartbeat has slowed again, and the air is coming easier, which is such a relief that I don't even think about what I say next.

"Death is *totally* fair," I say.

Clayton's eyebrows furrow together. I *really* shouldn't have said that.

"Sorry, I—"

"No, no." He puts his paintbrush down and folds his arms. "Go on. Please."

I clear my throat. "Well, we're all living with a death sentence. It takes equally. Takes everyone. What could be fairer?"

It feels strange to say these words out loud. The ones I used to think about while lying in bed, listening to my faulty heart. The ones I think about in bed now, listening to Mia's.

I don't usually share those morbid thoughts. People like to talk about death in the abstract, not with the *dying* girl. But I'm not the dying girl, not here, not with him. I'm just a girl—Mia's weird ukulele friend. And that feels, I don't know, kind of nice. Kind of free.

Clayton's looking at me from under the brim of his hat, an unreadable expression on his face. He turns slightly to finish up a spot where the wall meets the roof, dabbing his paintbrush into the corner. I try not to notice how his shirt rides up a little.

"I don't buy it," he says with his back toward me. "You're saying the fact that some people get to grow old while others check out while hiking a slot canyon—that's fair?"

"No, that's definitely unfair. But death is not the villain."

He turns to me.

"Then what is?"

"Life. *Life* is the one serving up the crappy hands, willy-nilly, with no rhyme or reason." I look at the collage again. "The injustice isn't that Mia died, it's that she got shortchanged. By life. Arbitrary, reckless, completely unfair life."

With those last words, I point my paintbrush at him with a little more force than I mean to. Purple paint splatters across his face.

"Oh—oh, I'm sorry," I say, reaching out to wipe it off. My

fingers swipe down his cheek, leaving two little purple trails. "Oh, um, I'm making it worse."

I reach up again, this time with the palm of my hand, but Clayton grabs my wrist.

And doesn't let go.

I've read about moments like this a million times in my books. Moments where the boy grabs the girl's hand, and the girl feels something. A spark. That's what they always call it. As if some sort of electric current could jump from one hand to another.

But I swear, here, right now, in this tiny tree house, my hand feels like it's on fire, shuttling little jolts up my arm, into my hand-me-down heart. And my breath is tight again, not in a panic way; more like this Clayton kid is making me feel hungry for air.

"Are you done?" he says, meeting my eyes square on so that I notice his eyes are not *just* hazel. A glimmer of gold sparkles right beside each pupil.

"Done?"

I can feel my face burning red, and I don't know if it's because I've shared too much or because of his hand on my skin or the way he's looking at me. Or because, for the first time in my life, I'm just a girl, and he's just a boy, and this isn't happening in the pages of a book but to me, right here, right now.

"With your soliloquy. Because I'd like a chance for rebuttal."

"Oh, yes, I'm done," I say. "Totally done."

Clayton lets go of my wrist, which is about the worst thing that's ever happened to me in my entire life, and turns toward the photos.

"Maybe you're right. But this project, finishing this for her, doing the things she wanted to do, feels like what she would want. Feels like cheating death"—he pauses—"or life—out of a small part of its arbitrary, reckless, completely unfair victory."

His answer is incomplete. It's obvious by the tone of his voice, like he's trying to convince himself. The way he clenches his jaw as his eyes linger on the photos. He's holding something back, another reason he needs to do this. And I'd bet my life that it has to do with what Tanner told me.

But one thing is clear: he's a little bit broken, a little stitched together, just like me.

So I don't ask for more, because maybe he needs us to be just a boy and a girl for a moment, too. Who am I to take that from him? From either of us?

"Well, I think Mia would like that," I say.

"We finally agree," Clayton says, and he gives a slight smile that's . . . rusty. Like the muscles in his face aren't used to it.

And I'm *definitely* rusty at being a normal teenage girl, so I'm not quite sure what to make of the fact that even though he's not touching me anymore, the electricity is still there. It feels like—

The sun's gone down. As soon as I realize this, I pat my pockets, but my phone's not there. I must have left it in the car with my clothes.

"What time is it?" I ask.

"Little after eight," Clayton says, looking at his phone.

My pill. It's past time for my pill.

"I have to go," I say.

"Right now?"

"Yeah, *right* now." The heartbeat in my ears is getting louder, faster. I've *never* missed a tacrolimus. "Can I return the overalls later?"

"Anytime," he says. "Bring 'em to our next vision board outing."

He dips slightly in a bow and gestures toward the photos. "Lady's choice."

Even though I *have* to go, I scan the photos, all the dreams Mia never got to finish. Since I have no idea what most of them even mean, I close my eyes, spin myself around twice and then point.

When I open my eyes, my finger's pressed into the photo of the lake with the NO TRESPASSING sign.

"Well, Grave Girl, hope you have a suit," Clayton says. "'Cause we're going swimming."

CHAPTER ELEVEN

8:15 P.M.

Fifteen minutes late on my tac.

I swallow the tacrolimus along with my other PM pills as soon as I get in the car.

How could I miss it? I've *never* missed it.

My breath is heavy again, and even though I tell myself it's just a combination of paint fumes and overexertion, full-on panic courses through me. I'm so far from home, and no one knows where I am except Clayton, who has no idea *who* I am or that only four months ago I had my heart ripped out of me.

I look out the window of the car, where the sun is setting behind the western hills.

What am I *doing* out here?

The alarm I set on my phone for tac time is still going off from somewhere in the back seat. I rifle through my clothes to find it. My parents have sent a bunch of texts. I fire a quick one back telling them I'm on my way, that I'm totally fine.

Because I am.

Fifteen minutes isn't going to kill me.

Right?

I lay my head back and listen to Mia's heart. It beats, strong and steady, against the fingertip I push against my neck. I start up the car and pull away, still paying close attention to the rhythm in my chest. It doesn't help that my whole body feels a little jumpy. I blame it on the Clayton of it all.

But just to be safe, I check my pulse one more time.

By the time I get home, I want to lie down in bed, maybe take my blood pressure and pulse ox reading, but my parents are waiting just inside the front door. Mom gives me this massive, almost desperate hug.

"Are you *okay*?" She stands back to scan me head to toe. "You didn't answer our texts."

"Oh, I put my phone on silent," I say. That's when I notice the kitchen table, set and waiting. "Oh, sorry, I found this little spot across the highway and just kind of vegged. Read my book."

"For six hours?" she asks. There's an edge to her voice.

"Kind of lost track of time."

"You took your pills?" Mom asks as we sit at the table.

I nod.

"On time?"

"I know how to take my pills."

Dad sits up straighter in his chair.

"Your mom's just worried, Syd. This is new, for all of us."

Mom's staring at her salmon, which she learned how to cook last summer because fish are full of heart-healthy omega-3s and antioxidants. A wave of guilt hits me.

"I'm sorry, Mom. I should have checked in. I will, next time."

Mom puts her hand on mine and gives it a little squeeze. Thankfully, Dad starts talking about something that happened at the college today, and Mom seems super interested in it, which means I can just nod along without much brainpower.

Because all *my* thoughts keep going back to today. The way Clayton's hand felt on mine, the look on Tanner's face when he said Clayton got Mia killed; but above it all is the vision board. After I pointed to Mr. Johnson's swimming pond, Clayton said we should go tonight.

"As in *tonight,* tonight?" I asked.

He said, "If I've learned one thing this year, it's that tomorrow's not guaranteed."

And damn, if I didn't feel that in my bones.

So against my better judgment, I told him maybe. He *almost* looked like he might smile for real and said he'd be there at midnight, with or without me.

But my parents are already kind of spiraling about *a drive.* No way they'd let me go swimming at midnight with a boy I just met. And if they knew that boy was my suspected donor's best friend who also may or may not have had a hand in her death, they'd shut the whole thing down.

I'd have to sneak out.

*   *   *

After dinner I lie down on my bed because, if I'm being totally honest, my breath is feeling funny again. I try not to think about how I was late on my pill.

Buzz. Buzz.

So you in or out?

My phone says it's nine p.m., which means I have three hours to make up my mind: in or out?

Today was stupid. That much I know. My heartbeat *is* still a little jumpy. The last thing I need is to trigger a rejection episode. And what about Clayton? Maybe that electric feeling between us was all in my head, a symptom of reading *way* too many novels featuring horny teens, but it felt *very* real—which is *very* dangerous. Because *nothing* could ever happen between us. He was her best friend. I have her heart.

If I were smart, I wouldn't even be thinking about going.

So I must be a total idiot, because all I can think is how Clayton said he wants to *make things right.* And maybe Clayton *did* have something to do with Mia's death, but I spent the last two years wishing on candles and in prayers and on shooting stars—hoping that the right person would die in the right way for me to live.

And I got my wish.

Whatever Clayton did, it can't be worse than that.

Maybe it's time for me to make things right, too. To do more than just find out who Mia was. To make some of her unfinished dreams come true.

So what if it's a little risky? Don't I owe her at least that?

These kinds of questions are too big to ponder alone. I flop on my bed and dial Chloe. Her mom answers my FaceTime. Tells me they're at the hospital for tests.

"Everything okay?" I ask.

Her mom smiles the same big, when-life-gives-you-lemons-throw-a-margarita-party smile that Chloe does.

"Oh, darlin', you know Chloe. She's *always* okay. I'll tell her you called."

I say thanks and hang up, wondering why Chloe didn't tell me about these *tests* herself. I watch her latest post on TheWaiting-List. She's in a hospital bed, with an industrial-grade air cannula up her nose and a hideous hospital gown with clowns on it instead of her usual vintage tees. Hundreds of people from around the world have already left comments. She ends her video like she ends them all: *"This is Chloe Munoz. Let the beat go on."*

Maybe it's best she didn't answer. *Tests* are never good news, and the last thing she probably wants to hear about is my new-heart dilemma.

I stare into my closet, hoping to find the answer in there. I pull out a hideously yellow one-piece bathing suit with pineapples on it. The tag says size fourteen, which means this suit is from eighth grade, before my boobs and hips and sick heart made their illustrious debuts. I squeeze myself into it and turn sideways in the mirror. *Way* too small. And too revealing. Clayton would for sure see my scar.

Nothing fits right anymore.

I take it off and toss it in the trash bin. It lands half-in, half-out. Maybe that's why I can't decide what to do with my future *or* tonight—nothing fits.

I turn to my *Guide to Life After Transplant* booklet. The

precautions-after-surgery section says I'm fine to swim by four months out as long as my scar is healed, but I have to be careful not to snort a bunch of nasty lake water up my nose. For a *Guide to Life*, it's woefully unhelpful.

When I toss the brochure back on my desk, the back cover catches my eye. It's some ad for the cardiovascular center with the words *Follow Your Heart* in bright red letters.

I stare at my reflection again.

Follow your heart.

But which one?

My old heart would probably have told me to forget this whole thing. To not trespass into a pond. To not lie to my parents about where I'm going or to Clayton about who I am. To play it safe, and keep this heart safe, too. It would say I should be content that I've hit the mother lode of information about Mia and be done with this whole charade.

But what would *her* heart tell me?

I take off my robe. My transplant scar bisects me with a deep purple line running from just under my collarbone to just above my navel.

After more than sixteen weeks, it's less Frankenstein's monster than right after the surgery with all the black stitches holding me together. Back then, I'd have nightmares about it opening, the skin just zip-zip-zipping wide open and this new heart tumbling out.

I run my finger down the purple line that splits me in two. To remove your heart, the doctors break you in half, cracking your rib cage like a wishbone.

Once you're open, they take out the diseased organ. For a few minutes, you're heartless. Lifeless. The only thing standing between you and death is a bypass machine. I try not to think about this too much. Me, all sorts of open and exposed, my new heart half-sewn-in, my old heart—well, actually, I don't know. I'm not sure what they do with the old heart. Throw it away, maybe? Some janitor takes out the hazardous waste before clocking out and chucks all the used-up hearts into some medical dumpster?

The lifeless strings of the bathing suit in the trash can catch my eye. And there's something about the sad, limp way it's half-hanging out of the bin that sends me the clearest message so far tonight.

My old heart is gone.

I can't follow it anymore.

I smash the bathing suit fully down into the trash, and then I grab some shorts and a T-shirt with a high collar. I pack a small bag with a change of clothes and a towel and shove it under my bed.

Then, I wait for midnight.

Because even though my old heart would have told me to stay, this new one, the only one I still have, is telling me to go.

CHAPTER TWELVE

AT NIGHT, MAIN STREET IN RAWLINS RIDGE FEELS LIKE A graveyard. It's eerie and quiet and dark except for a few flickering streetlamps.

The directions Clayton gave me take me all the way to the foothills where the town butts up against the mountains west of the valley.

As I pull up, my headlights shine on Clayton leaning against a massive oak tree next to a very serious barbed wire fence with numerous NO TRESPASSING signs. Beyond that, Mr. Johnson's infamous pond.

"You came," Clayton says.

"I came." I make no mention of the intense internal battle that preceded my decision, how this heart—*her* heart—told me to come or how I'm counting on this gamble to *make things right* for me, too.

"Opening's this way," he says, waving me after him.

"Thought you'd never done this," I say, eyeing the big yellow sign right above it: TRESPASSING IS A CLASS B MISDEMEANOR. SIX MONTHS JAIL OR $1,000 FINE.

"I haven't. But I've heard the rumors." He leads me to a tiny gap in the fence. "Always figured Mia and I would do it before we left."

"Left?"

Clayton clears out some loose brush and tumbleweeds covering the entry. "Mia was always too big for this town. No way it could keep her."

"Where was she gonna go?"

"Somewhere not here. I promised to get her out of here, someday." He holds the wire of the fence apart for me to crawl through. "Guess we ran out of somedays."

He says this matter-of-factly, like it's not the saddest thing I've ever heard. Sad enough that I ignore the intimidating sign and squeeze myself through the hole. I'm careful not to let the pointy ends of the metal scrape me as I go through. Sneaking out of the house was easy enough thanks to the dull roar of Dad's sleep apnea machine, but my parents will kill me themselves if I come home with a tetanus infection.

Clayton contorts through the fence after me. I follow him down to the pond, where he shucks off his shirt. The moonlight casts shadows on his chest. Let me just say right here, it's not like Clayton is some muscled-up beefcake or something, but it's the only boy body I've seen up close since eighth grade, when most of my male peers were all knees and elbows and fart jokes.

And right now, with the moon making everything all kind of soft and beautiful and mysterious, it looks good. *He* looks good.

I jerk my eyes away and focus on taking off my shoes, reminding myself that if I'm going to do this vision board, it's got to be about Mia, and *only* Mia. Giving her back a piece of what I stole. I'm not going to let my just-a-boy-and-a-girl fantasies run away with me again. No sparks. No noticing eye color. No losing my breath. Period.

His eyes rove up my body as I stand there barefoot in my T-shirt and shorts.

"Activity-appropriate clothing really isn't your thing, huh?" he asks as he reaches out his hand toward me without waiting for an answer. When I don't take it right away, he adds, "It's just a little steep getting in."

It's just a hand, Syd. Get a grip.

I take his hand and try to ignore the electricity where he touches me. He leads me down to the water, pushing aside a bunch of willow reeds forming a fluttery border around the edge of the pond. The muddy incline *is* steep, and squishy. The bottom of the pond squelches up between my toes.

I giggle involuntarily.

"You okay?" Clayton asks.

"Totally. I just, well, I just can't believe I'm doing this. What if we get caught?"

Clayton lets go of my hand as we clear the steep bank, and a part of me wishes he'd hang on longer. But he pushes out into the water, his arms sending ripples into the glassy surface.

"Then we run." He flips over so he's facing me. "Don't worry. Mr. Johnson doesn't usually shoot to kill."

"Oh, I feel so much better now."

I stand in the shallow water, glancing back toward the shore one more time. I really *cannot* believe I'm doing this.

My mind ticks back to the *Guide to Life After Transplant* brochure, all its warnings about lake water and bacteria and overexertion and the million other risks to someone like me. Plus, the way the moonlight is gleaming off Clayton's chest as he glides through the water, slow and quiet, like he's whispering a secret to the night?

Definitely risky.

But standing on the edge of the water, another thought hits me. The brochure is about *life* after transplant. I've spent so much of my life trying not to die. What if tonight, I don't?

What if I just . . . live?

That's what Mia would do. She was clearly the kind of girl who would dive right in. No second thoughts.

I close my eyes, take a breath and sink into the water.

The feeling is one I'd almost forgotten. The chill of the water as it overtakes me. How my body goes weightless. It's . . . incredible.

I guess swimming is one of those things you don't have time to mourn when you get sick, the mundane pieces of life that are just *poof,* gone. Like running and biking and hanging out at Randy's on Friday nights. Or being able to eat whatever you want without worrying about infection or drug interaction. Being able to imagine growing old.

I let the water pull me in.

I kick onto my back like Clayton does, careful not to get my head under. Above me, the night sky is showing off, the stars beaming like spotlights.

Clayton's quiet for a long time. Eventually the water rolls us together, our shoulders bumping every so often.

"Mia ever tell you her star theory?" he asks.

"I don't . . . I don't think so," I say, as if I'm thinking real hard about what Mia did or did not share during our fakity-fake friendship.

"She saw a documentary once. Couldn't shut up about it. How everything we are, every piece of this earth, started in those stars, forged in their intense heat," he says. "The calcium in our bones, the oxygen we breathe, the iron in our blood, every piece of carbon in us, all of them have been around since the beginning of time. We're all made of pieces of the past."

He's standing above me now, his face blocking the stars. "Oh, hold still, you have a bit of Einstein in your hair." He pretends to pick something off me. "And a little bit of Aristotle right"—he flicks something off my forehead—"got it."

I laugh. "Okay, that's a little creepy."

Clayton shrugs.

"Mia believed we're all just borrowed stardust."

Mia's heart beats loud into my ears, my own borrowed pieces reacting to Clayton's words.

"Well, that part's kind of beautiful."

"I guess," he says, floating on his back again. "But I think it's just something people tell themselves to make death less scary."

"Death isn't all that scary."

"Ah yes, I forgot." He gives my shoulder a little shove. "I'm talking to the death expert."

"I'm not an *expert*," I say, and maybe it's the spell of the starlight or Clayton sharing something kind of personal, but I decide to take another risk, to share something, too—a small piece of myself. "But I *did* almost die one time."

I don't tell him about my heart, just that I was sick a lot as a kid.

"One time was pretty bad, and long story short, doctors said they'd done all they could do," I say.

Clayton is dead silent as I talk. The water has moved him next to me so his shoulder is pressed up against mine. I don't move away.

"And that didn't scare the crap out of you?" he asks.

"At first. I was scared for my parents. I was scared it was going to hurt. I was scared of the unknown. I was pretty fond of living."

I leave out the part about how, when I first realized that *this was it,* I cried like a baby.

"But then, it was like my body and mind accepted it. And the funny thing is, when you've been scared of something so long, holding the fear so tight, letting go is kind of, I don't know, a re-lief. And all that was left was calm. Peace. I was floating, just like this." I splash my fingertips in the water. "I was free."

Clayton lets out a big breath.

"I hope it felt like that for Mia," he says.

"Me too."

And at least that much is true. Because whenever I think about that night, I think about her, in a hospital bed just like mine, hooked up to machines. Did she have a central line to her heart, too? Was her room filled with balloons and teddy bears and *Get Well Soons*? What moments flashed before *her* eyes?

I think about how, when the doctor came into my room with *the news,* there was confusion, then joy as we understood: I was going to live. We hugged. We cried.

But what about *her* family? A doctor delivering *their* news: their daughter wouldn't wake up. They probably hugged. They probably cried.

And while they mourned, we celebrated.

"Were you there?" I ask. "When she . . ."

Clayton shakes his head.

"Not at the very end." His voice cracks. He tries to hide it by clearing his throat. "Her dad didn't want me—"

He stops cold. He's avoiding this conversation again—the one about the past. Except the way he talks about Mia, I can't help but think Tanner's wrong about whatever role he thinks Clayton played in Mia's accident.

"But we were talking about *you,*" he says.

I can feel him looking at me so I turn to look at him, his face floating in the water, his eyes never leaving mine.

"What?" I ask.

He searches my face. "Are all the city girls like you? So . . . I don't know, deep?"

I stand up in the water, suddenly aware of how much of my past I just shared with this boy who I *really* don't want finding out about my past. I try to change the subject, and fast.

"First of all, I'm from Cherry Hill. Not quite a booming metropolis."

He smirks as he stands up next to me, whipping his dark, wet hair out of his eyes. "You got a Walmart."

"That does *not* make me a city girl."

"Oh yeah?"

He splashes water up at my face. I splash him back, harder, and I'm not even sure why except that it seems like the thing to do in this moment.

"Yeah."

And the next thing I know, we're splashing each other like our lives depend on it, and I'm laughing so hard that I lose my footing in the mushy mud. Clayton grabs me before I go under.

With one arm around my back, he's holding my wrists with the other so I can't splash him, and we're face-to-face, that little smirk playing on his lips, his breath on my skin.

"You know what?" he says.

"What?"

"I think you might be right. Beneath that city shine, you've got the heart of a country girl."

I pull back from him.

"What? How—"

"Because no city girl could commit a Class B misdemeanor *and* look this good doing it."

I realize that he wasn't talking about my *actual* heart at the same second I realize that he's flirting with me, which leaves me so discombobulated with both relief and worry that I just kind of stand there, frozen. My face must give me away, because he immediately pulls his hands off me, putting them up like a busted criminal.

"I didn't—I'm sorry, I just meant—"

"No, no, *I'm* sorry, I thought—"

We both stutter our way into silence and stand there looking at each other, the playful moment from before drowned in a sea of awkwardness.

"I'm doing this for Mia," I say.

"Right, right. Of course." He moves away from me, raking his fingers through his wet hair. "Me too."

He seems like he might say something else, and the only thing I can think is *tell him. Tell him the truth. Tell him why nothing can happen between us. Tell him who I am.*

But I don't get the chance. A gunshot rips the night in half.

Clayton's eyes go wide in the dark. In the distance, someone cocks a shotgun and yells some select obscenities in our direction.

"What do we do?" I whisper.

"Run."

We swim toward the shore, and when it's too shallow to swim, we slog through the mud, our feet sliding. When we get to the steep entry, I think, or maybe I imagine, that Clayton reaches out his hand to me for a split second before putting it back by his side. I grab a bunch of reeds instead and hoist myself out of the water.

He holds the fence hole open for me, and then we run.

Another gunshot fires into the air, ringing through the dark. My body is freezing in the night, but it feels good—alive. I haven't run like this in years, but just like with swimming, my body remembers. The cold air rushes past my face, my lungs gasp for breath, the muscles in my thighs strain.

By the time we get to our cars, I'm breathing so hard that I feel a little woozy. But it's not the kind of breathless that makes me want to take my pulse ox reading and hook up to my air tank.

This is the kind of breathless that reminds me that death *didn't* win in that hospital room.

I did.

I steady myself on Clayton's truck. And then I'm laughing. So hard that I lose my breath all over again.

And that's when I realize Clayton's laughing, too. The sound of it bounces off the water, off the clouds above us, off the moon.

"What was that about death not being scary?" Clayton says.

And for the first time since we met, Clayton smiles—a real smile. A grin so wide and open it creates little wrinkles in the corners of his eyes. A smile so bright it lights up the dark.

A smile I never want to stop.

"For what it's worth," he says, "I'm glad you didn't die, Grave Girl."

"Why? So you could get me shot?"

"No, no, I swear!" he says, still kind of laughing, that little dimple by his mouth going wild. But then his face falls serious. "It's just, well, I promised Mia the world, and I'm just a boy with some pictures. But at least we can give her those." He watches his toe dig into the dirt. "It's like you said, that's the reason we're here, right?"

"For Mia," I say, holding my hand out in the space between us.

He shakes it like we're striking an official deal, holding on to each other for a second or two longer than is strictly necessary.

"For Mia."

I smile all the way home.

Partly because my blood is still pumping and adrenaline is

still coursing through me, raw and alive and exhilarating, from running, from swimming, from coming this close to getting shot or jailed or whatever.

But also because Clayton's given me an idea. One that makes me feel giddy, like I'm not just an impostor here. Like maybe there's a way I can contribute, a way to turn this project into something bigger, something that Mia deserves.

Because Clayton may not know how to give her the world, but I do.

CHAPTER THIRTEEN

MY PARENTS ARE STILL ASLEEP WHEN I SNEAK BACK INTO
the house, Dad's snoring machine blocking out the world.

Thoughts of tonight buzz through my brain—the thrill of
running, the gunshot cracking the air, how Clayton looked at
me in the water, his smile lighting up the night. And above all
that noise, there's the idea for how I'm going to share Mia's vision board with the world.

But I can't do it alone. Which is why my first call in the morning is to Chloe.

She answers, her hair tousled into a quasi rat's nest.

"Time difference," she whispers, her voice scratchy. "It's only
seven a.m. here. This better be seven-a.m. important."

"It is, I promise," I say. "But first, since when do you go inpatient without telling me?"

"No big," she says, starting to wake up. She sits up in her

hospital bed, and I can see the exact second she sees herself in her FaceTime reflection. She starts trying to tame her hair. "Just a little tune-up."

"Don't lie to me, Chloe Munoz. I can see your posters."

Behind her bed hangs a demotivational poster. Chloe has a whole collection of them to mock the inane inspirational ones you see in hospitals, espousing empty platitudes like *Hope is the only thing stronger than fear.* When she's in for a long inpatient stay, Chloe always hangs one behind her bed. Today's has a picture of a bristly porcupine with the slogan *ATTITUDE: If you can't handle me at my worst, you deserve to also know it's my best.*

She also hangs her favorite Chloe original—a painting of a heart and the ocean, Chloe's favorite place on earth. The heart, an anatomically correct replication with veins and chambers and everything, hangs over the ocean like a setting sun. Below it, the words *dum spiro, spero,* Latin for *while I breathe, I hope.*

The point is, if the posters are already on the wall, this is definitely more than a tune-up. And I can't help but think that her *not* calling me has something to do with my brand-new heart.

"Seriously. What's going on?" I ask.

"Too early for med talk," she says, waving her hand in the camera. She's given up on her hair. "Cut to the chase. What couldn't wait until after my beauty sleep?"

I sigh, extra dramatic so Chloe knows I'm onto her diversion skills. Getting Chloe to talk about her heart when she doesn't want to is a losing battle.

I tell her everything—every last detail. About how Clayton

texted me and I went to the tree house to learn more about Mia. I text her a picture of the vision board. I tell her about committing my first misdemeanor last night.

I leave out the part about how when Clayton touches me, I feel kind of buzzy all over. She'd make a whole *thing* about it, and this is not a thing. It's a nothing. Just a silly girl who has read too many rom-coms.

"In a *lake*?" Chloe says when I get to that part. "Are you out of your mind? Do you know how dangerous—"

"I know," I say, cutting off her lecture. "But look, I'm here, I'm fine."

"You got *lucky*," she says. There's an edge to the word.

I smile, trying to lighten the mood. "What? I've cheated death before. It's kind of my thing."

Chloe grimaces. "Now you're being reckless *and* cocky."

I sigh. "I'm being *normal*, Chlo. And so what if it is a little dangerous? It's working. Clayton's already told me so much about Mia. Like how they used to hide out in this old tree house. She seems like she was a really good friend. And fearless—enough to want to trespass into a shotgun-guarded pond. She was like this force of life, fun and brave and deep, and honestly, perfect."

Chloe gives me a disapproving glance through the screen.

"And human," she says. "Don't forget that little detail. She was a girl, not a saint."

I wave my hand to brush off her comment. Chloe doesn't know what it's like to have someone else's heart beating inside you. To feel like their legacy—everything they were, everything they could have become—is now part of you.

"Point is, each picture is telling me more. And next time—"

"*Next* time?" Chloe holds the phone closer to her face all dramatic. "Please tell me I heard that wrong. That there's some faulty Utah-to-California cell reception or something."

I don't answer, which is answer enough for her.

"Sydney! You wanted to find out about your donor. Mission accomplished. Move on."

"I know. I *know*. But there's been a slight change of plans."

Chloe gives me a smile.

"It's the boy, isn't it?"

"No!" I say a little too defensively.

Chloe's still smiling like she knows there's more to the Clayton story—and she's right. But this isn't one of the works of fiction on my nightstand. This is *real* life, and it's complicated, and people could get hurt. That's all that matters. Not the funny little way Clayton's mouth turns up at the corners when he tries not to smile or the freckles on the bridge of his nose or the fact that when I'm with him, I'm not the sick girl.

A nurse comes in before I can explain all that. She starts wiping down Chloe's arm with antiseptic and waves to me from the side of the screen.

Chloe doesn't even wince when the needle shoves into her arm. Poking and prodding—another staple of life on the list.

We wait for the nurse to finish before we keep talking. What we're discussing is against about a gazillion confidentiality rules. It's not like they'd take the heart back, but I would be in *loads* of trouble and Dr. Russell would convene my transplant committee for sure.

When the nurse finally leaves with her Chloe samples, I continue: "It's not about the boy. At all. It's because of something the boy said. About how if we finish this vision board, it'll make things right."

Chloe puts her hand up to her head like I'm giving her a headache.

"We're already making things right, giving people hope. On a little thing called TheWaitingList? The channel you've *abandoned.*"

"Well, actually, that's kind of why I'm calling," I say, treading lightly because our channel is Chloe's baby. I've always just kind of been her sidekick. "Our site gave me an idea. An idea to turn Mia's vision board into something bigger. Something people all over the world could see."

Chloe's eyes light up.

"You want to do a post about this vision board!"

"Exactly. But just, well, not for TheWaitingList."

Her hand flies to her chest. "You're cheating on me?"

I take a big breath. Here goes nothing.

"I want to start another page. A new one. One *just* about Mia, where people could do her vision board with us."

"So do that on TheWaitingList."

"I can't. What if Clayton finds it? He'll see me on my old videos. It won't take him long to put it all together. It has to be totally anonymous. So even if he finds the new page, he won't find the old me."

Chloe smirks.

"Ah yes, secrecy, the foundation of any healthy relationship."

"Again, there is no *relationship*. But if he finds out, this whole thing will be over."

"Which would be a good thing, if you ask me. That cowboy of yours deserves the truth."

"Trust me, Chlo. *This* is what Clayton wants. And also, I think it's what Mia wants, or what she would have wanted."

Chloe balks, but I keep going.

"And it's like, living on the list, we're—we're parasites. We take to live. Sucking fake air from tanks. Stealing time and money from the people we love. Literally ripping the beating heart from someone else's chest. This is my chance to give back. To repay my debt to her, to the universe, to everyone."

"Okay, can we dial the drama down like ten volumes, please?" She sighs and leans back on her pillow. "If you're determined to do this, go ahead. Start your own site. You don't need my permission to—oh." Chloe looks directly into the screen. She's figured me out. "You sneaky little minx. You need my subscribers."

"I just need to borrow them," I say. "I don't have months to build my own. Maybe you could post on TheWaitingList, direct your peeps to my page?"

Her face tells me I've crossed a line. She doesn't get it. Any of this. She's still on the waiting side. She doesn't know how it feels to carry the weight of someone's death.

I make one last-ditch effort.

"I can't explain it, Chloe. But I need to do this. And I need your help. *Please.*"

Chloe slouches back into her hospital bed with a big sigh. Her face softens slightly.

"Pull on my shitty heartstrings, why don't ya?"

She's looking up at her ceiling instead of at me, flicking the tubing of her air cannula while she thinks. Finally, she points at me through the screen.

"For the record, I'm against this whole thing," she says. "But I do respect a boy who can make Sydney Wells commit a misdemeanor. . . ."

Chloe smiles, and I know she's in. I squeal. "Ah, you're the best! And I promise, when this is over, I'll be back, full-time, posting so much on our channel that you won't be able to keep up."

"Believe it when I see it," she says. The nurse has come back in and is messing with all the tubes hanging from the IV tree by Chloe's bed. "Send me the link to your adulterous page when you've got it up and running. And, Sydney, just so we're clear, you *so* owe me."

As the nurse starts wiping down her arm again, I blow her a kiss through the screen.

"Join the club."

I'm on my bed with my laptop, "resting" and staring at an Instagram page. I name it @TheMiaProject, and I leave my name totally off it. I'm grateful that my name isn't on TheWaitingList, either. Mom didn't think I should have my real name on YouTube, so there's little chance Clayton will find either site if he happens to Google my name or something. There *is* a slight chance my parents will see Chloe's post about it, but it's small. They stopped watching our channel once I stopped posting. All in all, I'm pretty safe.

In the page description, I write, *This account is dedicated to a friend who died too young. She didn't get to finish her bucket list, but you can.*

I post the first photo, one I took of the tree house after we painted it. The caption reads: *Where did you feel safe as a kid? Your hideouts, your refuge from the world? Revisit it. Post a pic and tag with—*

I stare at the screen for a long time, trying to figure out the perfect hashtag to complete my first post. I try out #bucketlist, #visionboard and #MiaProject, but they don't feel quite right. It has to be something that gets to the heart of what I'm doing here.

I pull up the picture of Mia's tree house collage on my phone. All the plans she had. All the life she didn't get to live.

The life that beats in me.

I start typing as the words come—*#ForMia.*

CHAPTER FOURTEEN

Monday at 2 . . . my house? I've got a lead on the photos.

Will there be shotguns?

I make no promises. Just bring your detective skills. I'll bring my houndstooth jacket

Whoa whoa whoa, why do YOU get to be Sherlock?

Wait, is he not the devastatingly handsome one?

and also kind of a douche

Oh Watson, chin up. We've got a case to crack!

I reread our texts five times to make sure there was no flirting on my end. It's been five days since I've heard from Clayton, and I'm sure my quasi rejecting him in the pond has something to do with it. But as long as we make this all about Mia, no one gets hurt.

I was glad for the break, honestly. Between painting and a midnight swim, my body's tired, but in a good way—in a way that means I've been doing something with my days. It's a feeling I didn't even realize I missed.

I pull up my new Insta page, TheMiaProject. Chloe made good on her promise and got a bunch of her subscribers all excited about my #ForMia missions. Already, I have 1,200 followers and ten new posts using the hashtag. I scroll through a few of the replies to my call for pictures of childhood safe places. A girl from the East Coast posted a picture of a creek bed with a rope swing.

Haven't been back in years, but all the feelings came right back! #ForMia

A boy posted about a family cabin. He said they sold it years ago but are going camping nearby this weekend #ForMia. A mom of three says she doesn't have a picture but she always felt safest with her dad.

Gonna drop by and surprise him. Share a bottle of Coke! #ForMia

Even though I'm not sure if I believe the whole memories-stored-in-hearts theory, I can't help feeling like this is where Mia's heart has been leading me all along. These people—these strangers—are responding to Mia's unfulfilled dreams.

I post Mia's picture of Mr. Johnson's pond next.

Take a risk. #ForMia

When Monday rolls around, I realize I'll need another excuse to go out. I can't keep *going on drives.* So around one-thirty p.m., I find myself launching into a story about how I reached out to my old friend Bree.

Luckily Dad is at work, so I only have to convince Mom, who is *thrilled* that I took her advice and that I'm going to the mall with Bree, just like old times. Of course, she has lots of concerns about crowds and germs and *doing too much,* but her excitement that I'm doing a normal teenage girl thing with another normal teenage girl outweighs all that, and she hands me some sanitizer and gives me a tight hug.

"Before you go, there's something I wanted to talk to you about." She's grinning in this kind of uncontrollable way as she goes into the kitchen. She comes back waving a stack of brochures. "I was waiting for your dad to get home, but I just can't."

She presents the stack to me with a theatrical "Ta-da!" The picture on the top brochure has a big stone building on it.

"College?" I ask.

There's a little knot in my throat, just like when Dr. Russell gave me the calendar and when I first saw Mia's vision board.

Mom gives my shoulder a little nudge. "This is a *good* thing, Sydney. This was the plan, right?"

Yeah. *Before.*

"What would I even study?" I ask, thumbing through the pamphlets that tell me *THE FUTURE IS BRIGHT!*

Mom grins and pulls out one of the brochures.

"Whatever you want!" She points to a page with a stage on it. "Like look here, a theater program! Remember how much you loved doing plays?"

"I was thirteen."

"Yes, but you're still you."

"Debatable," I mumble mostly to myself.

Mom sighs.

"You don't have to decide right now," Mom says, her grin faltering. "You've got time, Syd. That's the wonderful thing about all of this—you got more time." She reaches out and holds my hand. "So what do you want to do with it?"

I close the brochure. These plans—these dreams—belong to someone I don't know anymore. I can't waltz back into my old life, or onto a stage, like nothing's changed. I can't just pick up where I left off.

I check the time on my phone. Clayton's waiting. I don't have time to think about the future right now. Besides, working on this project—making things right with Mia—finally feels like I'm moving forward, just like everyone wants.

"I'll think about it," I say.

Another lie. I'm full of them these days. But it's for her own good. Otherwise, she'd fret about me *stalling my progress*, like Dr. Russell said.

Before I leave, I stick the college brochures in my desk drawer and slam it shut.

Clayton's pruning a bush in the front yard when I pull up. His baseball hat is pulled down low, so he doesn't notice me until I'm right next to him, standing above a shovel and bag of dirt.

He jumps a little and takes out his earphones.

"You almost gave me a heart attack." He looks at his watch. "I lost track of time."

I scan all the beautiful bushes and roses and immaculate hedges.

"Do you do all this?" I ask.

"Gotta earn my keep." He pats the top of the mound of dirt where he's just buried the roots of a very round, green plant. "Mums. Nana's favorite."

He brushes his hands off on his pants, leaving trails of dirt on his jeans.

"My car?" I ask.

He shakes his head. "We're walking."

The road is gravel, although it may have been asphalt at one point, probably ripped to shreds by years of summer heat and winter snow and two-ton tractors like the one that crawls along beside us before turning off into an alfalfa field. Clayton kicks a rock as we walk. He's unusually quiet, and I wonder if he's measuring each word for flirtiness, too.

Part of me wants to tell him about TheMiaProject, but the slight risk he might trace me back to TheWaitingList stops me.

"So," I say, eager to break the silence. "Tell me more about this lead."

Clayton gives the rock one final forceful kick. It ricochets down the street and into the weeds.

"Well, I was thinking we need to get as many eyes on this thing as we can. That's the only way we're going to figure out all the pictures. And that missing one in the middle. *That's* the one that's really got me. It's the biggest spot on the collage—

must have been important. Something Mia wanted more than anything."

We stop in front of a house, the only one visible on the same street as Clayton's. The house is worn a bit, the paint around the front door chipping and cracked, probably from the wind that is blocked by nothing but a few kind-of-straggly trees in the front yard. I'm beginning to think everything in Rawlins Ridge is a bit broken.

"They could use your green thumb," I say, careful to land squarely in complimentary territory while avoiding flirtation-ville.

Clayton pulls his baseball cap lower over his eyes.

"First, let's see if they even let me inside."

"Who?" I ask, but he's already knocking on the door, his eyes down like they were the first time I met him at the memorial. And I know the answer to my question.

But before I can tell Clayton this is a terrible idea, the door cracks open. And there, looking right at me, is the woman from the cemetery, the woman from the newspaper articles, the woman who I've thought about every time my own mother hugs me.

Mia's mom.

And I swear, this heart skips a beat.

CHAPTER FIFTEEN

UP CLOSE, SHE'S FRAIL, LIKE A STRONG WIND MIGHT crack her as easily as the outside paint.

She opens the door only slightly, but a big smile spreads across her face when she sees Clayton. I was not expecting *that*. It seems Clayton wasn't, either, the way he exhales like he'd been waiting for permission.

Before she opens the door all the way, Mia's mom pokes her head out, her eyes darting past us toward the driveway and then down the street.

"All clear," she says, letting the door swing wide.

Clayton's barely in the house before she wraps him in a hug.

"I was so happy you called. I've wanted to reach out . . . so many times, but, well, you know."

Clayton nods like yes, yes, he *does* know. She holds his hands in hers and lowers her voice, almost to a whisper. "I know you tried. I know that. But Jeff and Tanner, they just—"

"It's okay, Mrs. S." Clayton puts his hand on her shoulder. "We don't need to talk about it."

His eyes dart in my direction, seeing if I picked up on anything. I act oblivious, like Tanner didn't totally spill the beans that he blames Clayton for Mia's death.

"This is Sydney," Clayton says. "Ukulele buddies with Mia."

Her mom hugs me. It kind of knocks the wind out of me. Well, it's either the hug or the lie I just let Clayton tell. I know lying is always a big fat no-no, but somehow, doing it to Mia's mother feels extra immoral.

So does standing in her house.

"Come, sit." She ushers us in. "The boys are at the store. Shouldn't be home for a few hours."

We sit in the front room, a stuffy sort of space with a small flowered couch and an armchair. And as much as I feel like I should *not* be here, I'm also fascinated. This is where Mia *lived*. I scan the room, feeling a little . . . let down by it all. The Mia I've created in my head doesn't fit here.

In my mind, her life was always full of light and color and possibility. But this dimly lit house is dark and kind of sad, and there's a palpable claustrophobia within the four beige walls. It's not what I imagined. I suddenly realize how much of the girl that was Mia is my own creation, put-together pieces of articles and photos and eulogies.

I still don't know her at all.

Clayton launches into an explanation of the vision board. He shows Mia's mom a picture of it.

"Mia and that camera," she says, shaking her head and dabbing at her eyes with a cloth handkerchief from her pocket. I get the feeling it's taken up permanent residence there.

While Clayton talks, my eyes land on a series of photos hanging on the wall in matching wooden frames. Mia as a toddler, a baby boy who must be Tanner in her lap. Mia singing with a fake microphone. Mia in a tutu, Mia on Christmas morning, Mia with a backpack on, waving back to the camera as she gets on a school bus.

Mia, Mia, Mia.

My breath feels catchy again.

"You okay, dear?" Mia's mother asks. I pry my eyes from the walk down memory lane, but not soon enough. Mrs. Stoddard's eyes follow mine to the photos. "Jeff says I should take them down. Says it makes it worse. All these reminders."

She hands Clayton back his phone with a sigh. "And I'm afraid I'm not going to be much help on *these* photos, either. Mia wasn't in the habit of telling me much lately. You know how she could be."

Clayton nods. I do, too, even though I have zero idea *how she could be.*

"Well, maybe we could look at her phone?" he asks.

Mrs. S shakes her head slowly.

"It was never recovered."

Recovered. My chest tightens at the word.

"Okay, then just take one more look," Clayton says, pointing at the empty space at the center of the collage. "What do you think that was going to be? Was there something Mia wanted to do? Something big that she talked about?"

Mia's mom shakes her head again.

"Honey, she talked to *you* more than anyone around here."

Clayton sighs. "Is there *anything* that's familiar?"

She looks at Clayton and then at the phone one more time and then, finally, points to the pancakes.

"Well, I don't know for sure, but this one," she says. "There was a day, a couple of years ago. We had that huge snowstorm, remember? What did they call it? Snowmageddon?"

I remember it. All the roads closed down for two full days. Mom kept calling the hospital, worried that if a heart came in, we wouldn't be able to get there in time. *We've come too far to be stopped by* snow, she kept saying.

"I bet Mia didn't even remember this, but we were stuck in the house," Mrs. Stoddard continues. "And she got this idea to make her grandmother's slapjack recipe. We all just kind of ended up in the kitchen." Her eyes drift to the photos on the wall again. "The pancakes turned out awful. Gooey on the inside, charred on the outside. But oh, how we laughed. For that one afternoon, things were good."

Her eyes catch mine.

"Anyway, she always said we should try the recipe again. But we never found the time to—"

She cuts herself off and emits a deep sob that rockets right through me.

Because I recognize it. It's the same kind of cry my own mom let out the night I almost died—a sound that is painful in its depth. Endless in its grief. Hearing it makes me wonder: If I had died that night instead, would my own mother still be making that sound? Would she carry a handkerchief around in her pocket? Would Dad tell her to take down all the reminders of *me*?

Clayton puts his hand on Mrs. Stoddard's knee. His fingers still have dirt under the nails, and I don't know why I'm noticing that except that I'm desperate to notice anything besides the guilt that's making Mia's heart pound.

Guilt for lying, for living—I'm not sure which.

"If it's too hard to talk ab—" Clayton says.

She waves her hand in the air.

"No, no, I like talking about it. About her. Heaven knows, nobody else around here does. Jeff thinks it's going to *trigger* me. As if I'm not already thinking of her every second of every day." She sighs. "He didn't even want to read the letter."

Her head snaps up like something's just occurred to her. "Oh! I should show you the letter!"

She leaves us sitting there, and we can hear her rifling through some papers in the next room, and then she's back, waving one at us.

"The lady from the hospital sent it. Said we might get more, but it's just this one so far, from the—let me see. . . ." She pulls the letter from the envelope and scans it. "Yes, the liver."

Clayton's still looking at her, kind of confused. But I'm not: it's an organ-recipient letter, the kind Dr. Russell says I should write to my donor's family. The kind of letter I've written and deleted so many times because I don't know how to say thank you without hurting them. Do they really want to hear that I'm alive and well when Mia is not?

And now I'm sitting in this living room, talking about Mia's dreams, pretending to be someone I'm not to the very people I was trying to protect.

Mrs. Stoddard flaps the letter at Clayton. "Go ahead."

Clayton shakes his head. "No." His voice is sharp. He immediately follows it up with a softer "Thank you."

She pushes it toward him again. "Oh, I know, I know, I was apprehensive at first, too. But really, it's not so bad. It's, I don't know, lovely in a way."

"In *what* way?" Clayton asks.

"Just that something good came from all this. That a piece of Mia is still here. I guess that's silly. Of course, I know she's gone, but . . ." She holds the letter to her chest.

Clayton's staring at the letter in her hand like he's trying to burst it into flames with his retinas.

"It's just a liver," he says, clenching his jaw. Mrs. Stoddard steps back, and there's something so sad in her eyes and so sad in this whole house that even though I should probably most definitely shut up right now, I feel like I have to say something, anything, to help. If things had gone differently that night, *my* mother could be the one searching for signs, for connection with the daughter she lost.

"Actually, I think Mia would agree with you, Mrs. S," I start, trying not to make eye contact with Clayton or Mia's mom as I lie through my teeth. "She told me once that one of the reasons she was an organ donor was because she'd read this article about how our organs have memories."

Clayton and Mia's mom are staring at me like I've grown a second head, but I can't stop now.

"So when you transplant those organs, you also transplant

pieces of their original owners. Like some people have person-ality shifts, or they suddenly like McDonald's or can even have dreams about things only the donor would know."

The silence in the room is palpable as I try to remember why I started talking about this in the first place.

I lean back on the couch. "So, yeah, I think Mia would say you're right. It's not *just* a liver."

Mrs. S puts her hand on my arm. She holds the letter out to me.

"Would you like to read it?"

"No, I don't—I think that's just for you," I say.

Mrs. Stoddard nods like she understands. She keeps a tight grip on the letter as she walks us to the door. Before we go, she runs back to the kitchen again, returning this time with an index card with red writing at the top: *Grandma's Secret Slapjacks.*

"Our family could never quite get it right, but maybe you could," she says. "I'm sure Mia would like that. And I'm sure she'd like *you* to have this."

She turns to me and brings a bright blue ukulele out from behind her back.

"Oh, no, I couldn't," I say, a riptide of shame washing over me.

"I insist," she says, pushing the small instrument into my hand. The front is adorned with stickers, one of an ocean wave, another with a hibiscus flower and the words *UKE CAN DO IT!* "It's just sitting here. Mia would want someone to play it."

Clayton's watching all this, and I don't know how to say no again without raising suspicions. I *am* the avid ukulele player, after all.

I thank her and let her hug me one more time. Clayton sticks the recipe card in his back pocket as we're leaving. We're only two seconds out the door when Clayton turns to me.

"What was *that*?"

"What?"

"That whole wacko story about Mia living on in some kid's liver? Mia never told *me* about that."

I shrug. "She seemed so sad. I just wanted to help."

Clayton mutters something, and I stare at the bright blue instrument in my hand. The stickers that Mia put there. Stickers that meant something to her.

I just wanted to help.

But somehow I'm carrying Mia's prized ukulele, which I basically just swindled out of her mom, who lives in a house that looks nothing like I imagined, down a street I don't know, with a boy who doesn't know *me* at all, and I just made up a whole-ass story about his dead best friend, who may be nothing like I've imagined her to be, and how did things get so out of hand?

It's all too much.

I can't take this.

And I can't keep lying. Chloe was right—I'm being reckless. Not just with my heart, but with everyone else's, too. Clayton deserves the truth. They all do.

I stop walking. "Clayton, I need to go back."

"Because of the letter?"

"No," I say. "Well, sort of. You see, that letter—"

Clayton dips his head back and groans.

"Sydney. Mia is gone. Period."

He walks ahead a few steps to where he's left his shovel in the grass. He picks it up and tosses it into the wheelbarrow. It clangs loudly.

"So what's reading it going to do? Are you going to be happy for this person? Happy Mia died so *they* could live?" he kind of yells back at me. "I sure as hell am not ready to be happy about that. Not now. Not ever."

His words stun me into silence. He must notice the tears building in my eyes, because he walks back toward me, pulls his camo hat off and combs through his hair.

"Crap," he says. "I shouldn't have said all that."

"No, you're right. It's stupid."

"Agreed." He rocks on the backs of his boots, his eyes never leaving my face. "But if you believe Mia's living on in some liver, let's go back."

I take a breath, trying to steady my nerves. Inside my chest, Mia's heart is going crazy. I want to tell him, but I can't seem to get the words to come. If he knows the truth, he'll hate me.

Everyone will.

I hate me, too, if I'm being honest. I hate the way Clayton's looking at me, softer now, like he feels sorry for me. Because I have tears in my eyes and he thinks I'm having some vulnerable, grieving moment about my dead friend.

I hate that there's a selfish part of me that doesn't want to tell him the truth because then I'll be the sick girl again, the transplant girl. The girl who's alive because Mia's not.

"No, no, it's okay," I say, blinking back the tears along with the truth. "I'm not ready to be happy about it, either."

Clayton pulls the index card out of his back pocket and taps it against the palm of his hand.

"How about pancakes? You ready for that?"

He's grinning at me now from beneath his hat brim, trying so hard to make *me* smile that it's impossible to stay upset. That smile of his drowns out any thoughts of how careless I'm being. Because the only way out of all this is by finishing this board for Mia. Maybe then, if Clayton ever *does* find out the truth, he'll forgive me.

For the lies.

For who I am.

Maybe I'll even forgive myself.

I grab the card from his hand.

"I'm *always* ready for pancakes."

CHAPTER SIXTEEN

CLAYTON'S GRANDMA IS HALF HIS SIZE AND TWICE AS sassy.

The first thing she says when we walk into the house is "You must be Clayton's new girlfriend." My face flushes hot.

"Ignore her," Clayton says, putting his arm around his grandmother's small shoulders. "She thinks she's funny."

She swats at him. "I *am* funny."

Clayton gives his grandma a big side squeeze. She's small next to him, her white hair only coming to his pecs.

"This is Sydney. A *friend*," he says.

"Well, friend Sydney, I'm glad you're here." She sticks her thumb toward Clayton. "This one's been a bit of a hermit since—"

She cuts herself off and then gives me a side hug.

"It's just nice to see him with someone besides his old nana." She holds up her hand in front of her mouth and whispers to Clayton, "And she's every bit as pretty as you said."

Now it's Clayton's turn to flush bright red. His grandmother laughs and slaps him on the chest. "Serves ya right." She reaches out and grabs my hand like we're in cahoots. "Gotta keep this one humble, don't you agree?"

I nod. "Definitely."

Clayton waves me into the kitchen after Nana says she'll "leave us to it."

"My grandmother didn't—I didn't . . ." He sighs and leans against the counter. "My grandmother's crazy."

"Seemed perfectly sane to me. Except what was that part about a *new* girlfriend? Is there some sort of rotating cast of women in your life?"

He opens the pantry door and fake laughs.

"Sadly, Nana is the only lady in my life anymore. Had a mom at some point. Used to have a best friend."

"Wow," I say, taking the bag of flour he hands me. "That got dark *real* fast."

Clayton plops a bunch of ingredients on the counter—eggs, sugar, chocolate chips. He clangs a metal bowl onto the island and hands me a measuring cup.

"What about you?" he asks as I scoop flour into the bowl. "What's the boyfriend sitch in Cherry Hill?"

The stack of books on my nightstand—the closest I've gotten to a love story or a first kiss—flashes into my mind.

"Been going through a bit of a dry spell," I say. "Okay, maybe more like a drought."

"I find *that* hard to believe," he says. He adds in the baking powder, sugar and salt. I crack an egg on the rim of the bowl and then pour in the milk while he stirs it all together.

"I've just been, I don't know, waiting," I say, pouring in the chocolate chips.

Clayton plops some batter on the griddle. It spits and bubbles.

"On what?"

He's pretty close since we're both standing above the griddle, and the smell of the pancakes wafts up to me as I watch those little gold specks in his irises dance.

"Honestly?"

"No, lie to me," Clayton jokes.

"Then honestly, I have no idea."

We both reach into the bag of chocolate chips to sneak one. Our hands touch. For a second, we make eye contact, and if we *were* in one of the books on my nightstand, this would be the moment we realized something deep and meaningful about each other. And then maybe we'd follow it up with a flour fight that ended with us making out on the counter.

But back here in reality, we both pull our hands out of the bag, guilty.

"Sorry, I didn't—" he starts to say at the same time a burning smell reaches us. Clayton swears as he turns back to the griddle, where our first row of pancakes has been charred to bits. He scrapes the burned pieces off.

"Botched it," I say, shaking my head.

"Well, *you* keep distracting me."

Clayton pours out another row. He keeps his eyes on them until it's time to flip. When they're done, he slides the spatula under each pancake and slings them onto the plate I'm holding.

"Perfect," I say.

I drench mine in syrup before taking a big bite. Carbohydrates never tasted so good. Mom's been pushing the whole-grain, low-fat, low-salt, heart-healthy diet for so long that I almost forgot how yummy the bad stuff is.

Clayton's staring at me again.

"What?" I say, trying to stop this heart in my chest from doing the little dance it does when he looks at me like that.

He points to his cheek, right near his upper lip. "You've got syrup on your face."

I swipe at myself. "Did I get it?"

He laughs. "Sorta."

He reaches out to wipe it for me but stops, and I know he's trying to keep things platonic, too. And as much as I wish he would have just touched my face, it's better this way. Safer, for everyone.

I wipe again with my whole forearm until I'm sure I got it.

"So," I say, trying to get the focus back on the vision board and not on the flirtation land mines we're both trying to avoid. "Why do you think Mia cared about these pancakes?"

"You know how she could be," Clayton says, echoing what her mom said earlier.

"Right, yeah," I say. "But like *how* exactly?"

"You know, kind of obsessive. Stubborn. Wouldn't take no for an answer. She probably thought fixing those pancakes would somehow fix her life, or at least her family."

The Stoddards' depressing living room, so different than I imagined, comes back into my mind.

"So what exactly *is* the situation over there?" I ask.

"She didn't tell you?"

"No."

Clayton clears our plates, his eyes questioning me. "But she *did* tell you about her outlandish beliefs on organ donation?"

I focus my eyes on the dish rather than on him.

"Yep," I say.

At the sink, he hands me a towel while he starts washing.

"Mia's dad is a grade A prick. Doesn't mix well with alcohol. Mia's wanted to leave for years, but we were waiting to go together. And I couldn't leave Nana, not just yet. Not after all she's done for me."

"Where'd she want to go?" I ask.

He hands me a fork and leans against the sink, folding his arms with a shrug. "Always said the ocean was calling her."

"That's it!" I say, nearly gouging out Clayton's eye with a fork in my excitement. "The last photo? Maybe it's the ocean."

"Maybe," he says, drawing out the *a* to make it clear he doesn't think my idea's a winner. "But all the rest are things she wanted to do here, in Rawlins. The ocean doesn't really fit."

I stack the final plate on the counter, feeling a bit deflated. For a second, I thought I might finally be of some use here.

"Okay, so until we figure out the missing photo, what's next?" I pull up the photo of Mia's collage on my phone and point to the picture of one of those big four-wheeler machines on a hill. "What about this one?"

Something about the big, shiny ATV makes my stomach drop. Riding something like that would *definitely* be reckless, just like Chloe said about going in the lake. But I'm still here, aren't I?

Clayton shakes his head.

"We don't have to worry about that one."

"Why not?"

"Just don't." Clayton shoves the cleaned plates back into the cupboard with an unnecessarily loud thud. "Can we drop it?"

"Dropping it," I say, but I can't stop looking at the picture or thinking about what it would feel like to ride one or why it made Clayton's face tighten up so fast. I want to ask more, find out what it has to do with Mia or what Tanner said about Clayton. But we have a deal: the past is the past.

So I point to the picture of a girl's hand strumming a string. "How about this one?"

"You're the ukulele expert." Clayton's voice is still a little rough. He takes a breath and his eyes and tone both soften. "What do *you* think it means?"

"Maybe . . ." I pause, drawing out my word to buy myself some time. What would she have wanted to do with her ukulele? Get better? Learn a new song? "Maybe she wanted to perform somewhere? Like in a show?"

"Did she tell you that?"

"Yes?"

"Is that a question?"

"No?"

"Sydney. Yes or no?"

"Yes, definitely yes." I avoid his eyes when I tell yet another lie. "She wanted to perform. For people."

"That's"—he scans my face as I wait for the verdict. Is he buying any of this?—"surprising."

Crap.

"She never played for other people," he continues. "Not after the talent show fiasco. I'm sure she told you about *that*."

"Remind me?"

He narrows his eyes at me but keeps talking.

"She *made* us sign up for this stupid school talent show, her on the ukulele, me on the piano. Anyway, her dad had a bad morning, which meant *she* had a bad morning. Mia froze in front of the whole school."

The pancake recipe is on the table, covered in flour. I pick it up and blow it clean.

"So maybe it's like the pancakes," I say. "Maybe she wanted a do-over."

"She *was* talking about second chances a lot in the last few weeks before she—"

He pauses and swallows hard.

"See, there ya go," I jump in so he doesn't have to finish. "You just need to find a show or something where you could play."

"Where *we* could play."

"What now?"

He picks up Mia's ukulele from where I've laid it on the counter.

He shoves it at me. "You heard me."

I shrink back, trying not to take it.

"It's not gonna bite ya," Clayton laughs, practically forcing it into my hands.

I follow him into the living room, carrying the bright blue, four-stringed lie detector with me, panic rising with every step.

It won't take more than one stroke for Clayton to know I made the whole ukulele thing up. And the rest of my lies will unravel from there.

"You know 'Clair de Lune'?" He pulls up the bench and places his camo hat on top of the piano. "Mia's favorite."

Before I can answer or do what I really want to do—run out of the room, out of the house, out of the county, as far from this ukulele as I can get—he starts playing. Slow at first, soft, his wrists lifting lightly after each note. The melody of his fingers fills the room with a haunting sound, beautiful but sad at the same time, just like Mia's pictures.

I can't tear my eyes away from him. As the music picks up and his fingers start cascading across the keys, he leans in toward the music, then out again. Like his body is part of the song. Without his hat, his dark hair has fallen in front of his eyes, but it doesn't matter because they're closed anyway, and I wonder what he's seeing—who he's seeing.

Standing there, watching him play, I know I'm in trouble. Mostly because I have zero idea how to play this miniature guitar in my hands, but also because, right now, it's very clear that even though I've told a bunch of people a bunch of lies since I met Clayton, I've been telling the biggest one to myself.

Because I like the way he looks at me. How his fingers make my skin feel alive, and how they're skimming over the keys now. I like that he spends his nights with his head in the stars and his days with his hands in the dirt. I like how he talks about Mia—like she mattered, like she still does. I even like that he has secrets, just like me, things too close to his heart to share.

How he makes me feel new again. Because we're new to each other. No grief or loss or guilt weighing us down—no past defining us. For the first time, I'm not the sick girl or the waiting girl. I'm just me.

I like how that makes the future feel wide open—even if there can't be one for us.

I like *him.*

Seeing him there, playing Mia's favorite song, makes me ache. And right then, I know Tanner's wrong. He has to be. Clayton couldn't have hurt Mia. Even if I don't know what happened that night, I know *that.* I wish I could tell Clayton that, and also that I'm haunted by Mia, too. That as much as I keep trying to deny it, this heart seems to be reaching out for him.

As he hits the final high-pitched note, he lets out a big sigh and opens his eyes. For a second, he just stares at the keys, but then he turns to me.

"So," he says. "Let me explain something about a duet."

"I didn't want to ruin it." I sit on the bench next to him. He scooches over to keep a bit of space between us. I lean over to him and whisper, "I have a secret. I suck."

"You can't be *that* bad. Come on, play something. Anything you want."

What I want is *him,* and since I can't have that, I want the next best thing: to help him. So he can move on, too, from whatever it is he can't tell me about Mia's death.

"I'll make you a deal," I say. "I'll play—"

"Excellent."

"—*after* we do the ATV."

He leans his head back and groans.

"Is *that* dropping it?"

"Clayton, we can't just pick and choose—"

"She wanted to learn how to drive it, okay? But I don't ride. Not anymore."

I give the ukulele a little strum.

"Then I guess you gotta get back on."

Clayton shakes his head.

"This is extortion."

"*This* is a fair exchange. A photo for a photo." Then I add, just to tip the scales, "For Mia."

"You're a pain in my ass, Grave Girl." He grabs his hat off the top of the piano and fits it over his head. "But you've got yourself a deal."

CHAPTER SEVENTEEN

MY UKULELE SKILLS PUNCH A PRETTY BIG HOLE IN THE inherited-traits-via-transplant theory.

I've watched this YouTube video "Learn Ukulele in 15 Minutes" at least five times and I still have no idea what I'm doing. The long-haired guy in the video keeps encouraging me to *feel the music,* but all I feel are my sore fingertips from plucking the strings.

When my phone lights up with an incoming FaceTime, I'm more than happy to put the hideous thing down.

Chloe's face is pale—well, paler than usual.

"Josh died."

She says it just like that, no small talk or hello or anything.

"The liver kid?"

"Yeah."

I wasn't particularly close with Josh Who Was Waiting on a

Liver. He joined the group just a month or two before I got Mia's heart. He seemed nice enough. I mean, definitely nice enough not to die before being able to legally rent a car.

"I'm sorry, Chloe," I say. Chloe always takes deaths in the Broken Hearts Club hard. Like they're personal attacks instead of an inevitable risk of starting a club with a bunch of sick kids with questionable life expectancies.

"We're having a special meeting. Sort of a memorial," she says. "You're coming."

"Oh, I don't know. I really didn't know him, and I haven't been there in so—"

Chloe shakes her head, the air cannula hanging from her nose whipping back and forth.

"Sydney. This is nonnegotiable."

I sigh. "What time?"

"Tomorrow. Eight p.m."

"Oh."

"Oh what?"

"I'm, well, I'm supposed to meet up with Clayton." He texted me last night, saying we should create an original score for our performance. "We're, well, I'm learning the ukulele."

Chloe doesn't say anything, and she doesn't need to. The look on her face tells me all I need to know.

I try to explain. "I know, it sounds silly, but—"

"But nothing, Syd. Josh was one of us. Of all people, you should be there. You owe him this."

"I *owe* him?"

"Yes."

We stare at each other, the beating of her failing heart broadcasted by the telemetry machine.

Beep.

Beep.

Beep.

"Because I got a heart?" I ask.

Chloe flicks her eyes downward.

"Because you're one of us, too. At least, you *were*."

"Is this about the new web page? Are you mad at me?"

"No."

"Chloe."

She stares me dead in the eye through the screen.

"I'm sad, Sydney. My friend just died. And I'd like my *best* friend to be there at his memorial. Is that so ridiculous?"

Behind her, I notice her demotivational poster's gone. I notice something else, too: she's got an arterial line going into her, just above her wrist. A long tube connects her to a clear bag hanging from the IV pole next to her.

"Are you in the ICU?"

"Moved in this morning."

My chest tightens. "What's going on?"

She flattens her lips into a thin line.

"It's just a thing. A thing I can deal with. You know how it is. I'll be fine."

"But—"

"But if you *want* to help me, be there tomorrow. Eight p.m."

She hangs up before I can say anything else. I lie back on my bed and digest the conversation. I know she's sad, and even though Chloe won't talk about it, she's scared. Being at the hospital is one thing, a pretty routine thing for us. But the ICU? The whole place reeks of death. And it only means one thing—Chloe's heart is not doing well.

Could be an uncontrolled infection, or the meds aren't working right, or her failing heart is hoarding blood and nutrients like the selfish little beast it is, so her other organs are shutting down. Really, it could be one of a million complications that got her upgraded to the ICU. And every time someone goes in, there's a chance they're never coming out.

This liver-kid situation isn't going to help. When someone in the group passes, everyone has the same thought: who's next?

It's all probably put Chloe on edge. Still, I *owe* him? I barely *knew* him. But there it is, the reminder of this massive debt I owe everyone for living. My whole life is a predatory loan.

Rather than replay the whole convo over and over again in my head, I open up TheMiaProject.

The picture I posted of Mr. Johnson's pond and the mission to *take a risk* already has a hundred likes and a handful of comments.

This is such a cool idea. Gonna dedicate a song to Mia tonight at karaoke. Usually I just listen, but tonight, I'm going for it!

Thanks, Mia, for getting me off my butt. Here's a pic of me and my boys rock-climbing. Always wanted to try but never had the guts. Thanks for the kick in the pants!

Likes and comments are coming in from who knows where, and I wouldn't have a tenth of these followers without Chloe. I'm still not sure I owe the liver kid anything, but I do owe Chloe. And she wants me at that memorial.

> Hey, gotta bail on music practice tomorrow

Got a funeral to stalk?

> kind of

Oh. You okay?

> I think so

Found us a venue for our musical debut?

> Working on it. Ridden your ATV?

Working on it

> good night, Clayton

g/night, grave girl

I hold the phone to my chest, trying to picture his face when he said good night. I wonder if he's holding his phone, too, still thinking about me. I wonder if he wants to tell me his secrets, about the night Mia died, as badly as I want to tell him mine.

About my heart. About Josh, who died waiting on a liver. About the expression on Chloe's face, like I was scum for even *considering* not going to the meeting. How my chest felt like it was being squeezed by a vise when I realized Chloe was in the ICU. How if anything ever happened to her, I'd be lost.

But since I can't fix Chloe's heart and I can't come clean with Clayton, I do what I *can* do. I post a picture of Clayton stuffing a huge forkful of pancakes in his face. Underneath, I type: *Resurrect an old family recipe. Make it with someone you love.*

Delete, delete, delete.

Someone you care about.

Better.

The likes start coming in within a few minutes. People from around the world, breathing life into Mia's dreams.

I can't give Clayton the truth, but I can give him that.

CHAPTER EIGHTEEN

I SPEND THE ENTIRE NEXT DAY DREADING BROKEN HEARTS Club.

It doesn't help that Clayton keeps sending me updates on his original score, which doesn't seem to be going so well.

> No way Mozart did this more than 600 times

> Could really use your ukulele skillzzzzzzzz

> About to give up. Need any company at your thing?

A little before eight p.m., Mom knocks on my partially open door. "Friday night! *Breakfast at Tiffany's.* You coming?"

"Can't."

Mom's face falls. It's been years since I've missed a Wells

family classic-movie night. Even during hospital stays, Mom and Dad would squeeze into my bed with me and we'd watch on my laptop.

"Josh died," I quickly add.

Mom's hand goes to her mouth.

"Oh, Syd, I'm so sorry."

"I didn't know him that well."

"But still, it could . . ." She stops herself, but I already know what she was going to say: *It could have been you.*

And I know Mom means it as a good thing, but it makes me feel like a brat. Like I should be waking up every morning and singing show tunes and pooping rainbows and seizing the day or whatever—making the most of this *gift.*

What they don't tell you is that it's not *really* a gift; it's a trade. You exchange death for a lifetime of guilt.

Mom squeezes my hand and gives me this *you're a brave soldier* look that only makes it worse.

After she leaves, I click on the Zoom link Chloe sent me. The last time I joined in on our group was a week before my transplant. I was in the ICU. Things were not looking good. Mom did most of the talking for me, telling everyone how much I'd appreciated being part of this community. Everyone blew me kisses and said they'd be praying for me.

I didn't even know Josh had gotten so bad. Who else is worse? And how are they going to feel about me being there, all stitched up with a healthy heart and a stack of unread college brochures in my desk, greedily hoarding a future they could only dream about?

The Zoom screen blinks on with four little squares staring

back at me. Attendees have come and gone over the years, but as of four months ago, there were five of us: Chloe; me; Sariah, the girl with cystic fibrosis; Brody, the boy with half a heart; and then Josh.

"Sydney! You're here!" Sariah exclaims as soon as my video feed appears. She's skinnier than I remember, which is not a good thing in the CF world. She's been waiting on a set of lungs for almost a year.

"Hello hello!" I say, so upbeat that I immediately regret it.

I rack my brain for something meaningful to say. Something that says, *Hey, I'm still one of you guys. I may not be dying anymore, but we're still the same. Right? RIGHT?*

"Girl! Spill! What's life like off the list? How's the heart? I want all the deets," Sariah says.

She and Brody rapid fire questions at me.

"Can we see your scar?"

"Did you wake up feeling completely different?"

"Is it *so* weird?"

"Any rejection?"

Before I can answer, Chloe chimes in.

"Tonight is about Josh."

Sariah nods, amply scolded. I'm grateful to get off the hook, but also, Chloe's voice still has an edge to it. I'm here, aren't I?

"Brody, go ahead," Chloe says. More tubes and wires have been added to her since yesterday. She's beginning to look like an electrical outlet.

"Oh, uh, sure," Brody says. He looks pretty healthy. There are a few tells in the heart-transplant world—bluish lips, cannula, cough. Brody doesn't have any of them. If I didn't know he'd already had a heart transplant as a baby and is going for his second attempt, I wouldn't even think he was sick.

Brody talks about Josh and how he was super into marching band. About how he was always a good friend to him.

"My *best* friend," he says. "Which is funny because we never met in person."

I try to make eye contact with Chloe, but she doesn't notice, or at least she's pretending not to. She's clearly still upset with me, and I don't even know why.

I look at the picture of Josh she's posted in our chat. The boy in it is all smiles, holding up a tuba on a sunny day. He definitely doesn't match the yellowed, puffy-faced kid I knew with cirrhosis of the liver, which sounds like something only a sixty-year-old man who'd been drinking his way through a midlife crisis would get. But it hits kids, too—kids who would *love* the chance at a midlife crisis.

After Brody's speech, Chloe says a few words about how Josh was always such a big supporter of TheWaitingList. I swear she gives me a serious dose of side-eye when she says it.

After everyone's spoken, Sariah and Brody start with the questions again.

"Do you know anything about your donor?"

"Have you written *the* letter yet?"

"Oh man, what would you even say?"

Chloe interrupts. "She's practically dating her donor's best friend."

"Chloe!" I yell.

"What?" Chloe shrugs like it's no big deal. "It's Broken Hearts Club. Safe space."

Sariah's eyes are wide. "Wait? Are you serious?"

"No, no, she's not," I say. "We're not *dating.*"

I give Chloe a *what are you doing?* look that doesn't seem to faze her.

"But she *is* hanging out with him. Finishing her donor's bucket list," she says.

"Whoa," Brody says. "Does he know you have her heart?"

I shake my head.

"Ballsy," Sariah says. She's put on her AffloVest now, a contraption CFers use to literally beat the snot out of their lungs, so she kind of has to yell over the electric hum.

"I think the word you're searching for is *stupid,*" Chloe says.

"You can't say that. You don't know," I say. "You don't know what it's like to have someone else's heart."

Everyone in the chat goes silent, the churning of Sariah's AffloVest the only sound besides the echo of my words in the ether.

"No, no, you're right. I don't," Chloe says. Her voice is tight, measured. "Thank you, Syd, for that reminder."

The three of us stare blankly at her, Brody looking like he feels awkward as hell and Sariah's vest just humming away and me wishing I could rewind.

"Well, if no one has anything else, then I guess that's that," Chloe says before the screen goes blank.

Mom comes in before bed to check on me.

"How was group?"

"Weird," I say. "I'm not sure I belong there anymore."

The truth is, Chloe and I became friends when we were sick. Now there's this big, bright divide between us.

Mom scoots next to me on the bed and strokes my arm.

"You're just all in different places right now," she says. "That's bound to happen. It's *supposed* to happen."

"I guess," I say, and I'm surprised by the squeaky tightness in my throat. "But then, where *do* I belong?"

Mom's fingers glide up and down my arm. Mom can be uptight about my pills and doctor's appointments and, well, keeping me alive and all, but she also knows that sometimes, arm tickling is the best medicine.

"What about Bree? Was it nice seeing her again?" she says, nodding to a framed photo on my desk of Bree and me the summer after seventh grade, backstage before opening night of *Les Mis*, all toothy grins and excitement. "Is she still doing theater?"

"Not sure," I say, skirting the whole hanging-out-with-Bree question.

Mom chuckles. "You got *so* into everything French that year, remember?"

"How could I forget?" I say, gesturing to my room, which Bree and I decorated during our hideous Parisian phase. She was Young Cosette in the community theater's play and I was Young Éponine, and we bought every last Eiffel Tower painting and cheesy *Je T'aime* sign at Hobby Lobby.

All those same decorations are still here, a time capsule to the questionable taste of perfectly healthy thirteen-year-old me who thought the world rolled out in front of her like a map.

That girl died with my diagnosis.

"I don't even belong in my own room anymore."

"We can redecorate," Mom offers.

"No, that's not . . ." I sigh. "Never mind."

Mom props herself up on her elbow.

"Have you had a chance to look at those college brochures?"

"Not yet. I've been busy," I say. "I'm teaching myself the uku-lele."

"Oh, *that's* what that sound is." Mom raises her eyebrows, extra dramatic. "I thought you were slaughtering kittens in here."

"Mom. It's not *that* bad."

"Well, it's not good."

We both laugh. Lying there together like we have so many times, part of me wants to tell her what I've been doing with Clayton, how I've learned that Mia was a musician, a dreamer, a risk taker. And how working on this Mia project has given me a purpose again. I want to tell her that Chloe's mad about it, even though I don't really understand why.

For the past three years, Mom's been my go-to person. And now there's this whole part of my life I'm not sharing with her.

But I can't. Partly because she'd tell me it's all massively inap-propriate, but mostly because I know she'd make me stop. And that's the one thing I can't do.

"I'm sure I'll figure out what I'm doing with my life at some point," I say as if I believe it. "Gotta make this all worth some-thing, right?"

Mom stops tickling my arm.

"Sydney. This heart, this life, it's a gift—no strings attached.

Go to college. Play the ukulele outside the bus station for spare change. I don't care." She lays my arm back by my side and looks me in the eyes. "You're here. That's more than enough for me."

After Mom leaves, I realize Clayton has sent me a final update:

Done. Just had to find the right inspiration

I pull up the sheet music he's sent me, and I try to play it through.

Mom's right, it does sound like I'm murdering cats. I run my fingers across Mia's stickers, across the wood grain, imagining how she must have made this baby sing.

And me? I'm just an off-key echo.

I put the ukulele down and fire up my computer to do something I'm *actually* good at: internet super sleuthing. I scour websites and social media pages, searching for any sort of upcoming talent show or performance where Clayton and I could do our duet. I even stumble on the Cherry Hill High School theater page, and there, front and center, is Bree, taking a bow on a stage. I pause for a second, like I've opened a portal to my past.

I click off the page.

I may not know where I fit in anymore or what I want to do with this *gift* I've been given, but I know what Mia wanted. And maybe, for now, that's enough.

Finally, I find what I'm looking for on the Rawlins Ridge City Facebook page: *Fourth of July Variety Show. All Acts Welcome.*

Bingo.

CHAPTER NINETEEN

TWO WEEKS.

That's all I have to get ready for the show. Clayton reassures me that my part is mostly chords. *Piece of cake,* he texts me. *Even if you* do *suck.*

Yeah, maybe for someone who actually plays the ukulele. I spend almost the entire two weeks practicing, watching long-haired YouTube guy tell me where to put my fingers.

Mom and Dad tell me I'm getting better, but I'm not so sure. It does sound less like expiring felines, though, and that's not nothing.

Exactly two days before the Variety Show, I meet Clayton at his house for a run-through.

"Bad news," I tell him when he opens the door. "I still suck."

He laughs. "Don't tell me you're backing out."

I sit at the chair that he pulls out for me next to the piano. "Just managing expectations."

"Consider me managed."

He sits on the bench, facing me, a look on his face that can only be described as *waiting to be wowed.* I wish he'd quit.

I strum the first few chords, taking my sweet time transitioning from one to the next, and I keep my eyes locked on my fingers. When I hit the last chord, it's quiet for like an eternity.

"Well, that was," Clayton says, stretching out the *s,* "something."

"I warned you."

"That you did, Grave Girl. That you did." Clayton turns to the keys. "Maybe listen to me play it through once?"

The piano melody starts out slow and low, hauntingly sad. But then it gets lighter and higher as it crescendos into a dazzling display of sharps and flats and runs.

His fingers move effortlessly, so much easier than mine on the strings, like they instinctively know where to go. He hits the final note, the music lingering around us.

Clayton taps his fingers on the top of the piano, thinking.

"Let's have you try it again," he says. "But first, we gotta fix your body."

He stands up and walks around back of me. "You're holding this thing like you're afraid of it." He takes the ukulele from my hands. He holds my left hand up and slides the neck of the ukulele back into it. Then he places my right hand on the strings. He pulls back my shoulders.

"Now try," he says.

I start again, fumbling this time over the chords because I'm concentrating on how I'm holding the ukulele and also on the weight of Clayton's hands on my shoulders.

"Wait, wait, wait. You're still not trusting it, Syd. Play the instrument. Don't let it play you." He sits back on the piano bench, one leg on each side like he's riding a horse. He taps the seat in front of him. "Sit."

I hesitate.

"Oh, settle down," he says. "I'm not trying to cop a feel." He pats the seat again.

I straddle the bench. He puts his arms around me, one hand on each of mine. My breath catches.

"Now, *feel* the beat." His breath is hot on my neck. A little shiver shoots through me. The only beat I can feel right now is the one in my chest, pounding. "Don't think. Just feel."

We play together, the pressure of his hands on mine making me forget about getting the music right. And somehow, the more I forget about that, the easier the chords come. Not perfect, by any means, but still, easier.

"How was that?" he asks, his breath making the hair on my neck stand up straight.

"Good." I swallow hard. "But Mia was better."

I know it's true even if I never heard Mia play. His arms are still around me, loosely, his hands still on mine. His voice is soft in my ear.

"Mia was Mia. And you, Sydney Wells, are you." I twist slightly so I can see his face. He looks at me like he wants to say something else. What is he holding back? If only he knew how much I'm not saying, either. How much I want to tell him. How much I can't.

That's when it happens: his eyes go to my lips. I see it, and he knows I see it, and a flash of something sparks between us—

energy, white-hot and alive, like I could catch it in my hands. My heart—Mia's heart—beats like it's going to burst out of my chest.

"Sydney," he says, half question, half declaration. And somehow, I just know, by the tone of his voice, his eyes on my lips, the energy between us and some sixth sense I didn't even realize I had—he's going to kiss me.

I move back quickly.

His face falls. The space between us extinguishes the spark. He brushes his hair from his eyes but doesn't look at me.

"I'm sorry, that was totally inappropriate," he says. "I'm so sorry. I don't know what—"

"It's fine." And in that moment, I curse all the books on my nightstand, all the *un*realistic fiction that makes love seem so easy—simple, uncomplicated.

"*Here's* a question," he says, still looking down. "What happens after all this?"

I shrug. "I don't know. It's a Fourth of July festival, so probably some sort of hot dog–eating contest. Country folk are super big into showcasing their digestive abilities on national holidays, right?"

Clayton kind of, sort of smiles, but his eyes aren't in it.

"No, I mean after we finish the vision board. What happens with"—he wipes his palms on his jeans, still not meeting my eyes—"us?"

Us.

My brain rolls the word around, feeling the weight of it. But the other part of my brain, the practical part, stops it in its tracks. There is no *us*.

Because I fell for the one boy who's so off-limits it's not even funny. I got the heart, but I can't use it.

"I don't know. I mean, there's not really a reason—"

"Right. Got it," he says, standing abruptly. He whips the sheet music off the piano.

"Are we done practicing?" I ask.

"It's good enough."

"So . . . I held up my end of the bargain," I say, rocking back on my heels awkwardly. "We made a deal. For Mia."

He gives me a *you've got to be kidding me* look but then walks to the front door, swings it open and gestures for me to go out.

He walks quickly, me double stepping to keep up as I follow him around the house, to a red four-wheeler parked under the carport. The lower half of the machine is caked in mud, mud that's clearly been hardening there for a long time. And I know pretty much nothing about recreational equipment, but I'd bet good money Clayton hasn't touched this ATV in months.

"Get on," he says.

I swing one leg over the seat. He cranks the keys in the ignition, and the machine roars to life beneath me. He pulls a joystick-looking thing from the P position to the D position and then points to a little lever on the right handlebar.

"This is your gas. Push in to go. Ease off to stop." He squeezes a little lever on the left handlebar. "These are your brakes."

He folds his arms and steps out of the way.

"Give it a go, then."

With my thumb, I push into the gas lever. The machine lurches forward and stops.

"Ease into it," he says, still not making eye contact.

I try again, this time going slow, and the machine creeps forward in the dirt, out of the carport and into the gravel driveway. I squeeze the brakes to stop.

"Now what?" I ask.

"Now consider yourself taught."

I sit up straight in the seat, still clutching the brake.

"That wasn't the deal. Mia's picture is on a hill. A *big* hill. You are supposed to teach me to drive up there. We're supposed to do it together."

Clayton hits the joystick so it goes back to P.

"No. No hills. Lesson's over."

"That's not what Mia wanted, and you know it."

"Oh, all of a sudden *you're* the expert on what Mia wanted?"

I dismount the ATV seat and stand on the footwell, so I'm a good twelve inches taller than Clayton.

I cross my arms. "Well, I for sure know she'd say you're being a total chickenshit."

He laughs, but it's fake, full of hurt and anger.

"Right. *I'm* the coward here."

"What's that supposed to mean?"

"Nothing. It means nothing." He yanks the keys out of the ignition. "None of it means anything."

I get off the footwell, standing face-to-face with him.

"What are you so afraid of, Clayton?"

"Me?" he says. "What about *you*?" He takes off his hat and rakes his fingers through his hair. "I don't get you. Sometimes, you look at me, and it's like, well, like there's something there. But other times you're so, so . . ."

"So what?"

"So oblivious!" He mashes the camo hat between his hands, the little muscle in his jaw flexing and releasing rapidly. "Except you're not, are you? You're the kind of girl who notices things, who thinks deep thoughts about death and life and who hides in tombs rather than be something you're not. You're not oblivious at all."

He looks up at me now with a weak laugh that's not really a laugh but more like he's realizing something that's downright hilarious in its *not*-funniness.

"Which makes me the jerk who can't take a hint, huh?"

"No, that—"

He steps back when I step toward him.

"Just tell me this. Am I crazy? Is this whole thing in my head? This . . . whatever it is, between us."

I shake my head.

"You're not crazy."

My voice is small, and he replies just as quietly, all the anger from a minute ago washed away, transformed into something almost honest. As honest as we can get, anyway.

"I get it. I didn't expect any of this, either." He gestures between us. "The last thing I need is to care about someone again. But as hard as I tried to fight it—and trust me, I tried—I can't help it. I care about you. A lot."

It's my turn to avoid his eyes. I'm afraid if I see them, then I might not be strong enough to push him away.

"Well, you shouldn't."

He takes a step toward me. "Is it about your pills?"

I move away from him.

"What?"

"I saw them in your car. That first day. A whole bunch of them. Are you sick?"

"That's none of your business." Tears are building in my eyes, either because we're fighting or because a little bit of truth—a small corner of reality—just snuck between us. I blink the tears away, wishing I could blink away my lies as easily. "You don't know anything about me."

"Then tell me!" Clayton says. I stare at him, a million different reasons why I can't swirling in my head, but they come down to this: I'm afraid of what I'll lose if he knows the truth.

"It's not like I'm the only one with secrets here," I say instead.

Clayton puts his hands up like he's busted.

"Okay, you got me. I haven't ridden that ATV at all since our deal."

"That's not what I'm talking about," I say, bolder.

He squints at me.

"What else do you want to know? My whole tragic back-story? How my mom chose meth over me. And all my dad left behind was this," he says, holding up his camo hat.

"Clayton, that's not—"

"No, no, let's get it out, shall we?" he says, his voice rising and his words coming out with a sharp edge. "I don't fit in a family or in this town, and the one person—the only person—who made me feel like I belonged is gone. Does that about cover it? What else do you want to know about?"

I don't know what to say, but I know we're too far into this conversation to turn back now. I inch toward him.

"Mia," I say softly.

"What about her?"

"How she died. And why Tanner thinks . . . well . . . he thinks you got her killed."

Clayton's face drains of color.

"He told you?"

I nod.

He won't look at me. He shakes his head at the ground. "You believe him?"

"*Tell* me what to believe." I move closer, until I'm within arm's length, close enough to feel the emotion rising off him. "Tell me he's wrong and I'll—"

"I can't!" he yells, meeting my eyes. He shakes his head and lowers his voice. "Don't you get it? I *can't*. Because he's *not* wrong."

His words hang between us.

"So whatever you're hiding," he finally says. "It can't be worse than that."

He's looking at me like he's waiting for a reaction or maybe a confession of my own, all the secrets I've been keeping.

I say nothing.

He nods with the saddest smile I've ever seen before turning and walking away. He stops on his front porch, the swinging screen door half-open.

"Maybe you're right," he says, facing me again. "Maybe we *don't* know each other."

The door closes behind him as he disappears into his house, leaving me all alone with the words I can't say.

*　　*　　*

I'm a terrible person.

That's all I can think the whole drive home. I should have come clean with Clayton. I shouldn't have turned the tables on him, pried out his deepest secrets to protect mine.

How did it even get like this? I wanted to do something good—something meaningful. Something that would make my life, the one Mia saved, worth saving.

Instead, I've made a mess.

When I walk through the door, Mom's pacing in the front room. Dad's behind her on the couch, a solemn expression on his face. Mom's face is twisted in this weird, unreadable way.

They know.

Because of course that's what I think, because that's what a terrible person would think—all about herself. But Mom turns to me, her hands kind of gripping each other like she's wringing out a wet towel.

"Oh, honey," she says, her voice tight. "It's Chloe."

CHAPTER TWENTY

THERE ARE A MILLION WAYS TO EXPLAIN HOW A SICK heart feels.

Like a fish flipping around in there. Kind of a ka-thud. A weird pressure in my neck. Like shoes going around in the dryer, but in my chest. An uneasiness under my ribs. Like something's just not right.

I've had them all.

But nothing has felt the way it does when Mom says Chloe's name.

It's like this heart in me freezes, midbeat, shooting little icicles into my bloodstream that harden my arteries all the way to my fingers and toes. Like my whole body turns glacial in an instant.

Chloe.

My frosty veins make my body heavy and numb, but

somehow I make it to my room. Her mom answers my Face-Time. Her eyes are puffy and red.

"She's been waiting for you," she says. There's a catch in her voice that makes my throat feel funny, too.

There's a bit of rustling, and I catch a glimpse of a hospital bed and a stack of uneaten pudding cups on the tray next to it. In the corner of the room, *Get Well Soon* balloons float above a bunch of cards, opened and displayed facing the bed.

The screen rights itself and Chloe appears. Well, a version of Chloe. Her lips are dusky. Her face is swollen. I'd bet she's rocking some massively puffed-up ankles, too, from all the fluids building up in her. The nurses have swapped out her air cannula for an oxygen mask connected to a ventilator. She moves the mask down to her neck to talk.

"One-A status, baby. Let's go!"

Her voice is scratchy and faint, but she says this like it's a victory. And maybe it *is,* in a way. Getting bumped to 1A means she's top of the list if a heart comes in, but it also means if she doesn't get a new heart, the doctors think the one she's got only has a few weeks left—maybe less.

I stumble over my words, trying to find the right thing to say, which is all sorts of stupid because I've been on the other side of this phone call. I've been the one in the bed with the wires and the tubes and the nurses coming in and out, being extra nice and bringing the extra pudding cups, which is *never* a good sign.

So I know there is nothing to say that will change any of it. Nothing to say that will make this particularly jagged pill any easier to swallow. Because when you're seventeen and *this might be it*, nothing makes sense.

"Well," I say finally. "You look atrocious. And I can't even see the cankle situation."

Chloe laughs, all the tubes and wires protruding from her jiggling. Her laugh quickly turns into a cough, and in the space of a heartbeat, she's sitting up in bed, her mother tapping her on the back, telling her to "breathe, baby, breathe."

Through the phone, across six hundred miles, I watch my best friend struggle to live.

All around her, the signs of end-stage scream at me. Her cough because her lungs are backed up with blood. Her wall of pillows to keep her propped up so her lungs won't drown her in her sleep. The medicines flowing through tubes, electrolytes and beta blockers and heart cocktails to keep that sucker pumping just a little bit longer. The uneaten pudding cups because she's not hungry; her stomach isn't getting enough oxygenated blood. It's shutting down.

She's shutting down.

Above her bed, the nurses have allowed her to put up one of her posters (bending the rules: also *not* a good sign). This one has a snowflake on it: *Failure. When your best just isn't good enough.*

Looking at it, I get the same feeling I did when I was where Chloe is now. I felt . . . greedy.

I wanted more. More Mom rubbing my arm. More Dad quoting impossible-to-understand poetry. More Friday night shakes at Randy's.

More life.

And right now, all I want is more Chloe.

More *this.*

More time.

She leans back on her cascade of pillows. Her face is red and sweaty.

"Chloe, about the other day, in group—" I start, but she shakes her head.

"Uh-uh. We're not doing that. No deathbed repentance here. One, because we don't have to. We're best friends—we get pissed and then we move on. I was a brat, you were a brat, it's over. Capeesh?"

She continues, "And two, this is *not* my deathbed. *Dum spiro, spero,* remember—*while I breathe, I hope.* And I'm still breathing." She winces, probably from the pain of the pressure in her lungs. "So tell me something else, anything else. Something that has nothing to do with how much urine I'm putting out or how much oxygen I'm taking in." Her face has kind of sunk back into the pillows. "Tell me about your cowboy."

"You don't want to—"

"Syd. Just give a dying girl what she wants."

I don't want to talk about Clayton right now. I want to talk about Chloe. And if I didn't acutely remember what it was like being in that bed, wishing someone would treat me like *anything* besides the dying kid, I'd tell her no.

But I do remember, every heart-failing moment of it.

"My cowboy is a disaster," I say. "We had a fight. He likes me."

Chloe rolls her eyes. "Only *you* would see that as a problem."

"And I like him."

"News flash of the century."

"Do you want to hear this or not?"

"Okay, okay, shutting up." She slips her oxygen mask back on and gestures at me to go on.

"But we *can't* like each other. We have *way* too much baggage. He has secrets. I have secrets. The truth will only hurt him."

"You mean hurt you."

"What?"

She takes the mask off again, all the way this time, unloosing it from behind her head.

"You're afraid if he knows the truth, he'll reject you. Because your existence and Mia's are mutually exclusive." She pauses and takes a deep, ragged breath. "And what if he wishes Mia were the one who lived? And your worst fear will be true—you won't be enough."

She stops again, gathering more air.

"That's what this is all about, isn't it? Your obsession with Mia, doing this project with Clayton? You want to prove to yourself that you deserve this heart." Chloe's voice is all raspy now. She stops to take another big breath, but she's running out of air faster than she can talk. "But you don't have to earn your place in this world."

Chloe flips over onto her side, holding the phone out in front of her.

"Swimming in lakes. Sneaking out. Lying. You're taking all these risks," she says. "But you're scared of taking the biggest one. The only one that matters."

She's small there, amid all the machines and pillows and wires. She closes her eyes a minute like she's summoning all her strength. When she opens them, she looks me dead in the eye, and even though she's in another state, I can feel the weight of it like she were right in front of me. Oh, how I wish she were.

"There's a reason they call them rib *cages*," she says. "Because our hearts are wild. And that one in your chest may have been someone else's once, but it's *yours* now, Syd. Listen to it. Set it free." She stops to catch her breath. "You deserve that. And you know, in the bottom of *your* heart, that boy deserves the truth."

Chloe's eyes shift off camera as a mix of voices enters the background. She snaps her oxygen mask on quickly.

"My pit crew has arrived," she says with a groan. "Talk later?"

"Of course. Call me anytime. Day or night."

Chloe bites her bottom lip, and it's hard to tell with her oxygen mask on, but I think I see her chin quiver just slightly.

"One more thing," she says, her breath fogging up the mask. "It's just, well, if the docs are right, I may not—"

"You will."

"But if I—"

"Chloe Munoz. I'll see you soon. When you're not being quite so dramatic."

She smiles at me from behind the mask, and then, she's gone. The screen freezes for a second with the image of her, a look in her eyes that I remember all too well, one that's full of uncertainty and fear and an unquenchable desire for *just a little more.*

It's not more than ten seconds after the screen goes blank that I think of a million other things I wanted to say to her. What if that was the last time I talk to her? Does she know how much I love her? How she's the only reason I survived these last few years?

I press redial, but the phone just rings and rings. Her voice-mail picks up.

"Hey, you've got Chloe. If you're calling about a heart, keep talking. Otherwise, send a text like a normal person, ya savage."

I hang up at the beep.

I get on TheMiaProject, hoping for a distraction from the ache in my chest, all the things left unsaid. I read the latest comments on doing family recipes.

A woman who finally convinced her grandmother to teach her the secret family lasagna recipe says, *thanks Mia! We reminisced all night.* There's a teenage girl from Idaho who made chocolate chip cookies with her family. She's posted a picture of them in the kitchen together, stirring and smiling.

And I don't know if it's the posts or all the things I wish I had told Chloe before she hung up, but I decide right then that I don't want to leave things unsaid with anyone. Especially not the people I love.

I find my parents in the kitchen, Dad in his chair, Mom curled up next to him like it's big enough for two.

"Oh, honey," Mom says. "How's Chloe?"

"Not good." I swallow the emotions building in my throat. "But do you guys have plans Saturday night?"

Mom pushes her hair behind her ear with a smile.

"You seem to have us confused with two people with social lives."

I take a deep breath. "Well, I'm playing my ukulele in a town festival. Over in Rawlins Ridge. Would you want to come?"

They look at each other, and then at me.

"Rawlins Ridge?" Dad asks.

"It's a long story."

"One you're going to tell us?" Mom asks.

"No," I say. "But I'd really like you there."

Dad puts his book down.

"Then we'll be there."

In that moment, my chest feels lighter than it has in years. So light that I don't even think before saying the words that come next.

"Good, because also," I say, "there's someone I'd like you to meet."

CHAPTER TWENTY-ONE

THE RAWLINS RIDGE LIBERTY DAYS CARNIVAL IS SMALL-town Americana at its finest (or worst, depending on how you see it), complete with hordes of kids running around shoving pink cotton candy in their mouths, families waiting in lines for rides with names like the Corn Catapult and a plentitude of boys with jeans tight enough to satiate even Chloe's Levi's lust.

Chloe. While I'm out here, her heart is giving up in a hospital room. I check my phone for any updates, but like the last two days: nothing.

Mom notices me checking and puts her hand on my arm.

"Anything?"

I shake my head and try to focus on today's task, which I have at least *some* control over. We find the stage, and I scan for Clayton, part of me wondering if he's going to show. We haven't even talked since our fight. I almost texted a bunch of times, but I didn't know what to say.

I still don't.

So when I finally spot him, walking toward us, my brain and stomach twist into knots.

"You came," he says. He has a hint of surprise in his voice, too, and I wonder if he's been replaying our conversation, too, wondering if we were done for good.

"I came," I say.

Mom kind of arches her eyebrows up at me like *it's a boy?*

"Mom, Dad, this is Clayton," I say. Clayton reaches out to shake my dad's hand.

"Nice to meet you," Dad says, giving me the same suspicious/embarrassing eyebrow raise Mom did. "We've heard absolutely nothing about you."

Mom shoves him not so discreetly with her elbow.

"Don't pay any attention to him," she says. "Now, where *did* you two meet?"

"Mutual friends," I say before Clayton can even open his mouth.

Mom buys it.

"Oh, we've been so happy that Sydney's been catching up with her old friends. Didn't know she had them all the way over here in Rawlins, though!"

Clayton seems confused but smiles anyway. After my parents are seated in the folding chairs in front of the stage, I tell him I'm sorry.

"I haven't exactly told my parents about Mia's list," I say. "And I know what you're going to say about me keeping secrets but—"

"No," Clayton says. "You don't *have* to tell me anything. The other day, I was wrong about that. And I wanted to text you to tell you that, but as you so astutely pointed out, I'm a chicken-shit." His eyes meet mine. "But, actually, I do want to tell *you* something. If that's okay. Maybe after?"

"Okay," I say, and all I can hear are Chloe's words: *That boy deserves the truth.* I decide I can give him a small piece of it.

"My friend is sick," I say. I take a deep breath and surprise myself when my eyes start filling with tears.

"How sick?" he asks, concern etching his brow.

I try to answer but can't seem to make the words come out. Clayton's eyes shift toward the audience that's filling in the chairs now.

"We don't have to do this," he says. "We can wait."

"Uh-uh," I say, shaking my head. "Chloe never waited on life. I'm not going to, either."

"Chloe?" he asks. "That's her name?"

I nod, and somehow, hearing him say her name feels good, like he finally knows a piece of me, the *real* me.

"Chloe Munoz," I say just as the loudspeaker overhead calls out our names.

I follow Clayton onto the stage, Mia's ukulele tucked under my arm, her heart suddenly catapulting into action. I didn't think there'd be so many people, and I'm a little rattled by it. It's not stage fright—I've been on a stage before, lots of times. But in all those plays, I was in character; I was playing a part. Here, I feel exposed—like all these people can see directly inside me, to the secrets I'm keeping.

I close my eyes, run my fingers over the wave sticker on the wood and try to channel Mia—her bravery, her joie de vivre, all the things she was that I'm not. Because right here on this stage, I need to be a little more Mia and a lot less me.

When I open my eyes, Dad winks at me from a few rows back. Mom holds up her phone to let me know she hasn't forgotten to record it for Chloe. In the back corner of the audience, I see Mia's mom. She gives me a smile but doesn't wave. Mr. Stoddard is leaning against the outer wall of a game booth with a red Solo cup in his hand. Tanner's next to them, arms folded, scowling at us.

Clayton takes a seat behind the electric piano while I sit on a barstool by the mic. Before he starts, Clayton leans across me toward the microphone.

"This performance is dedicated to Mia." He winks at me. "And Chloe."

He begins to play. I wish I could just listen to him, the way his fingers make even that chintzy-looking keyboard come to life. But I thrum the chords when I'm supposed to, even though my fingers are shaking.

I notice Mia's family leave about halfway through. I force my eyes toward Clayton rather than stare at the space where they were or at the audience, all the people who probably knew Mia.

Clayton meets my eyes, and it's like he pulls me back from the dark places my brain was trying to go. He nods, and somehow, he makes the audience—and the fear—melt away. And we're just playing for each other, and suddenly, it's like I'm back, standing on the community theater stage, feeling the thrill of performing.

I'd forgotten how much I love it. How it makes me feel . . . alive.

And even though I'm sucking it up on this ukulele, at least I'm here, I'm doing it. I think Chloe would be proud.

And maybe, somewhere, somehow, Mia is, too.

After, my parents ooh and ahh.

"Seeing you on a stage again, well, it was just . . ." Mom waves a hand in front of her face. "And you," she says, turning to Clayton rather than finish the thought that has her on the verge of a breakdown. "You are incredible!"

Clayton's face flushes red

"Thank you, ma'am."

Mom slaps him on the shoulder.

"Oh no you don't. I was just starting to like you," she jokes. "But if you're going to start ma'am-ing me . . ."

"Sorry, ma'am, er, Mrs. Wells." Clayton shoves his hands deep into his pockets. "Would it be okay if I show Sydney around? Rawlins Ridge doesn't do much very well, but they *do* know how to throw a carnival."

My mom gives me a knowing look that's so cringe I want to hurl myself in front of the Corn Catapult. Dad stares at Clayton like he's just asked for a million dollars.

"What? Alone?"

Mom turns to Dad. "Didn't you say something about wanting to win me a teddy bear?"

"I did?" Dad says.

Mom gives him a serious death stare.

"Oh, right, I did," Dad says, finally catching on.

"You two just do, well, whatever it is you do," Mom says, still giving me that knowing, embarrassing look. "Meet you by the fun house in, say, an hour?"

We decide to ride the Ferris wheel first.

"Sorry about my parents," I say while we wait in line. "They don't get out much."

"They were cool," Clayton says with a laugh. "But what did your mom mean about seeing you on stage *again*?"

I shrug. "Oh, I used to do plays and stuff. When I was younger. It was no big deal."

"Seemed like a big deal to her," Clayton says, giving me a sidelong, curious glance. "You don't do it anymore?"

"Nope," I say, anxious to get off the topic. "Kind of outgrew it."

We shuffle forward in silence a few turns. When we reach the front, the ride guy buckles us in and then lurches us into the night sky.

And then we stop. More people get on. Go. Stop. Go. Stop. Eventually we make it to the top of the wheel. Below us, Rawlins Ridge spreads out to the mountains to the west and the highway to the east. Far, far in the distance, I can make out the bright red-and-white water tower of Cherry Hill.

I lean over the railing as far as I can.

"There's the tree house," Clayton says, pointing a few streets away.

"Wow," I say. "That *is* one purple eyesore."

Clayton laughs. "Mia would love it. And over there"—he points to a spot up on the mountains, a shadowed crevasse— "that's the slot canyon."

We both fall silent. It's the first time he's mentioned the slot canyon to me. A flash flood. Mia hit her head.

"I should have told you," he says, like he's reading my mind. "The night Mia di—"

"Clayton, it's okay. You don't have to—"

"No, I do. I do. I want you to know everything. Because, well, what's the best way to say this?" He hesitates. "The song I wrote . . . it was inspired by you."

"Me?"

He wipes his palms on his jeans nervously. "I was trying to capture this feeling, like the one you get swimming. And you need air, and your lungs burn so bad that when you finally reach the surface, it feels like you're reborn. Like that breath restarts the world.

"That's how you make me feel," he says. "Like I can breathe again."

Funny he's talking about breathing, because right now, I can't.

"I told you, since Mia, I don't really fit anywhere." His eyes search Rawlins. "But then you came along, and I want you to know everything because I want you to know *me*."

The wheel lurches again so we're teetering right at the top, our bucket swinging. My stomach falls a bit from the height and also because I'm trapped here with Clayton, who is clearly about to spill his soul to me.

I try to imagine I can see through the mountains, all the way to California—all the way to Chloe. I picture her in that hospital bed, stuck there while I'm up here.

Listen to your heart, she said. *Set it free.*

For the last three years, people have been telling me about my heart. What's wrong with it. What it needs. What it can do—what it can't.

And now, *my* heart is talking back. It's telling me I better tell this boy the truth *before* he divulges his darkest secrets. Chloe's right: he deserves it.

"Wait," I say. "Just wait." The ride has started spinning in earnest now, whipping us downward. We circle around, passing the man at the gears and then making our way back up to the top. "I need to tell you something first."

"Right now?"

"Yes, right now. Before you say anything else."

I shift over in my seat so I can see him better. The wind is blowing his hair wild. The carnival lights blur behind him.

"First off, I didn't mean for things to get this far. I didn't know I'd have feelings for you."

Clayton smiles. "You have *feelings* for me?"

"Clayton, I'm being serious."

"You have *serious* feelings for me?"

"Clayton! Just listen, okay? You know my friend Chloe?"

He nods, still grinning.

"Well, she's not normal sick. She has a problem with her heart. She needs a new one."

Clayton tries to say something, but I plow ahead because I know if I stop, I won't get through this.

"That's how we met."

I tug down the top of my blouse, just far enough to show a few inches of my scar. Clayton scoots over toward me.

"Holy crap. Are you okay? What happened?"

"I met Chloe in a support group, for kids waiting on hearts. For sick kids."

"The pills," he says, but he's still looking at me like he's more worried about my scar than what I'm trying to tell him. He's not getting it.

"I was dying, Clayton. Until five months ago." I swallow hard. "When I got my new heart."

I can see the exact millisecond he understands. Something changes in his eyes. His whole body shifts away from me. He shakes his head.

"No."

My words start coming fast, panicked.

"I only went to the cemetery that day because I wanted to know about her. But then I met you, and you told me about the vision board, and I just, I don't know, got caught up in it all. But I didn't expect to feel like this, about you. I didn't expect any of this."

"No."

"I should have told you, but I didn't know how, and the longer it went, the more it felt like I *couldn't* tell you. And I'm sorry. I'm just so sorry."

We whiz through the night in silence, all my words spilled out around us. The ride bumps to a stop and then starts going backward. Someone in the bucket above us screams.

"That's why you were there, in the grave that day?" he asks, not looking at me.

I nod, biting my lip to keep my tears from pouring down my face.

"I wanted to tell you. So many times."

"You didn't know her," he says, more to himself than to me, and the world is whizzing by behind him and I think I'm going to be sick. "I thought you cared about her. That *we* cared about her."

"I did. I do. And I wanted to do something for her. Like she did for me because—"

"Was any of it real?"

"I'm real," I say. "I'm still me."

His face turns sour, like all the pieces have finally fallen into place.

"And *who* is that?"

The ride comes to an abrupt halt when we're only a few feet off the ground. A bright red firework flashes into the sky.

Clayton yells to the man at the gears.

"I need to get off."

"Everything stops for the fireworks," the man says. "Have you down in a minute."

Clayton still won't look at me. He's staring straight ahead, his jaw tight. And the silence threatens to break me all over again.

"I just wanted to help," I say, but I know it's not enough.

Clayton turns to me, finally, his eyes cold.

"You want to help? Then stay out of my life. Like you were supposed to." He unlatches the bar holding us in. "Screw this."

He jumps down to the ground, landing on all fours. And then

he's up and walking away, quickly, without so much as a glance back in my direction.

The man at the gears yells after him and then turns to me, his eyes drifting down to where my shirt is still pulled down, exposing the stitched-together, Frankenstein-creature parts of me.

I try to cover it up, but it's too late. The truth is out.

I'm a monster.

CHAPTER TWENTY-TWO

I'VE ALWAYS HATED WHEN A GIRL IN ONE OF MY BOOKS falls to pieces over a boy. Like really? Get yourself together, girl.

But that was before I had anything to lose.

Except I don't exactly fall to pieces after the carnival, either. It's more like I fall backward. Like Mia and Clayton never happened. Walks around the cul-de-sac with my parents. Poetry readings with Dad.

It's every bit as reclusive and pathetic as it sounds. Mom and Dad could tell something was wrong the second they picked me up at the fun house. I told them I was fine, but it doesn't take a super sleuth to notice that I don't leave the house for a week.

I try to call Chloe, but her mom tells me she's not up for talking.

"I'll have her phone from now on, okay, hun?" she says. "If

you need something, call me, but otherwise, we'll call you. Chloe needs to rest."

Mom and Dad tiptoe around me. Mom keeps giving me these sidelong looks of pity and asking me why I don't call up Bree or something.

"She's out of town," I say. Oh, and also I haven't seen her since eighth grade and I'm a big fat prednisone-faced liar.

On our walk one afternoon, Mom tells me how much stronger I seem.

"Remember when you first got home?" she says. "How you could barely make it past the mailbox?"

I nod, trying not to think about how being with Clayton, doing all the things we've done together this summer, is the reason for my burst of cardiac conditioning.

"Just tell me this," Mom says, clearly noticing my pout. "Is it about Chloe or Clayton?"

"Both," I say.

She loops her arm through mine.

"Well, I can't say much that will help with what Chloe's going through, but I do have some experience with boys," she says. "And the good news is, the heart's the toughest muscle in the human body. It's not like a bone. It can break—and it will, a bunch of times in your life—and it bounces back, stronger than before."

This is anatomically incorrect on so many levels, but I let her have her metaphor.

And I wish I could give her more than that. I wish I could tell her the mess I've gotten myself into. How I've lost the one person who could see me for *me*, not my diagnosis. How I've hurt the one person who made me feel like maybe I'm worth this heart.

But I've told too many lies to come clean now.

"You're new to heartbreak," Mom adds, patting my arm. "But trust me, it doesn't last forever."

Except this week seems to. Every day is longer than the last. I don't even have it in me to read. I'm not feeling the rom-com vibes, and all my heart-related medical books make me worry about Chloe.

By the end of the week, I haven't heard from her mom again, which means Chloe's heart is still beating. It's pretty much the only good thing to happen in the last seven days, but it's also kind of torturous. I check my phone constantly, a knot of dread in my chest each time.

And a small, selfish part of me is also hoping that maybe Clayton will text, too.

When I close my eyes at night, all I can see is the look on his face when the truth finally clicked, like I was a supervillain peeling off my rubber mask. I fantasize that we'd met some other way, some meet-cute like in my books. Would I have introduced him to my parents and blushed when my dad said, *Have her home by midnight or else*? Would I have let him kiss me on that piano bench?

That's when I remember I have one last bucket list item to post. I open up Mom's video of Clayton and me playing on the stage. I zoom in on him. His fingers are flying over the keys, but his eyes are on me. I scroll back through the video and watch from the beginning. His eyes are on me the entire time. And for some reason, it makes everything hurt more.

I save a screenshot from the video but pause before posting it. I'm obviously not going to be working on the vision board anymore. That was finished the second Clayton knew who I was.

I pull up TheMiaProject and read through the most recent comments. They remind me this was bigger than whatever Clayton and I were or weren't or could never be. This was me taking Mia's dreams to the world—giving her a small piece of the second chance she gave me.

I upload the photo along with a mission: *Put yourself out there. Any way you'd like. Even if you suck.*

I scroll through the past posts, and it feels like I'm looking at a close friend's dreams, not a stranger's. I was getting to know this fearless, hardheaded country girl who didn't quite fit—and I liked her.

And now, it's over.

I pick up her ukulele and strum a few chords. Even though I'm still trash at it, it makes me feel like I'm doing *something*. I play it so long that my fingers hurt. So long that one of the strings pops off, zinging loudly as it breaks.

"No!" I yell.

Mom and Dad come running.

"I broke it," I say, desperately trying to get the string to loop back around the little tuner thingy.

Dad kneels beside me.

"We'll take it in," he says. "We'll get it fixed."

"*I* can do it. I broke it; I can fix it."

Dad puts his hand on my shoulder. "Honey, honey, it's okay—"

"I'll fix it!" But the string won't stretch. No matter how hard I try, it won't go back the way it was.

I decide to take a drive. I take the ukulele with me.

I drive the familiar path to Clayton's house, part of me hoping he'll be outside and I can be all casual: *Oh hey, just cruisin' around with your best friend's broken ukulele and recycled heart. What you been up to?*

But I don't stop at Clayton's. I don't stop until I get to Mia's. Tanner answers the door. I hold out the ukulele to him.

"This belonged to Mia," I say.

He grabs it from me.

"Thought I recognized it at the carnival," he says. "Guess you didn't take my advice, huh?"

It takes me a second to realize he's talking about Clayton.

"You're wrong about him, you know," I say. "He loved Mia."

Tanner kind of smirks and then holds up the ukulele.

"It's broken," he says.

The loose string hangs off the instrument all sad and lifeless. I choke back the tears that are threatening to erupt again.

"I—I couldn't fix it."

I turn to leave because what else can I say? The last thing I see as I'm driving off is Tanner, still in his doorway, holding the broken piece of his sister in his hands.

At home, I curl up under my covers even though it's only

three p.m. I haven't had an honest-to-goodness afternoon nap since before the transplant. Back then, my energy used to bottom out after lunch like I was a toddler. But my heart *is* feeling a little fluttery, and besides, what else am I doing with my life?

Chloe's heart is in free fall. Clayton hates me. And I never made things right with Mia.

I'm beginning to think moving on was a terrible idea.

Or maybe, that it's not even possible.

Might as well sleep.

I sleep deep, so deep I don't even register the ding on my phone the first time. It sounds like a far-off alarm somewhere in my dreams. It's only on the second ding that I realize it's real. I fish my phone out from where it's sunk down into the covers.

Meet me at the tree house?

CHAPTER TWENTY-THREE

THE RED FOUR-WHEELER IS PARKED UNDER THE TREE house. The afternoon sun glints off the paint, sparkling clean from top to bottom. Clayton's sitting on it.

"You washed it," I say, repressing the urge to ask a gazillion questions about whether he hates me as much as I hate me and whether we're still friends or more than friends, and are we doing Mia's vision board anymore or have I irrevocably screwed everything up?

He hands me a helmet. "Word is I owe you a lesson."

The helmet is heavy, like it's built for major, traumatic-brain-injury-causing crashes. *Reckless.* That's what Chloe says I've been. With this life. With my heart.

I pass the helmet back and forth between my hands.

Clayton reaches for it.

"If you don't want—"

"No." I yank it back from him. "I want to."

Not just because Mia would have done it, but because Chloe's lying in a hospital bed, death taunting her. The least I can do is laugh in its face, the way she would.

This isn't reckless.

It's revenge.

I fasten on the helmet. He pats the seat for me to get on behind him.

"Hold on," he says. I don't see any handrails or anything, so I grip my seat. Clayton side-eyes me. "To me." He grabs my wrist and pulls my arm around his waist.

His T-shirt is thin. I can feel his stomach muscles beneath it, just like I can feel the heat radiating from him. He smells like grass after rain.

Clayton eases the ATV forward, asking if I'm okay about five times before we even hit the main road. He picks up speed as we drive through town, past Stoddard Hardware, where Tanner is outside, mad-dogging Clayton as we drive by.

By the time we reach the edge of town, the wind's whipping me as he picks up speed. I duck my head behind his back. He turns onto a dirt road and we head steadily upward into the foothills.

"Still okay?" he yells over the wind and the roar of the engine.

"Still okay," I yell back.

I'm *more* than okay. I cling to him as we cut through the wind, and if I close my eyes, it feels like we're flying. And just like when I stood on that carnival stage again after so long, a life-affirming breathlessness courses through me. My heart picks up, beating in my ears—

I'm here.

I'm here.

I'm.

Still.

Here.

The ground flashes by as we climb the mountain. The path is so narrow that I can see down the side, which is all sagebrush and rocks and is so steep that it makes my stomach do a double flip.

But I'm not scared, not with Clayton. I just hold on tighter.

On the top of a hill, Clayton stops the ATV. The heat of the engine rises up my calves. I realize my arms are still tight around him.

Even though I don't want to, I let him go.

He yanks off his helmet. Below us, Rawlins Ridge spreads out.

"Best view's from up top," Clayton says, pointing away from the town, to the mountain behind us. When I follow his gaze, Mia's heart does that flip-flopping fish thing.

The slot canyon.

Ice spreads through my veins.

He's brought me to where she died. Why? To make me face it? To punish me?

Sitting on the ATV, Clayton stares into the canyon for a long time. It's a thin crevasse between two massive, sheer rock walls cut into the mountain. The canyon slithers back into the rock with a thin path following the cliffs on either side. They're notoriously dangerous. Small spaces. Jagged rocks. No cell service. Flash floods.

Finally, Clayton talks, his back still toward me.

"I want to know everything."

"What?"

He puts the machine back in park but leaves it running. "About your heart. How you got Mi—your new one. I need to know."

"What? Just spill my guts, right here, right now?"

He turns slightly to face me.

"You've been lying to me since the moment we met. So yeah, tell me something true. Something real. Right here. Right now."

He seems like he means it, so I start talking. "I was diagnosed with heart failure when I was fourteen. By the time I was fifteen, I was on the transplant list. I waited two years."

"Two years?" Clayton asks, finally turning off the engine.

"Two," I say, "that felt like a hundred."

"What was that like?"

"Waiting? It was . . . well, it was torture."

With his back to me, I can't see his face, but I can feel his body, tense, listening, waiting for more.

So I tell him about those years. How I jumped every time the phone rang. How I heard sirens in the distance and hated myself for wondering if tonight would be *the* night. Knowing that my life depended on someone's death—but wanting it anyway.

I tell him other things, too. How my body betrayed me, little by little. How Dad's face looked that night in the ICU, when reality came crashing down.

"Facing death like that—giving up hope—it changes you. It changed me," I say. "I gave up on life before it had a chance to give up on me."

He's still facing away from me, and I'm glad, because I don't know if I could say all this if I could see his eyes.

"But then," he says quietly, his words half carried away, "one night . . ."

"Everything changed. My whole life. Just like that."

"You got a heart."

I nod. "Mia's."

Clayton's shoulders stiffen, and he gets off the ATV. He walks to the foot of the canyon, which is getting harder to see as the sun goes down behind it. And maybe he's heard enough, but I'm not going to leave anything unsaid. Not this time.

And then, if I lose him, at least he'll know the truth.

I get off the four-wheeler and stand behind him.

"Can I be honest?" I ask softly. I half expect him to turn and say, *I don't know, can you?* But he just stares straight ahead into the jaws of the canyon.

"At first, that night, when the doctor said there was a heart, I didn't know whose it was. And I didn't care," I admit. "I just wanted to live."

Part of me desperately wants to reach out and touch him again, connect with him. I fold my arms around my waist and squeeze myself tight instead.

"But when I woke up, and this heart—*her* heart—was beating inside me, I *did* start thinking about where it came from . . . and what it cost. It was *all* I could think about. And even though I'd been handed a brand-new life, it felt like I was still waiting. To wake up. To feel like this life, this heart, was mine.

"That's why I went to the memorial that day. To learn about her. But I met you, and it was like you handed me this gift, this way to finally make the guilt go away—to make it right."

Clayton keeps looking into the canyon, his hands pushed down so far into his pockets that I can see the outline of his fingers, balled into fists through the fabric.

"And I thought," I continue, "well, it seemed like maybe we both needed that."

Clayton digs the toe of his boot into the dirt. He still won't face me, but he starts talking.

"We'd had a fight," he says. "That night."

"Clayton, you don't have to—"

"She showed up to my house. I could tell she'd been crying. Wouldn't tell me why, just asked me to take her up here. I said no. It was raining. It wasn't safe."

He swallows hard.

"She was so mad. Told me if I wasn't man enough to leave this town with her, I could at least do *this* for her. I told her to grow up. Told her I'd take her another time. That the whole wide world didn't revolve around her. And then I slammed the door." He hits the side of the ATV with his palm. "I didn't know what she was up to until I heard the engine. Came out in time to see the taillights."

He stares at the ATV, and I wonder if he's seeing her disappear again into the dark.

"I took off after her in my truck, but the road only goes

partway. I had to run the rest. By the time I got there, water was pouring out of the canyon." He bows his head and shakes it like he's trying to shake off whatever he's seeing. "It just kept coming and coming. I couldn't get through. I tried getting to higher ground. I knew she was in there. I just couldn't reach her."

His voice goes high before cutting off. I stay quiet, even though I want to tell him to stop. That he doesn't owe me this. He doesn't owe me anything.

"When the water finally started going down, I went in. She was there. I couldn't tell if she was breathing." He closes his eyes, leaning back on the ATV, his arms folded across his chest. "I loaded her up and drove like hell to get her home. But the creek was so high. The rock was so slick. It was awful. Half of me screaming *Slow down!* and the other half screaming *Faster! Faster!* And the whole time this horrible feeling that I was screwing up, that I was losing her. By the time I got her to her parents, she was all but gone."

I can't stay silent any longer.

"So her family, they think you took her up there?"

He nods. I take a step toward him.

"Then tell them the truth. That this wasn't your fault! You *didn't* do anything wrong."

Clayton waves his hand in the air, brushing off my empty words.

"Except I did, didn't I? Every action I took, every action I didn't take, they're *my* fault. Who else's would they be? I could've just driven her like she asked. I could have convinced her not to go in the canyon. I could have driven faster. What if I could have gotten there in twenty minutes instead of forty? Could the doctors have saved her, then? What about fifteen?" He punches his thigh, just once, sharp and angry. "And why didn't I just wade in after her? I *should* have gone after her, even with the water. Maybe that would have been better. For everyone."

"What? If you'd *died*?"

He doesn't answer. He doesn't have to. He looks into the canyon again, deep this time, as if he's daring the waters to come, to hit him full force. His words—the expression on his face—are ones I recognize, ones that can't be fixed with empty platitudes. You can't talk someone out of guilt that's wedged into their heart.

"You're right," I say, staring into the darkness of the canyon with him. "No matter how many times people tell me it's not my fault my donor died, that won't change the fact that every breath I take is one she won't."

Clayton looks up at me, *finally.* And in that look, I let myself hope, just a small glimmer, that maybe the truth wasn't the ultimate wrecking ball. Maybe, just maybe, it's the one thing that could save us.

"How do you live with that?" Clayton stares into my eyes. "How do you ever move on?"

"I wish I knew," I say. "All I know is I feel it, too."

"Feel what?"

"The shame of being the one who lived."

Even in the gathering dusk, I can see his face change—soften. His eyes catch mine and there's something in them, an understanding, an appreciation of how that night, this place, changed both of us—forever.

I inch toward him. "But I do know one thing," I add. "With you, it doesn't feel like I'm waiting anymore. The future feels wide open. It feels—possible."

Clayton turns toward me for the first time today.

"I thought so, too. This summer, doing the vision board with you, it was like—like my memories of Mia weren't haunted anymore," he says. "I stopped feeling guilty every time I smiled."

He glances back at the ATV as if he's debating hopping on and riding off.

"But then you told me the truth, and all the guilt came rushing back. And I told myself this was over—*had* to be over. I'd just . . . stop thinking about you. Stop *feeling* about you."

"Probably best," I say, even though what I really want to say is *Don't go, don't do this, don't throw this away because of the Mia of it all. See me, right here, right now. Let me be enough.*

"But it turns out . . . ," he says, turning toward me again. I glance up at him, and he's looking straight at me, like he's in some kind of pain. "It doesn't work like that. You can't just decide not to care."

He digs into his pocket for his phone and holds it out between us.

"So I went looking. For you. The *real* you." He taps a few times and then holds it up toward me. "I found this."

On his screen is TheMiaProject.

"It's yours, isn't it? You did this?" he asks.

"How did you find it?" I ask in return.

"Started with your friend Chloe. Wasn't too hard from there."

His tone is indiscernible. Is he angry? Happy? I try to think of a way to explain myself.

"You wanted to give her the world," I say.

Clayton touches my chin with his finger, gently lifting my face so I have to meet his eyes.

"I can't believe you did this for her."

"And you. I did it for you, too." I take a breath, steadying the beat in my chest. "Mia gave me a heart. But you? You gave me the chance to use it."

Clayton meets my eyes now, the little golden specks glowing in the setting sun.

"I'm still mad at you," he says.

"I'm still mad at me, too."

"You lied to me."

"I know."

"And you have her heart, Sydney. Her *heart*."

The truth hangs between us.

"I was fine before you," he says. "And I'd be fine again—eventually. I've gotten pretty good at losing people. But here's the thing." He moves closer to me, so close that our bodies almost touch. "We don't always get to choose who or what we lose in this life." He reaches out and touches my hand. I open it and he slides his palm against mine. "But sometimes, we do."

The only thing I can think is of this time in the ICU when I coded. Dad said the doctors had to shock me back to life. That's what Clayton's skin feels like on mine—a resurrection of flesh and skin and hope.

We sit, hand in hand, as the sun goes down, neither one of us speaking, letting the energy between our bodies say it all.

In the dark, his eyes drift down to my collarbone.

"Can I? Can I see it again?" he asks.

I undo the top button of my shirt, slowly, not sure if this is such a good idea. Last time he saw this, the raw and real evidence of Mia's sacrifice, things didn't go so well. Still, I want to be open, about everything—hold nothing back.

I undo the second button, and then the third so he can see all the way down, past my bra, to where the scar stops just above my belly button. I open my shirt wider so he can see all of it—all of me.

He reaches out and touches the top of it with his fingertip.

"Okay?" he asks, meeting my eyes.

"Okay."

He traces the pink, puckered skin all the way down.

"Does that hurt?"

I shake my head. "You want to listen?"

His eyes kind of go wide, but then, slowly, softly, like he's afraid he might break me, he lays his ear to my chest.

"I hear it," he whispers, like he's passing a secret.

In the fading light, we sit, skin to skin, our fingers intertwining, my hand in his hair, holding him to me. His cheek is warm on my scar, his breath steady on my body.

While inside, Mia's heart—my heart—goes wild.

CHAPTER TWENTY-FOUR

THE NEXT DAY, CLAYTON PICKS ME UP AT MY HOUSE.

No clandestine meeting at the tree house. He's here, standing in my living room, shaking hands with my father, who is asking him where we are going. Mom and I are eavesdropping from the kitchen.

"Sydney isn't like other kids your age," Dad says. "It's important that you understand that."

"I do, sir," Clayton says, and the way he calls my dad *sir* melts me.

"If I could slap a Handle with Care sticker on her forehead, I would," Dad continues. "But I can't, or at least she won't let me, so I'm telling you instead. Be careful with her. Make sure she's careful with herself."

I decide they've had enough alone time.

Clayton stands up when I come in, like this is some sort of

formal prom situation. And even though we're just going out on his ATV again, I guess it kind of is a big deal. There's a *boy* in my living room. A cute one. One who knows who I am and what I am and came anyway.

Dad winks at me when I catch his eyes. And even though I'm still hiding plenty about what I've been doing these past five weeks, it feels good to let them in on a part of it.

Mom has lots of concerns vis-à-vis the ATV situation—speed and incline and my prednisone making me susceptible to sunburns and general bodily harm, to name a few. Clayton knocks them down like he's playing a game of Whac-a-Mole. He shows her his ATV license, along with the sunscreen and ample water he's brought.

"And I read online that you have to be careful about dust, you know, for heart patients, so"—he whips a bandanna out of his pocket and hands it to me—"that should help."

Mom raises her eyebrows.

"I'm impressed," she says.

Clayton shrugs. "The *last* thing I want to do is hurt her."

He reaches out and holds my hand *in front of my parents.* My heart pounds in my chest, and Dad looks kind of pissed but also kind of proud. Mom wrings her hands together. But I think seeing me putter around here like an old maid last week made her feel sorry for me, because finally she says I can go. I give her the biggest hug I can muster.

"You're the best," I say.

"I'm a pushover is what I am," she says, kind of laughing.

"But you're *my* pushover," I say, squeezing her.

"You have your pills?"

I pat my pocket.

"Be careful!" she yells out the front door after me.

"Don't know how to be anything else," I yell back.

If last week was an eternity, this one is a blip, a blur of Clayton and mountains and dirt in my teeth and wind in my hair. He takes me out every day, letting me drive sometimes on the easier parts, him tackling the steeper hills.

And despite what I told my mom, out on the ATV, riding the mountains like anthills, I feel anything but careful.

After years of waiting, I finally feel alive.

Like death can't touch me here.

I feel . . . invincible.

Clayton's the one who keeps asking how I'm doing or if we're going too fast or if the trail is too bumpy. I remind him that Mia's heart is stitched in pretty tight—we're not gonna knock it loose.

"Just nervous," Clayton says, giving my thigh a little squeeze as he drives. "Precious cargo."

The truth is, I feel strong. My body finally feels like it's keeping up with this heart—like they're working together. As we fly down the mountains, my heart is in my throat, beating and living and feeling every minute of it.

I wish I could tell Chloe about it. Tell her I *know* her heart is coming, that soon she'll be out having adventures, too. We can have them together. Because out here, flying through these hills, it's like I know she's going to be okay. She *has* to be.

The sensation of the wind and Clayton on my skin stays with me each night. And I don't even care that I'm a cliché, a trope, a formulaic, swooning protagonist from one of my rom-coms.

Except they were all wrong. The real thing is *so* much better.

Mom's still a little nervous, though. She brings it up at my next appointment with Dr. Russell. Wants to make sure the good doctor approves of my *level of exertion.*

She does—as long as I stay up with my meds and get plenty of rest and hydration.

Mom jumps in. "It's just, well, as you know, her friend Chloe isn't doing—well, things can just change so fast."

Dr. Russell nods solemnly.

"I did hear about that, and we're all pulling for her. We know what she means to Sydney." She turns to me. "But it's okay to live your life. In fact, I'm sure that's what Chloe would want."

I've never loved Dr. Russell more.

"So this boy you're spending time with," she says with a playful smile. "Is he a friend or . . . ?"

"Something more," Mom says, and I want to die. Dr. Russell chuckles and congratulates me, which makes it *so* much worse.

"Syd. We gave you a strong heart," she says, beaming. "Use it."

CHAPTER TWENTY-FIVE

WE END THE WEEK AT THE SLOT CANYON.

We keep coming back to this spot after our riding lessons. Clayton's sitting behind me on the ATV while I drive. I come to a stop, and Clayton inches forward so he's holding me tight from behind.

"Consider yourself officially taught," he whispers.

My heart sinks. "No more riding?"

"We can ride," he says. "But I think we can also check it off the bucket list. Don't you?"

"And I'll post it on TheMiaProject."

I hop off the ATV and take a picture of Clayton, the pink-hued sky a perfect backdrop. He leans back on the seat, propped up on his elbow like he's in some sort of raunchy photo shoot.

"The Lusty Cowboys of Rawlins Ridge," he says in this mock-sexy voice. "That calendar would sell like hotcakes."

I take a picture and then swat him in the chest.

"Thought you weren't a cowboy."

"And that is *still* the truth," he says, grabbing me around the waist and pulling me toward him. "But if that does it for you, I'll be whatever you want."

"That so?"

"That. Is. So." He's got a goofy grin on his face, and his eyes shift to my lips. His hands pull me closer. And even though we've been touching like this for a week now, it still sends a shiver up my spine, a little jump start to my heart.

I glance at the slot canyon and pull away from him. His eyes drift up there, too. He immediately goes from flying-through-the-hills Clayton to thinking-about-the-past Clayton.

"I'll never understand why she had to go up there so badly," he says. "Nothing to see but this stupid town."

The serpentine rock walls that lead into the canyon tower above us.

"Maybe we should go up there," I say, walking toward it. "If it was so important to Mia, maybe it'll help us figure out the rest of the board."

Clayton grabs my arm and pulls me back.

"No way. It's not safe. Didn't you hear me promise your dad to be *extra* careful with you?"

He pulls me into a hug.

"I'm not *that* fragile," I say. "Don't forget, I've beaten death before."

"Still," he says. "Not worth the risk."

I give in and sit on the ATV seat instead to edit his photo before posting it on TheMiaProject.

"What's the mission for this?" he asks.

I look at the photo of the ATV, thinking about this last week, about flying over the cliffs with him.

"Do something that makes you feel alive," I say.

Clayton smiles, and the light in his face returns. While I have my phone out, I double-check to see if Chloe's mom has called. It's been more than two weeks since she hit 1A status. If that heart doesn't come soon—

I force myself not to finish that thought.

"Anything?" Clayton asks. He's used to my near-obsessive checking on Chloe calls.

"Nothing. But right now, *nothing* is what we want." I slip the phone back into my pocket. Not hearing from Chloe's mom means Chloe is still okay. "But we don't have to talk about that."

Clayton's eyebrows push together.

"She's your best friend."

"Right, but you know, she's waiting on a heart, and *you* probably don't want to—"

"I want to. She matters to you. She matters to me." Clayton pats his chest for me to lean against him. "I wouldn't be here if I wasn't okay with all this, Sydney."

I recline into him as he leans back on his elbows on the black seat of the ATV. He tilts his head up, toward where the first stars are coming out.

"Remember how I told you Mia's theory about how we were all born in the hearts of stars?" His hair dangles down and tickles the side of my face. "We all have pieces of each other. You just happen to have a bigger piece of Mia. And maybe that's okay. Maybe it's kind of amazing. Like my heart recognized hers."

I sit up.

"You recognized her *heart*?"

He chuckles and shrugs. "I know, I know, I sound like Mia, right? Spouting all this hippie-dippie stuff but—what's wrong?"

"Nothing," I say.

"Your face says *something*."

He tries to pull me back to him, but I resist. And I'm not even totally sure why, except that what he said felt . . . wrong.

"It's just, well, is Mia's heart the *only* reason we're together?"

Clayton's eyes go wide.

"No, no, I didn't mean that at all. I just meant . . . I don't know what I meant. It just sounded poetic." He reaches for me again. "It's a good thing, Syd. It's like we have this cosmic connection."

"So if it weren't for Mia, we wouldn't *have* a connection?"

"But we do have it."

"Because I have her heart?"

"Because you're you."

We stare at each other in silence, the tension between us so different than the usual freedom I feel up in these mountains. Clayton takes off his hat, running his fingers through his hair. I'm frustrating him. I'm frustrating myself, too.

"I don't understand what's happening right now," he says. "You were worried I wouldn't be happy about you having Mia's heart. Now you're worried I'm *too* happy about it?"

He's right, I'm being ridiculous. Maybe Chloe was onto something—maybe I'll *never* feel like enough, like I'm always in Mia's shadow. I let him hold me close again, chest to chest, and

I can feel his heart beating and my heart beating, and for the life of me, I can't tell where mine ends and his begins.

"I'm sorry," I say. "Sometimes I just . . . I just need to make sure you're here for *me*. Because of me."

Clayton gathers me to him and lays his forehead against mine, and I shut my eyes. His breath on my lips, his body tight against mine.

"I'm here for you, Sydney. For the way your nose crinkles up when you laugh. For how truly awful you are at the ukulele."

He leans back a bit so he can look at me—well, at my lips. He whispers into the space between us.

"For every piece of you."

I pull back, and it takes every tiny fiber of everything I am to do it. Because what I want more than anything is to feel his lips on mine right now, to reassure myself of our connection—one that has nothing to do with my heart.

"No." I look over to the slot canyon. "Not *here*."

Clayton deflates slightly, but I think he gets it. This is where she died. It's sacred space. Not somewhere for a first kiss. And I definitely don't want to have my first kiss *ever* in a place that reminds him of Mia.

"Then let's get out of here," he says with sort of a sad smile that makes me wish I had never said anything about anything.

I grab around his waist as he starts down the mountain. Behind us, the slot canyon gets smaller and smaller, but the worry inside me only gets bigger.

I was so afraid Clayton knowing about Mia's heart would be the end of us. What if it's the only thing holding us together?

I keep thinking about it even after I'm home, all through classic-movie night.

A cosmic connection.

Is that all we have? Is there even a *we* without Mia? Is there a *me*? My phone buzzes. I dig down to get it from between the couch cushions where I'm sitting, squished between my parents and a bowl of low-fat-low-salt-low-fun popcorn.

And all my worries about Clayton slip out of my head as the familiar ice slithers in.

[Incoming Call] Chloe.

CHAPTER TWENTY-SIX

I DON'T WANT TO ANSWER.

I don't want to know.

I feel like one of those military widows who refuses to open the door when some smartly dressed officer stands on the front porch, bearing news that will alter her life forever. As long as that door stays shut, nothing has to change.

I get up and walk away from the couch, watching Chloe's name light up.

If I don't answer, she's fine.

But on the fourth ring, I accept the call.

"Hello?"

"It's go time, baby!"

"Chloe?"

Her voice is unrecognizable, raspy and raw and so weak that I can barely hear it.

"My package has arrived," she says. "You better believe Amazon is gonna get an earful from me about the delay."

I fall onto my bed.

"Stop it. Are you serious?"

"As a heart attack. Doctor's on the way to get it right now."

I don't even realize I'm screaming until Mom and Dad show up in my doorway, white-faced and panting. I point to the phone and mouth the words: *Chloe, heart.*

Mom kind of falls into Dad, who leans against my door frame.

"Can you FaceTime?" I ask.

"No can do, amigo," she says, and I can hear a little bit more of my best friend now. "They're prepping me. I had to sell my soul to even make this call."

I can hear lots of people in the background. Even across state lines, the excitement is palpable.

"Will you do something, for me?" she asks.

"Anything."

"Tell the Broken Hearts Club I'm going in."

"Of course."

"And post on TheWaitingList. Let everyone know what's going on. Maybe send up a few prayers or candles or sacrifices to the great spaghetti monster that I come through this."

Mom's moved to the bed next to me and holds my hand.

"You will, Chloe. I know it," I say.

"Sydney?"

"Yeah."

"I love you."

"Love you. See ya on the other side."

And then, she's gone.

Mom and Dad and I hug for a long time in my room, nobody really saying anything. Mom and I are crying. Dad looks like he's trying not to but losing the fight.

I didn't realize how on edge we all were.

Just five months ago, it was us in that room, us caught up in the whirlwind of a new heart, the hectic pace of antibiotics and last-minute EKGs and Betadine showers and my parents signing a bunch of papers acknowledging this transplant could save my life but could also maybe leave me brain-dead or actually dead instead. It was a two-hour roller coaster of emotions from joy to fear and back again.

We never really got to just stand back and marvel, to bask in this moment.

But right now, in my room, we're quiet, holding each other and wondering at the miracle that's about to happen.

The miracle that's going to save Chloe's life.

I send a quick email to the Broken Hearts Club, letting them know what's going on. I realize I don't have a lot of details, but the most important one I put in the subject line: *CHLOE'S GET-TING A HEART!*

I switch over to YouTube. I haven't logged into TheWaiting-List in so long that I have to dig out the password from a Post-it note in the bottom of my desk drawer, buried deep under the still-unread college brochures. I look into the green recording light on my computer and think about the best way to announce this, especially when I've been MIA for so long. Before I decide, my phone buzzes.

we gotta finish the board.

My fingers hover over my phone. I want to tell Clayton about Chloe, but something stops me. It's one thing for him to know I have Mia's heart; it's another thing for him to see it from the other side in real time, all the rejoicing over someone else's death. I decide to keep it to myself, at least for now.

Isn't that what we're doing?

right. but we should do it soon

Why the rush?

it's holding us back

how so?

today at the canyon. you pulled away from me. Because of Mia.

This is about kissing?

No. I mean yes. That's a BIG part of it. Definitely sign me up for that. But it's more about US. We need to see who we are without her.

The thought of finishing the board gives me a little pit in my stomach. What happens when it's over? What will we even talk about? Or do?

But he's right: even though I'm worried about this whole *cosmic connection* situation, a part of me wants to see, wants to know, who we are without Mia between us.

The idea of an us—just us, no borrowed hearts or guilt—gives me the same feeling I have on the ATV. Like I'm flying. Like nothing could go wrong. Like the future is as wide-open as the mountains, open and free and miraculous.

Because today *is* a miracle. Chloe's getting a new heart. I have a Clayton. And for the first time, I don't just feel like I *should* be moving on; I want to.

Let's finish this sucker.

CHAPTER TWENTY-SEVEN

WE ONLY HAVE TWO PHOTOS LEFT—CLAYTON AND THE cornfield. And, of course, whatever Mia wanted to go smack in the middle. We decide to focus on that one. And we decide to start back at Mia's house.

I'm glad for the distraction. Chloe's surgery started early this morning, and her mom probably won't call until she's in recovery, so I have lots of waiting ahead of me. If it weren't for today's vision board outing, I'd be staring at my phone, driving myself crazy.

Not that my nervous system is doing much better standing on Mia's front porch again. My stomach is fluttering, and also maybe my heart a little bit. Those little butterfly wings in my chest have been showing up again lately.

"Hey, can we *not* mention the whole transplant thing to Mia's mother?" I ask before Clayton knocks.

"Sure," he says. "But I bet she'd like to know. You saw how she was with that liver kid's letter. Like it was some message straight from heaven."

"Yeah, I know, but I also see how her dad and brother treat you."

"That's different," he says.

"Afraid they won't see it that way."

Clayton reaches out and gives my hand a squeeze.

"Whatever you want."

Mia's mom hugs us both just like the first time. She looks even smaller than before, frailer if possible. And the dark circles under her eyes are worse, and the house itself is somehow darker.

"Haven't changed a thing," she says as she leads us to Mia's bedroom. There are clothes on the floor, the desk is piled with papers, and every wall is absolutely covered in posters or pictures or pieces of fabric hung with thumbtacks.

Even the bedsheets are crumpled up like someone's just slept in them. Clayton kind of jerks his eyes toward a half-drunk water cup on the bedside table. Someone *is* sleeping in here. I'd bet my last dollar it's Mrs. S.

She tells us to take our time but that her husband will be back around three, so be out of here before then.

"He just . . . well, you know Jeff. I don't think he'd love having people poking around in Mia's things," she says, as if it's not because her husband thinks Clayton took Mia up to that slot canyon. Her voice is almost as frail as her body. "Says I'm a silly old woman for keeping all this stuff."

She runs her finger across an old-timey record player perched on a dresser that's also home to about twenty bobblehead dolls from different TV shows.

"But it's, well, it's pieces of Mia. How can I get rid of it?"

She touches a little silver urn, the one from the birthday memorial, on the bedside table.

Seeing it—her *remains*—in the room where she lived makes me realize how bizarre this all is. Being in her bedroom without her. Going through her things. It's all so *intimate.* But then again, a piece of Mia literally beats inside my body. Doesn't get more personal than that.

So once Mrs. S leaves, I get over myself and get to work. I inspect the photo wall first. Like in the tree house, it's a collage of pictures; some feature Mia's hallmark soulful aesthetic, others are more candid selfies with Clayton, and most are magazine clippings of clothes or accessories or far-off vacation spots.

"What about one of these," I say, pointing to a photo of a piazza in Italy. "Maybe she wanted to travel? See the world?"

Clayton inspects the clippings.

"She did, for sure," he says. "But it's like your ocean theory—doesn't quite fit. The tree house mural isn't from magazines, they're places Mia had been. Pictures *she* took."

I keep searching while Clayton combs through Mia's bedside drawer for clues. So far he's found a collection of Carmex tubes in varying states of emptiness, a toenail clipper, a bottle of perfume and about a hundred ukulele picks. It's all so pedestrian, so . . . *human.* Nothing like the Mia of my imagination.

Clayton's rifling through a massive stack of movies next

to an old-fashioned TV and DVD player. He holds up *Casablanca.*

"Mia made me watch all these. But I guess it was worth it. Because that day, when I quoted this baby to you, I could tell— you were smitten."

I throw a stuffed elephant at his head. Then I hurriedly put it back with the others in this little hammock thingy hanging on the wall so I don't mess up the Mia shrine.

Because even though it's chaotic, there's something charming about it—freeing. In classic Mia form, she didn't care how things were *supposed* to be. She had her own idea about what mattered and what didn't, and she stuck to it. And every inch of this room, every photo and knickknack and black-and-white movie screams, *MIA!*

This is the room of a girl who knew exactly who she was. What would that even be like?

"So what about *your* room?" Clayton asks. "Is it just one big poster of me or like do you have other things, too?"

"My room is woefully boring," I say, thinking of the outdated French decor.

"I don't believe that for a second," he says.

Okay, maybe it's not *boring,* but it's a sick girl's room. My old green oxygen tank is still in the corner. The big, bulky oxygen concentrator is shoved right next to it. My dresser doesn't have bobbleheads; it's got medicine bottles and the massive whiteboard calendar Mom uses to track meds and doctor's appointments. The only evidence that there's a person beneath my diagnosis are my books and the outdated pic of me backstage during *Les Mis.*

Clayton's stopped searching Mia's room and is searching my face instead.

"Okay," he says. "Don't tell me, let me guess. You're a clean freak."

"Not sure I'd use the word *freak*—"

"Nailed it. And by your bed, you have . . ." He taps his chin, thinking.

"Books. I have *books* on my nightstand."

"What kind?"

My face kind of flushes. "Romance novels."

"Interesting," he says, a massive grin on his face. "Grave Girl is a closet romantic. I want to see it."

"What? My room?"

He nods.

"I'm telling you, it's a snooze fest," I say. "I can't play sports. I do school on my computer, and *this* right here, rifling through Mia's stuff, is pretty much my only hobby. And my only friend—"

I check my phone for any messages. I'll be hearing from Chloe's mom any time. Chloe should definitely be out of surgery by now, which means her old heart is already out. And her new one is in.

The thought makes me go all kinds of clammy and cold. I force myself to push thoughts of Chloe and operating tables and bypass machines out of my head. Worrying about it all day isn't going to make the time pass any faster.

"Everything okay?" Clayton asks. "Is it Chloe?"

"Yeah, no, everything's good," I say, feeling guilty not telling him that she's under the knife right now. "But yes, as I was saying, Chloe. Who lives in another state and is my only friend."

"Well, and me," Clayton says. He reaches out and grabs me by the belt loop of my jeans to pull me to him. His fingers touch me just slightly along my lower back. "And so what if your room is boring? It's yours. And I find *you* endlessly fascinating."

"Oh really? What is it you find *so* fascinating?" I ask, kind of laughing because I'm nervous to know the answer. What *does* he see in me beyond our cosmic connection?

He smiles. "Are you kidding? A girl who accelerates on the downhills? Who starts an Instagram for someone she never even met? Who's beautiful without even trying."

I feign offense.

"How do *you* know I'm not trying?"

"I'm just saying, I want to know more about *you.* And for someone who wants to make sure I'm here *for you,* you're pretty stingy with information on yourself," he says. "I mean, even on TheMiaProject, all these people write in with little pieces of their lives, but you don't. You only post Mia's."

"Well, it's *about* Mia."

He raises his eyebrows at me.

"Sometimes"—he gives me a look like I'm not going to like what comes next—"sometimes I think you're hiding behind Mia."

I try to squirm out of his arms.

"I'm *not* hiding."

"Exactly what you said when I first met you. And you were lying."

"Well, I'm not lying now." Except maybe I am, a little. It's hard to tell anymore. "It's just, Mia's *much* more interesting. The fun, spontaneous, loyal best friend with dreams and plans and artistic talent coming out the wazoo. She's, well, she's practically perfect."

Clayton frowns.

"Don't do that."

"Do what?"

"Put her on a pedestal because she's dead. Mia was *not* perfect."

"Right."

"Yeah. *Right*," he says. "She was about the most pigheaded person I've ever met. Couldn't apologize to save her life. Not to mention kind of judgy. A downright snob, actually. Thought this whole town was beneath her. Which is probably why I was her only friend. Do you see anyone else in these photos?"

He gestures to the wall, where it's just pics of her or her and Clayton. I guess I didn't really think about *why* she didn't have a lot of friends. In my mind, Mia's always framed in unattainable goodness and light. I start to get that sinking feeling again that the *real* Mia is just outside my grasp. Like I'll never truly know her *or* this heart.

"All I'm saying is she's a hard legacy to live up to," I say.

"Who says you have to?" He pulls me closer. His breath is sweet like Juicy Fruit gum. His body is pressed against mine. "I miss Mia every day. But you, Sydney Wells, deserve to take up space in this world, too. You're already taking up space in my heart."

I can feel Mia's heart beating loud and strong between us, resurrecting all my doubts about who we are without her. Clayton's focused on my lips again.

"Not here," I whisper.

He loosens his arms but still holds on to me.

"Right, yeah, of course," he says, like he's just realized we are standing in the middle of Mia's room. He shoots me a teasing grin. "But soon?"

I smile back. "We'll see what we see."

Clayton dips his head back and grabs his chest like I've mortally wounded him.

"Torturing me," he says. "Add that to your list of hobbies."

"Will do," I say as I open the closet door. On the floor, there's a suitcase, half-packed.

"Still sure my travel idea doesn't fit?" I ask, pointing to the evidence.

Clayton crouches down and rifles through the suitcase. A bathing suit. A pair of sandals.

"Could've been a family trip," he says. "Or just a weird Mia thing. She'd been threatening to run away since fifth grade."

We tackle the desk next. In the chaos, there are disorganized mounds of homework papers and flyers from months, years, ago.

"Jackpot," Clayton says, picking up a planner.

He cracks it open, flipping through the pages while I look over his shoulder. Mostly there are little doodles in the margins, but occasionally there will be an actual event penciled in.

Clayton stops in February. In one square, there's an address— *3432 Cozy Lane*—along with a name, *Tanner.* Next to that, in bright purple: *ROAD TRIP!!!*

Clayton looks at me, both of us coming to the same realization.

February 15.

The day of my heart transplant.

"The day after the slot canyon," Clayton says. His eyes land again on the half-packed suitcase. "Mia, Mia, Mia. *Where* were you going?"

CHAPTER TWENTY-EIGHT

WE RETREAT TO THE TREE HOUSE TO DEBRIEF.

"If she *was* going somewhere, she would have told me," Clayton says, tapping his finger to his chin as he studies the collage. "It just doesn't add up."

"Maybe it was a surprise? Maybe she was going to take you?" I say. "Maybe that's why you're on here, too. Taking you was part of the vision?"

"Maybe," he says unconvincingly.

On his phone, he Googles the address. A bunch of places come up, from Pennsylvania to one in England. Very unhelpful. Clayton groans.

"Dammit, Mia, why you always gotta be so difficult?" he says, tossing the phone onto the wooden-slat floor. "Fickle. That's another thing she was. How am I supposed to figure out what she wanted when *she* didn't even know?"

Above us, the twilight sky, which has a pinky hue to it, peeks through the big hole in the roof.

The sun going down reminds me how long it's been since Chloe went into the operating room. I *definitely* should have heard something by now. I check my phone again.

Nothing.

I'm sure everything's fine. It's *got* to be fine.

"What about Tanner?" I ask.

"What about him?"

"His name was next to the address. Seems like we should ask him about it."

"Right," Clayton says. "That's not the worst idea I've *ever* heard."

I step closer so I can see his face.

"Chickenshit," I say.

Clayton's face scrunches in mock anger. "How dare you?"

He tickles my sides, and I collapse to the floor, laughing. He follows me down until he's kind of over me, his legs on either side, pinning me down and tickling the crap out of me. I'm laughing so hard I can't push him off, not that I really want to.

"Ow!" I yell.

He recoils.

"What? Did I hurt you? Is it your heart?"

I pull out a little rock from behind my back.

"I rolled on this."

Clayton sits back on his knees, relief washing over his face. "Oh, okay."

"Clayton. Again. I'm not made of glass," I say.

"Right, I know, I just . . . I've been reading about the post-transplant period, and—"

"You've been *researching* me?" I say, mock horrified. Like I have any room at all to judge a little after-hours interwebz super sleuthing.

Clayton flushes pink. "I just worry, that's all."

"Well, don't," I say, giving him a playful punch in the stomach. "Now back to the address. If Tanner could help us, we gotta ask him."

Clayton stretches out on the wood floor, his hand behind his head, and gestures for me to lie next to him. His heart is beating hard, much harder than normal. He really was scared he'd hurt me, which is sweet but also kind of sucks. Part of me wishes for the days before, when Clayton was just a boy and I was just a girl, and nobody had to *be careful.*

He caresses the back of my head with his hand. His heartbeat starts to get back into its usual, measured rhythm.

"Fine," he finally says. "But I'm not facing him *and* his dad together. They'll be together at the store and at home."

"So what, then?"

He points to one of the pictures. It's pretty dark in the tree house now, but I know those pictures like the back of my hand: he's pointing to the cornfield.

"This Friday night, Tanner will be where he is every Friday night along with every other kid my age in Rawlins—the cornfield kegger. And I don't understand *why* Mia wanted to go to that phony-filled place, but at last we can check it off *and* we can see what Tanner knows."

"Sounds like a pl—"

My phone buzzes.

> This is Chloe's mom on her phone. Just wanted
> to let you know our girl is out. Doctors had
> to improvise a bit, so it took longer than they
> thought, but she did amazing. Should be waking
> up any minute. More details soon.

Instead of ice, a warmth flows through my veins this time, filling me up so full and so fast that it feels like my heart may burst.

"What?" Clayton says. "You're smiling like you just won the lottery."

"I kind of did," I say. "Chloe got a heart."

Clayton sits up, kneeling next to me on the floor. "No way. When's the surgery?"

"It's, well, it's done. It was today."

Clayton leans against the wall. "And here I am blabbering on about the cornfield kegger."

"No, no, it was a good distraction. But she's out. And she's okay."

Clayton's smiling, but it's off.

"What?" I ask.

"Well, I mean, it's just, we've been together all day. Why didn't you tell me?"

"Oh," I say. "I wasn't sure how you'd feel about it."

He looks like I've wounded him.

"When are you going to start believing me, Sydney? I'm *okay* with it. With everything." He opens his arm wide for me to scooch next to him. I snuggle into his side, both of us tilting our heads back to study the stars through the hole in the ceiling. "You know, I've watched all your videos on your YouTube channel with Chloe."

A little spike of dread goes through me. "You saw those?"

I can't remember exactly what videos I've posted over the years on there, but I know I look sick, really sick.

"Yeah," he says. "And I *loved* seeing it. All that stuff made you who you are. And in case you haven't noticed, I'm kind of falling for who you are."

His heartbeat picks up again next to me, and I can feel him take a deep breath.

"Except it doesn't feel like falling at all," he says. "It feels like coming home."

Clayton looks down at me, and our eyes lock together, and there's that electricity between us. And we're not just a boy and a girl, and that's okay, because he's right; the past made us who we are. Even the painful parts, the ones I want to forget, brought us here, to this tree house.

And maybe that's a cosmic connection or just life being life, but whatever it is, lying here with him, my heart has this going-to-burst feeling, because Chloe's okay and Clayton's here, knowing all of me. And even though Mia's vision board is on the wall and this was *their* tree house, their sacred space, it kind of feels like ours now, too.

Just like how this was *her* heart, will always be hers—but it's also mine.

And I'm tired of waiting.

So I close my eyes, and lean in.

CHAPTER TWENTY-NINE

EVERY DAY WAS WORTH IT.

Every second, every millisecond of waiting. Because all the romance books I've read, all the stolen kisses and passionate frenches and first-time nervous pecks are nothing compared to what happens right then, in that tree house.

When his lips touch mine, I'm reborn. Every nerve ending in my body sparks to life. As our mouths come together, he runs his fingers through my hair and pulls me closer, like he can't get enough.

I can't, either.

What starts out slow turns a little frantic. Because while my nerves are glittering up and down my body like sparklers on the Fourth of July, a hunger starts deep within me. A hunger to be as close to Clayton as I possibly can, to crawl inside him and set up a new home and fill out a change-of-address form with the US Postal Service.

And I know, without a doubt, I'd wait again, my whole life if I had to, for just one more kiss like this.

When we finally pull apart, his lips are red, his eyes a little wild.

"Worth the wait?" I ask, kind of breathy. And it's not the bad kind of breathless, the what's-wrong-with-my-heart kind. It's the kind that reminds me that my heart is more than valves and chambers—it's a powerhouse of electricity. I feel it zapping through me.

And I never want it to stop.

He smiles. "Every. Damn. Second."

We laugh, and the sound of it fills the tree house, fills me, fills the space between the stars, who are the only witnesses to this kiss of all kisses. Those stars that cradled us all those billions of years ago. The same ones that made Mia, that made us.

As they look on, Clayton pulls me to him once more.

My parents know something's up the second I get home.

"You're glowing," Mom says. "Something happened."

Not just something, Mom. The greatest thing in the history of mankind happened, and I will never, ever be the same. That's what I want to say, but I don't, of course, because it's my mom and even *she* doesn't want that kind of detail about my love life.

"Chloe's out of surgery!" I say instead. "Oh, and Clayton kissed me."

Mom's hands clasp together as Dad perks up from his armchair.

"What a relief!" she says at the exact second he says, "Was this a *first* kiss?"

"Daaaaad," I say, acting annoyed, except I'm not at all. "Yes, a *first* kiss."

"Well, then, huzzah!" Dad raises his fist in the air. "I like Clayton."

I can feel myself grinning like a goofball. "Me too."

Mom hugs me. "Oh, how wonderful! What a day!" Her eyes go wide. "A *big day*! I have just the thing."

Mom goes out into the garage, where I hear her opening the deep freeze. She comes back in with a Baskin-Robbins box holding a massive mint-chocolate-chip ice cream cake, my favorite. Mom used to get me one for every birthday, but ice cream and fudge are definitely not part of a heart-healthy diet.

"I got it when you told me about Chloe's heart," she says. "Just in case we had a reason to celebrate. And now we have *two* reasons."

She puts the cake on the kitchen counter and pops open the top of the box.

"Mom," I say. "Most kids don't get cake for first kisses."

Mom hands me a fork. "Well, you are not *most* kids."

We don't even divvy up the cake, we just all dig our forks in right there at the counter. Dad raises his bite up in the middle of us like it's a champagne goblet.

"To Chloe," he says. "And to the first kiss of love."

Mom and I look at each other. Mom shrugs.

"Lord Byron? 'The First Kiss of Love.' Please tell me you know what I'm talking about?" We shake our heads. Dad lowers his. "I've failed. As a poetry professor *and* a father."

He sighs this extra dramatic sigh and then launches into the whole thing, his bite of cake still outstretched like he's giving a toast.

"Away with your fictions of flimsy romance,
Those tissues of falsehood which Folly has wove;
Give me the mild beam of the soul-breathing glance,
Or the rapture which dwells on the first kiss of love."

He grabs Mom by the waist with his non-cake hand and plants a big old smooch on her. I cover my eyes.

"Impressionable children present," I say, even though I don't mind it at all. Actually, it's nice. Usually when Dad quotes poetry about life and love and everything in between, I feel like an outsider, an observer tapping on the glass.

But now I'm in on the secret.

We "clink" our cake pieces together and then I chomp into mine. It tastes like a little piece of heaven, and it's still only the *second*-sweetest thing to touch my lips today.

"Carbs and kissing? Not sure my heart can handle it all," I say, giggling like a little kid.

Mom smiles at me, her eyes dewy.

"Your heart can handle more than you think," she says.

I take another bite.

CHAPTER THIRTY

MY PILL.

The thought hits me at two in the morning.

In the dark, I find my tacrolimus. Can I take it now? Do I wait until the next one?

The bottle doesn't say. I find a bunch of guidelines online: If it's almost time for your next dose, skip. Otherwise, take the pill immediately. I do some quick math—six hours until my next dose. I'm smack-dab in the middle.

I should call my transplant coordinator. Or tell Mom. Get an opinion from someone other than Google.

But then Mom will reassume her role as medicator in chief. Probably tell me I need to focus more on my recovery than kissing.

I decide not to take it.

I lie back down, my heart racing. I put my hand on my chest. Does the beat feel a little funny? Was that a little skip?

I tell myself it's okay. I've been doing so well lately, and it's just one missed dose. Still, I stay up the rest of the night worrying about it. Taking my pulse. Wondering if I *have* become cocky about living. Sure, I beat death before, but that doesn't mean I always will.

When eight a.m. finally comes, I take my next tacrolimus dose, and I decide I've *got* to be more careful.

My first step is taking a few days off from riding. I tell Clayton I'm going to stay home and rest until the cornfield kegger on Friday.

> is this about the kiss?

> definitely not. The kiss was . . . everything.

> agreed. Still, you kiss a girl and then she won't see you, makes a boy wonder

> Just not feeling great

> What's going on? Do you need to go to the doctor? I can come right now. Forget the cornfield. You should rest

> Clayton. I'm fine. We're fine. Everything's fine. I'll see you Friday. Very excited for my first cowboy kegger party

> Ugh. Don't remind me. The battle of the oversized belt buckles. I'll never forgive Mia for this one

> We'll get in, get our answers from Tanner and get out

And if on the way home, we get lost on a back road somewhere . . .

> That's just the risk we'll have to take

I clasp the phone to my chest, wishing it were him instead.

"My boyfriend is *so* dreamy," Mom says from the kitchen table in this hilariously swoony voice.

"Mo-om," I say, even though I don't mind. I've waited a long time to have my mom heckle me about a boy.

"And how *is* Clayton?" she asks. She's got her medical-bill-paying glasses on and a bunch of envelopes scattered on the table in front of her. "How come you're not out with him today?"

"Eh, just thought I'd take a few days off," I say, trying to act casual, like I didn't miss a dose of the drug that every doctor post-transplant has reminded me is *the* most important thing I must do every day because my very existence hangs in the balance.

"You feeling okay?" Mom's put down the bill to study me instead. She stands up and comes closer, putting the back of her hand on my forehead.

"Totally," I say. "Just being careful."

"Smart," Mom says. "Temp feels okay."

"That's because *I'm* okay."

Mom eyes me as she sits back down at the table.

"Heard from Chloe?" she asks.

"Not yet."

I've texted Chloe a bunch of times since her mom said she got out of surgery. She's probably still waking up from all the drugs, and I know she's busy in all her post-op appointments with everyone making her sit up and walk around and answer *How we feeling today?* every thirty minutes until she's begging to be sent home.

Still, it's weird she hasn't called. A little seed of worry sprouts in my gut, but I try to distract myself with TheMiaProject. On my bed, I read the tagged posts, people talking about things that make them feel alive under the picture of Clayton on the ATV.

After that, I look around my room and decide it's time for some overdue cleaning.

I start with all the sick-kid paraphernalia I don't use anymore. I chuck the oversized hospital water bottles, thermometers and face masks into a bin. Mom leans against the door frame, watching me.

"What brought this on?" she asks.

"It's just time," I say, which is totally true, but the real truth of it is that Mia's room inspired me—*Mia* inspired me. "The dying-girl motif is so three years ago."

Mom chuckles as I hand her the oxygen tank.

She helps me take down my old room decor. I hold up a black-and-white picture of the Eiffel Tower in a red frame.

"We thought we were so cosmopolitan," I say with a chuckle. "We had this big plan to go live in Paris together and eat croissants on the Rue de Whatever."

"You still want to go?" Mom asks.

I haven't really thought about it. When I got diagnosed, time stopped, and so did all those dreams.

"Yeah," I decide. "Someday."

"Someday," Mom says, kind of to me but mostly to herself, like she's feeling the weight of the word on her tongue. "I like the sound of that."

I pause when I get to the framed picture of Bree and me backstage. It was the last play I did before I got sick, the last time I did something because *I* wanted to, not because a doctor prescribed it or Mia had it on her bucket list. I put it back on my desk rather than toss it into the donation box.

Once we've cleared out all the vestiges of thirteen-year-old me, Mom and I stand back, admiring the bare walls.

"So," Mom says. "What you gonna put in here now?"

"Not sure," I say, and for the first time since I woke up to this brand-new heart, this brand-new life, that doesn't feel so daunting.

It feels, instead, like a blank canvas—full of possibility.

After the room overhaul, I'm feeling kind of beat. I think about the missed pill again. Take my pulse and oxygen levels. All okay.

But my bed is sending out serious nap vibes, so I give it what it wants.

I wake to my phone ringing.

Chloe.

And then she's there.

The sight of her through my screen makes my eyes water. I blink the tears away before Chloe can laugh at me, but it's almost too much, seeing her all pink and alive. No more oxygen mask. Even her lips are full of color instead of the grayish blue of the last few weeks.

She's covered in post-transplant paraphernalia. IVs in her arms and neck. Electrode wires crisscross her hospital gown.

But even under all that, she looks like Chloe again. And running right down the middle of her, peeking out of her gown, is white gauze, covering her incision.

"Let me be the first to welcome you to the New Hearts Club," I say.

Chloe shakes her head, the neck IV jiggling hard.

"Maybe put the brakes on the whole welcome wagon," she says. Her voice is better, too—strong.

"What? Why?"

"Didn't you hear? I'm officially heartless."

I laugh even though I don't really get the joke. I chalk it up to the meds.

"Sydney. I. Didn't. Get. It," she says, enunciating each syllable. "I got *this*." She holds up a gray backpack with two tubes sticking out the side. It looks like a normal backpack, but I know better. Those tubes are going straight into her abdomen, connecting an artificial pump in the backpack to the artificial heart in her chest. "Say hello to my little friend."

"Wait, what happened? There was a heart. You said there was a heart."

She shrugs. "It was a dud."

"What do you mean 'a dud'? They were prepping you for it and—"

"Syd. Does it really matter *why*? It didn't work. And I was already open on the table, so the doctors made a game-time decision. They took my crappy one and stuck me with the TAH."

The total artificial heart: a machine instead of flesh and blood. A machine meant to bridge the gap until a real heart comes.

"It's good, this is *good*. This will buy you more time," I say, even though I *hate* when people try to put a positive spin on a crappy situation.

"Riiiight," Chloe says. "More time. More hospital visits. More waiting. Bottom line is, I got snaked. They turned me into the Tin Man." She kind of cranes her neck like she's trying to see something. "Hey, what happened to your room?"

I lift the phone so she can see the extent of my bare walls.

"What? No more hideous Paris decor?" Chloe shakes her head. "It's like I don't even know you anymore."

"So, this artificial heart, how long will it—"

"Sydney Wells. You know better than to ask that. It'll last as long as it lasts." She heaves a big sigh. "But they're keeping me pretty busy down here. Got an appointment later with a guy from Jiffy Lube." She gives a weak little laugh. "Anyway, so could you update YouTube again? Let my fans know I'm a robot or whatever."

I feel my face freeze. The video.

"I—"

Chloe gives me a death glare through the screen. "Don't tell me."

"I was going to. I emailed the group and I had the site open and everything and then—"

And then Clayton texted me. About the bucket list. Chloe can see it written across my face.

"Let me guess—Mia," she says.

"Chloe, I'm so, so sorry. I'll do it right now."

Chloe's lips form a tight line.

"Forget it. I know how busy you are with your new life and all."

"Don't be like that. It's just one video."

I shouldn't have said that. Judging by the look on Chloe's face, I *really* should not have said that.

"It's not just *one* video, Sydney." Her face is red, and while I'm happy her artificial heart is pumping enough blood to make her face *that* red, I've never seen her quite this mad before. "This page, these *videos* may be all I leave behind."

She sinks back into her bed a bit.

"You used to get that," she says, quieter now, which is worse somehow. "I'm not fighting for my life here. I'm fighting to make my short, stupid life mean something. And I may not have a bucket list like your precious Mia, but I needed your help with this—to care about *me* for one second."

"I do care. And I'll post, right now—"

Chloe lets out a barking, angry laugh.

"Forget it. You're clearly too busy doing whatever you're doing next for Mia. Maybe if I had died on that table, you'd give me half the attention you give her."

"That's not fair."

"Do *not* talk to me about fair."

Tears well up in her eyes, which makes them well up in my own. The six hundred miles between us has never felt so far.

"I gotta go," she says.

"Chloe, please, wait. I want to make this right."

She gives me a weak smile that's just about as hopeless as I've ever seen.

"When are you going to get it, Sydney?" she says. "You can't."

CHAPTER THIRTY-ONE

CHLOE WON'T ANSWER MY CALLS.

For three days I go straight to voicemail. My texts disappear into the void.

She asked me to do one thing, and I failed.

The guilt of that sinks deep in my chest. Because through everything, we could count on each other. She's the *only* one who understands what I've been through. I stare at my phone, hoping to see it light up with her name.

It doesn't.

I almost think about not going to the cornfield kegger on Friday night, partly because I'm still a little shaken up about my missed pill but also because maybe skipping it would prove to Chloe that she's still my best friend, that this Mia project hasn't replaced her—that nothing ever could.

But that's also why I *need* to go—finish this thing and put it behind me. And isn't that what Chloe keeps telling me I should do?

I try to rally. Clayton picks me up in his truck, but we go to his house first for a four-wheeler.

"Only respectable way to show up to a cornfield," he says.

He fastens my helmet and then says, "There was something else I'm forgetting. Ah yes."

He kisses me, softly, his hands on either side of my face, his teeth barely tugging on my bottom lip as we pull apart.

"Can't forget that," I say, the warmth of him spreading through me just like the first time. I try to muster a smile as he pulls back, but his lips on mine only remind me of how we were kissing when Chloe was waking up, a machine in her chest instead of a heart. The guilt rips into me fresh.

"Chloe didn't get the heart," I say. "Well, not a real one. It's a machine to keep her going until . . ."

I can't seem to say the rest. Because I don't know the rest. I don't know how any of this will end.

Clayton wraps his arms around me. I tell him how I didn't post on TheWaitingList. How I let Chloe down.

"She's your best friend," he says. "It'll be okay."

I check my phone again to see if she's written back.

She hasn't.

I climb on the back of the ATV and wrap my arms around him as he starts it up. And even though I know I messed up with Chloe, being close to Clayton, being out here on the hills together—my heart feels better.

With the wind whipping my face, I know Clayton's right— everything will be okay. I can *make* everything okay, somehow.

The cornfield is just beyond Mia's old house. Its massive

rows of tall green, not-quite-ripe corn stretch out in both directions as far as I can see. Clayton finds a little path on one side and starts driving straight into the middle.

Other ATVs have come this way recently, judging by the fresh tracks ahead of us. The path is narrow, so I fight off the cornstalks that thwap against me. And just when it feels like this cornfield couldn't possibly go any farther, we emerge into an opening.

A bunch of ATVs and pickup trucks form a circle. In the middle, kegs perch on the seats of four-wheelers and Tiki torches cast flickers of light and shadows across the field, as if it didn't already feel like a murderer with a hockey mask is *definitely* about to pop out of the corn.

Clayton helps me off the ATV.

"You ready for this?" he asks.

I nod. "For Mia."

"For Mia," he echoes.

It's painfully obvious that Clayton is not a usual here. The people already gathered around the kegs size us up as we walk in. Even a girl dancing in a very short denim miniskirt in front of a portable speaker stops to gawk.

Clayton's holding my hand tighter than usual, and his jaw is set. Seeing him nervous makes me nervous. But I hold on as he walks up to a guy sitting on the tailgate of a white pickup truck with a red Solo cup in his hands.

"Well, well, well, what do we have here?" the guy says. "Clayton Cooper in a cornfield. Thought you were too good for this kind of country shit."

"I'm here, ain't I?" Clayton asks. "You seen Tanner?"

"He's around, somewhere." The boy smiles this kind of half-cocked smirk. He hops off the tailgate, his eyes wandering all the way from my Vans to my boobs. "Who's your friend?"

Clayton kind of stands in front of me.

"Nobody *you* need to worry about," he says.

The boy cranes his neck to see me behind Clayton.

He smiles that nasty smile again. "You ever decide you want a *real* cowboy, you know where to find me."

He takes a big draw out of his cup as Clayton and I walk away.

"'Ain't I'?" I whisper to Clayton.

Clayton shrugs. "When in Rome."

Two girls run up to us. One is the girl from Mia's birthday memorial, the emotional one who cried into the mic. But tonight, instead of tears, her face is covered with enough contour to pass as military camouflage. She bats her massive fake eyelashes at Clayton.

"Clayton Cooper," she says. "Haven't seen *your* face in a while. Where you been all summer?"

I don't like the way she says it or the little flare of jealousy in me when her eyes flit up and down his body. Clayton touches the tip of his baseball hat.

"Clara," he says.

"Who's the new girl?" she asks, eyeing our clasped hands.

"I'm Sydney," I say, rather than wait for Clayton to answer for me like I'm incapable of taking care of myself. For some reason, I really don't want this girl to think that. "I was friends with Mia."

The girl slips her arm through mine in a movement so quick and self-assured that I don't have time to say no.

"Well, any friend of Mia's is a friend of mine," she says. "Let's get you a drink."

I shoot Clayton a look that's trying to say, *Please don't let me go*, but he nods like *It's okay*. She fills up a red Solo cup with beer from the keg, but I hold up my hand.

"Sober?" she asks.

"Something like that," I say, rather than go into detail about how alcohol interacts with my medicines and could kill my already vulnerable liver.

"Just like Mia," she says, taking a big sip from the cup herself. "Because of her daddy and all."

"You were close?" I ask.

"Used to be," she says, leaning against the ATV that holds the keg. "She used to sleep over at my house almost every weekend. In the summer, she basically lived there. Then, poof, one day she never talks to me again."

"What happened?"

She leans in closer. "I figured out what was going on with her daddy. I told some of the other girls about it. Mia didn't like that. Told me I should mind my own beeswax. Said I was gossipin'." She shakes her head. "I was *trying* to help. But you know Mia. Couldn't tell her nothing. But I'll never forget those summers together." She tips the red Solo cup back to drain the last few drops. She leans in close to whisper, "You know, one time, we even skinny-dipped in Johnson's pond."

I'm not sure I heard her right.

"The one with all the No Trespassing signs?"

"Uh-huh. We snuck in after midnight. Laughed so hard we almost busted a gut."

That doesn't make any sense. If Mia already snuck into Johnson's pond, why was it on her vision board?

"Oh, hell to the no."

Clara's looking over my shoulder when she says it. My eyes follow hers into the middle of the circle, where Tanner Stoddard has just driven up on an ATV. His lights are shining right on Clayton.

He dismounts. The Tiki torch flames distort his face, and I swear he's taller than he was in the hardware store. Tall and angry and, judging by the cup in his right hand, drunk.

"You got no business here, Cooper," he says.

I inch toward Clayton, who shields his eyes from the beams.

"I'm only here because of Mia," he says.

Tanner takes two giant steps toward him, his finger pointed in Clayton's face.

"Say her name again," he says. I can smell the beer on his breath. "I dare you."

Clayton's face is tight, but he makes no move to pull away from Tanner or his accusing finger. Instead, he cracks his knuckles together and stares right back at him.

"Mia."

He practically spits the word.

Tanner is on him in a half second. They're on the ground, rolling and grunting before anyone else can react.

Tanner's on top and he gets in a good punch at Clayton's face. I scream without meaning to. Then Clayton's rolled on top, and he's pinning Tanner down, and Tanner's trying to kick him off, the beam of the ATV lights showcasing them like a spotlight.

"She'd still be alive if she hadn't met your sorry ass," Tanner says between huffs. "You took her up there. You let her go into that canyon. *You killed her!*"

He yells this last part with hate so thick it bounces through the corn, and the rows throw it back at us, the accusation echoing in the night. Clayton's jaw is flexing as he struggles to keep Tanner on the ground.

"I just want to talk," he says through gritted teeth.

Tanner cranes his head back a little and then jerks forward to spit a huge loogie on Clayton, right in his face.

"*We* got nothing to talk about," he says.

And before I can think too much about it, I feel myself stepping forward.

"Then talk to me."

They both turn to me, Clayton still on top of Tanner, his mouth starting to bleed a little from the punch.

"It's important," I say. "Please."

Tanner gives Clayton a shove.

"Then get your dumbass boyfriend off me," he says.

Clayton hesitates, then moves off and reaches out a hand to help Tanner up. Tanner scoffs at it and pushes to his feet by himself. He gives Clayton one final shove as he passes.

"Five minutes," he says. "Then you can *both* get the hell out of my sight."

*   *   *

We walk away from the circle of gawkers, who have turned back to the music and each other. Show's over.

When we're a good distance away, surrounded by cornstalks, Tanner sits on the ground. He's holding his side.

"You okay?" I ask.

"Fine," he says, straightening up like it doesn't hurt. "Better get talking. Your five minutes already started."

I tell him, as quick as I can, about the vision board and the missing final picture. When I get to the part about finding the half-packed suitcase and the note on the planner, he stops me.

"You were in her room with that son of a—" He shuts his eyes and balls his fists, unable to even finish the thought. "When? Who let you in?"

"Oh," I say, remembering how nervous Mrs. S was that her husband or Tanner would find us there. "We just kind of . . ."

He leans his head back.

"Dammit, Mom," he says.

"Please don't tell your dad."

He stares at me, right in the eyes.

"You think I'm stupid or something?"

I shake my head. He picks up a rock from the dirt and chucks it hard into the corn around us.

"Go on, then."

"We think she was planning a road trip somewhere, and wherever it was, maybe that's the final picture. The last one we need to finish her board. And since your name was with that address, we thought maybe you'd know what it meant."

He chucks another rock into the night.

"Your boy doesn't know?" he asks. "Thought Mia told him everything. Forgot the rest of us existed, seemed like."

"That's not true," I say.

"And what do you know about it?" he says, an edge to his voice that almost hides the quaver in it.

"I know she loved you."

The words come out before I've thought them through. All I know is I need his help, and also, what's one more lie at this point?

He narrows his eyes at me, and I keep going.

"Said she had a little brother," I say. "Said he was her best friend."

"Used to be." Tanner stands up, gazing into the corn like he's seeing something there. All I see is row upon row of the tall green stalks, their leaves blowing in a light breeze. "She tell you we used to come here?"

I shake my head.

He points into the stalks. "Hid a blanket smack in the middle of the field. On the bad nights, we'd run outside, straight out the back door, all the way here without stopping. Hid some books and flashlights, too. We'd read until it was safe to go home."

He pitches another rock into the darkness, aimlessly. I stare into the corn where the rock hits with a muffled thud. It's almost like I can see them there—Tanner and Mia, hiding. And it's like for the first time I see something else, too: Mia. Not the made-up, perfect version I've been putting on a postmortem pedestal, but a girl, of flesh and blood, with flaws and talents and memories and regrets.

I touch the soil. She was scared here. She was running. And she dreamed of getting far beyond this town.

That was real.

"But then Clayton Cooper moved in. She started going to that tree house. With *him*." He jerks his head back toward the circle, which I can't see but I can hear, the music pumping through the corn. "I lived in that house, too. I *still* live there. But she chose him, an *outsider*."

The word makes me think about Chloe. About how we've grown apart since my transplant. How I relished those days with Clayton where my past didn't define me. Because sometimes you need someone who isn't part of the heartache.

"Maybe that's *why* she chose him," I say. "Maybe you were too close to it."

"Or maybe it's 'cause I learned to stay out of Dad's way. Mia never could seem to figure that out. She always took the brunt of it." Tanner considers the rock in his hand. "And I let her."

Then he looks at me, a glimpse of humanity on his face.

"To be clear, I will *never* help Clayton Cooper," he says.

"Understood."

"But you seem like you really cared about Mia."

"I did," I say. "I do."

"We got an uncle," he says, hefting the rock up and down in his palm. "Name's Tanner, too. My dad hasn't talked to him in years, some fight a few years back. Didn't even come to the funeral. Mia didn't tell me nothin' anymore, but I'd bet that's where she was going."

"And your uncle lives in . . ."

"California."

He bends down to pick up one last rock. He chucks it into the corn. It hits the dirt in the distance.

"On Cozy Lane?" I ask.

Tanner turns to face me, closed up tight again.

"Your five minutes are up."

CHAPTER THIRTY-TWO

CLAYTON DRIVES THROUGH THE MOUNTAINS INSTEAD OF straight home, faster than we've ever gone.

"I was right," I yell over the whipping night air. "It was the ocean. She was going to California."

I know Clayton hears me even though he doesn't respond. His eyes are set dead ahead, his knuckles white on the handlebars, his fight with Tanner still pumping adrenaline through his veins.

"Clayton, those things Tanner said . . ."

He doesn't respond, just keeps driving, zooming over the hills. I hold on tight.

A few rain sprinkles nip my skin as we fly through the night. Within a few minutes, big stinging pellets thwack my arms. Suddenly, Clayton swerves, clenching the brake so hard we fishtail in the dirt that's quickly becoming mud as the rain gathers in little streaming divots.

"We gotta get you home," he says, before turning the machine sharply, tipping a little as he takes the corner. The wheels splatter my legs with mud.

And then we're flying.

But I don't feel free or invincible.

I feel terrified.

The creek that's normally little more than a trickle is roaring now, sloshing into the road. Clayton hesitates for a second, the ATV slowing, but then he guns it, heading straight for the water. When we plow through it, a wall of water sprays us, but we make it through.

On the other side, the whip of the wind chills me to the bone as the ground whizzes beneath the wheels, and I'm holding on for dear life, praying that the traction on these tires still works on wet ground.

"Clayton," I yell. "Clayton!"

I pound on his back and he skids to a stop, the wheels trying to grip the dirt. Through the rain, he turns, an unreadable expression on his face.

"You're scaring me," I say.

"I—I—just—" And then it's like *my* Clayton returns from behind the mask of whoever this speed-demon maniac is, whoever has been here since Tanner yelled *You killed her!* into the night. "Are you okay?"

I nod. "Just scared."

He creeps the rest of the way home, checking every few minutes to see if I'm all right. When we get to his house, he parks under the carport, takes off his helmet and holds it in his hands, just staring at it. He shakes little drops of water from his hair.

"California, huh?" he says as if he weren't just careening down the canyon. "Then that's where we gotta go."

I wrap my arms around myself, trying to fight off the cold of my wet clothes.

"Technically, California is out of the question," I say.

Technically, I'm not supposed to travel out of the state or more than four hours away from the hospital in my first year post-transplant. It was one of the pseudo-promises I made to my transplant team. I'll take my meds. Come in for *all* my appointments. Let them make any major decisions about my heart. And I won't leave.

Not to mention that my mother, who has been astonishingly cool about the boy and the ATV, would absolutely draw the line at interstate travel. When I tell all this to Clayton, his face falls. He tries to cover up his disappointment with a shrug.

"So we wait," he says.

"For what, six more months?" I ask.

He looks at my arms holding myself tight and jumps off the ATV. He grabs a hoodie out of his truck and drapes it over my shoulders.

"We wait until it's safe. Until you're better."

Better. He says this like I'm getting over a virus or something. I'm not sure he fully appreciates that I'll never be all the way *better.*

"The future's not guaranteed," I say. "Isn't that what you said?"

"Yes, but I'm an idiot. Think I just proved that." He jerks his head back toward the mountain, now almost invisible through the rain and the dark. "I shouldn't have driven like that. Not with you." He rubs my arms up and down, trying to warm me. "I just, I saw the rain—the water—and I wanted to get out of there. Get you safe."

Except we both know it wasn't just about me. It was about Mia. He was seeing how fast he could go in the rain. He was still trying to save her.

"We have to finish this thing, Clayton. Put it behind us," I say.

The raindrops pelt the carport in steady staccato beats. I lean into him, the chill wiggling into my bones. He wraps his arms around me and pulls me tight just as Nana swings the house door open and appears on the porch, hands on hips.

"What are you two knuckleheads doing out here getting soaked to the bone?"

I stand up too quick, and my head feels like it's swimming. I blink away the little shooting stars of light on the periphery of my vision.

"Trying to decide something," Clayton says.

"Well, can you decide it under an actual roof?" Nana says. She ushers us in the front door and wraps a blanket around my shaking shoulders. "Now, what's all this about?"

"Just, well, there's something we need to do, but we're not sure it's the right time," Clayton answers.

Nana taps her chin.

"What's that thing all you kids say? YOLO?" she says.

Clayton groans. "Okay, that's it, I'm taking away your TikTok."

She laughs. "Well, it's true. You only live once. Better make it count."

By the time I get home, I can't stop shivering.

I keep shaking even once Clayton gets me inside and Mom shoves me into a hot shower. I hear Clayton asking what he can do to help. I hear him apologizing over and over. She tells him she'll take it from here. *Just go,* she says.

After my shower, Mom wraps me in a fuzzy blanket and gets in bed with me.

"We got caught in the rain," I say once my jaw stops quaking long enough for me to speak. I leave out the part about Clayton charging down the mountains like a madman.

"You gotta be more careful," Mom says, rubbing my arms hard and fast to warm me up.

"I will," I say. "I mean, I am. This just kind of happened."

"Things can't just *happen,* Sydney. Not to you," she says. "You can't just go running off like a normal kid."

There it is. A *normal* kid.

Mom and Dad will never see me as anything but the sick kid. The kind of kid who they'd *definitely* say can't go on a road trip to the ocean. Which is why I can't tell either of them I'm even considering it.

The one person I *could* tell is Chloe. After Mom leaves, I go to TheWaitingList and watch her newest video. She explains her new "heart" (she does air quotes every time she says it). She apologizes for not posting sooner, adding that she *tried* to. A little ache spreads in my gut. She unpacks the backpack, showing off the battery she has to keep fully charged at all times.

"Half woman, half machine, all badass," she says, putting her positive spin on it in her Chloe way. *"This is Chloe Munoz, reminding you to let the beat go on."*

Her cheeks are still pink. She looks strong. I hate that I can't just call her up and tell her that. I send a text instead: *Saw your video. Looking good, bionic woman.*

I pull my comforter up around me, burrowing into the dark, partly still trying to get warm, partly trying to ease the ache of Chloe ignoring me. There has to be something I can say. Something I can do to make things better.

My mind jumps back and forth between Chloe and California, trying to decide what to do about either one. Because Chloe's wrong; I *can* make things right. I know I can.

An idea hits me.

I type in the address we found in Mia's notebook, narrowing the search down to California this time. I find it near the coast, close to Newport Beach.

Only one hour from Chloe.

I could see her.

I could finish this vision board *and* show Chloe how much I care about her. I could show up on her front step and tell her in person—face-to-face—that she's still my best friend and I screwed up but despite the miles and hearts between us, I love her.

I can fix everything.

I just have to get there.

> I'm going.

Sydney! Are you okay? Your mom was so worried

> Worried is my mom's natural state. I got wet. I dried. I'll survive

I don't know what I was thinking

> You were thinking about Mia. Which is why you need to make this trip. I need to make it, too. So, I'm going, with or without you

you wouldn't

> I most definitely would. My best friend needs me. And I won't let her down again

what if you get sick?

> I won't

And your parents?

> What they don't know can't hurt them

Syd

> Don't Syd me. Don't you see? California is the *only* way forward. For both of us

It just feels risky

I look around my room, bare except for the stack of books on my nightstand. I've spent my teenage years playing it safe, reading about people doing things, stories of characters who follow their hearts and find their happily ever afters.

The girl who owned this ticker before me would go in a heartbeat.

So would Chloe.

> You heard Nana. . . . what's life without a risk?

CHAPTER THIRTY-THREE

TWO NIGHTS LATER, CLAYTON FLICKS OFF HIS HEADLIGHTS as he pulls in front of my neighbor's house so my parents don't notice.

His face is stressed, pulled tight at his mouth when I get in his truck.

"I'm still not sure about this," he says as I climb in. He probably wouldn't even be here if I hadn't threatened to go without him.

"That's okay." I shove my duffel bag at my feet, click the door shut, quietly, and meet his eyes. "I am."

Clayton's not convinced. "But *I* promised your dad I'd take care of you."

I pull the top of my shirt down slightly, revealing my scar.

"Look at me, Clayton. I've faced death. I've *felt* it. Been *this* close to it." I hold my thumb and pointer finger up, centimeters apart. "But I'm still here. A road trip isn't going to do me in. Not now. Not after everything."

He gives me a doubtful look. I slide my fingers through his.

"Besides, if you had a chance to see Mia, right now, wouldn't you go? No matter what?"

Clayton leans his head against the seat and groans.

"Going to be the death of me," he says, putting the truck in gear.

When we get to the highway, though, he doesn't turn north like the map to Newport Beach says he should. He turns south and tells me he's got to make a quick pit stop.

The pit stop is back in Rawlins. He pulls up to Mia's house, turning his lights off as we creep to a stop in front of it. He tells me to wait in the car, which I'm happy to do because I'm feeling a little woozy from the cough medicine I took before leaving my house. Since our ride in the rain, I can't shake this cold that's got me kind of run-down and my heart kind of jumpy. But it's nothing that's going to stop me from getting to the ocean *or* Chloe.

I watch from the truck as Clayton shimmies up the tree that towers over the Stoddards' house. I gasp out loud when he jumps from the branch to the roof and then runs up it like a cat burglar to the small west-facing window. He slides the window up, lifts up a leg and then disappears into the house.

I swear I hardly breathe while he's gone. My eyes flick from the window to the front door, hoping the Stoddards are all sound asleep.

And then, Clayton's back, climbing down the tree, using only one hand this time because the other is clutching something against his chest. He jumps to the ground, doing a half roll onto the grass, both arms protecting whatever he's holding. Then he's running back toward me, a wild grin on his face.

He plunks the thing on the bench seat next to me.

"Is that . . . ?" I start.

Clayton smiles from ear to ear. He pats the silver urn between us.

"Told her I'd get her out of this place one day."

The highway feels like freedom.

It stretches out in front of us, dark and empty except for the occasional bright lights and low growl of a Mack truck.

The double yellow line stretches out like it's showing us the way. I've driven this highway with Mom a million times over the last few years, the same road, the same yellow lines, all the way up to the hospital in Salt Lake, to the doctors who doled out my time in measured guesses.

But the road never felt like this.

"There's a metaphor here," I say, rolling down my window and sticking my hand into the night air.

"Where?" Clayton says.

"Here. This," I say, flicking my wrist to gesture to the outside. "The highway. It's like life."

Clayton chuckles. "Sorry to tell you this, but I think Tom Cochrane already beat you to it."

"Who?"

"Country singer. Wrote a little song called 'Life Is a High-way.'"

"Oh," I say. "Right. Well, he's not *entirely* correct. Life isn't *always* a highway, I mean, most of the time it's like a back road, like that one out to Johnson's pond. It's full of twists and turns and setbacks, and sometimes you end up where you wanted to go, and sometimes you don't." The air buffets my hand outside, flicking and bumping it this way and that. "But tonight, it feels like a highway. Like everything in the universe is conspiring to help us."

"Now you sound like Mia," he says.

"Well, she's in my blood."

And right now, I can't help but feel like Mia, leaving reality in the rearview. I'm taking the trip she never got to.

I think of the scared little girl in the cornfield as I tighten my grip on the urn. And I'm probably going to be grounded for life when I get home, but right now, I'm getting Mia out of this town.

I think about texting Chloe, too, letting her know I'm on my way. That I know we can figure all this out once we're together, face-to-face. But it will be more fun to surprise her. We've always talked about meeting in real life, but someone was always sick or on steroids or having *tests*. The business of staying alive always got in the way of living.

But not tonight.

"Chloe's artificial heart is going to burst," I say. "I can't wait to see the look on her face."

Clayton reaches out and puts his hand on my thigh, which is

exposed because I decided a sundress was the perfect escaping-to-California ensemble. Except this time, I picked one with a normal neckline, one that shows off my scar in all its glory. Because I want Chloe to see it, to see that it matches hers—that we're still the same.

"Okay, but I have one question," he says. "Why are you sitting so far away? You know they don't make these bench seats for nothing."

He doesn't have to ask me twice. I unbuckle and move to the middle seat. I kind of have to straddle the gearshift, and it's a little awkward because of the whole sundress situation and how Clayton keeps cranking between gears to pick up speed.

"Not hating the clothing choices this time," he says, his hand going a little higher up my thigh every time he shifts.

I laugh, and so does he, and the sound of it is like a warm blanket. I scoot even closer and lay my head on his shoulder, feeling his muscles flex and tense as he drives, the night air whipping in through the window and the highway pointing us toward the ocean and Chloe and exactly where we're supposed to be.

Outside, the world rolls out like a welcome mat.

CHAPTER THIRTY-FOUR

I WAKE UP DISORIENTED.

We're still on the road but it's nowhere I've ever been. Outside the window, a flat swath of dirt stretches out for forever, speckled only with the occasional sagebrush.

And the sky is different. There's a sliver of light on the horizon.

"Morning, sleepyhead," Clayton says.

"How long was I out?" I ask, wiping my forehead, which has gotten all sweaty in my sleep. My whole body feels kind of sticky. My foggy brain slowly remembers that this is real, that we're really doing this. We're taking Mia to the ocean. And I'm going to see Chloe, in real life.

"Four hours," he says. *Four* hours? That cold medicine knocked me out good. I don't even remember falling asleep. "PS, you snore."

"I do not."

"Like a buzz saw."

The more I wake up, the more I realize two things: my head is in a vise, and my bladder is going to burst.

"Can we stop at the next gas station?" I ask, pushing on both my temples, trying to ease the headache.

"Why, what's wrong?" Clayton asks, sitting up straight and looking at me instead of the road.

"Eyes on the road!" I yell as a truck whizzes past us, blaring its horn. "I'm fine. Just need some Tylenol."

"We should go back," Clayton says. "You're sweating like crazy."

"No, no. We should pull in right there," I say, pointing to a Shell station just off the highway. "I've just had this cold. Someone took me four-wheeling in the rain."

Clayton pulls into the parking lot.

"At least call your mom, then." He hands me my phone. "She's been blowing this up since like three a.m. I'll get your Tylenol."

He hops out of the car and I scroll through my missed calls. Mom has called like twenty times.

I thought we'd at least make it to the California state line before she and Dad woke up and saw I was missing. Why were they up at three in the morning anyway?

A little pang of guilt hits me, thinking about them going into my room, finding it empty. At least I left a note, a short one: *Going to California. Will explain more when I get back. This is just something I have to do. Be home in two days. Don't hate me.*

They probably think I'm off on some sort of teenage sex-cation with Clayton. But it's so much more than that. I run my fingers across Mia's urn. This is so much more than us.

Mom's texts get increasingly panicked as I scroll down.

> Syd. Please. Just call us.

> Where are you?

> You need to come home. Now.

There are other texts, too. Sariah from Broken Hearts Club texted at four a.m.

> My mom just told me. Sydney. I can't believe it.

Then another one an hour later.

> Sydney. Are you there? Can we talk? I understand if you don't want to.

Sariah and I don't really talk outside of group. And definitely not before dawn. The sharpness inside me digs deeper when I see there's one more, from just a few minutes ago.

> She was such a force of life. You just never think it can really happen to someone like that.

I check my call log again. Mom a million times. Sariah. But before any of them, a single call from Chloe's phone.

My chest tightens.

Clayton's back. He opens the car door and hands me the Tylenol and a pack of gum.

"I'm not gonna make you chew this, I'm just gonna say your morning brea—" He stops when he sees my face. "What? What is it?"

"I don't know," I say, except there's a part of me that does. And that part of me is making my heart squeeze so tight I can hardly breathe.

"Sydney, you don't look good. I'm scared," he says. "You need to call your mom."

He holds up my phone and dials it for me. Mom answers on the first ring.

"Sydney, baby, are you okay? Mike, Mike, it's her!"

Dad's on now, asking where I am. I don't know. The world is confusing. And it's kind of spinning, tilting, ever so slowly.

"I think . . . Nevada."

"I'll come get you, just stay put," he says. "Tell me how to get there."

"Wait, no, I'm okay. Clayton's here." I take a breath but can't quite fill my lungs. "Mom, is Chloe . . . ?"

I can't finish the question. There's silence on the line. Silence that says more than a thousand empty words.

"Just come home, baby, okay? Come home."

It's hard to piece together what happens next. I don't remember getting out of the car. Or putting the phone down. But suddenly I'm walking, away from Clayton, who's talking to my mom, away from the car, away from Mia in her silver urn.

I'm walking down the road, but it's not a road I know, and I don't know where I'm going or why I'm out here, and all I really want is what I wanted when I almost died before my transplant, when my heart was failing and my life was slipping: I want my mom. I want to go home.

And more than anything, I want more time.

A sharp pang hits me, right below the ribs. A stab so deep and swift that it buckles my knees. I fall to the gravel, the world still shifting like a Tilt-A-Whirl.

The last thing I see is Clayton's face above me. Filled with fear.

I hate myself for it.

Then, my heart squeezes.

And the world blinks out.

CHAPTER THIRTY-FIVE

I'M RUNNING AFTER A GIRL WITH PURPLE HIGHLIGHTS IN her hair. My thighs are burning. My lungs are screaming. But I keep running.

And then I'm inside a dark, tight canyon. My feet slip on loose rocks. I catch myself on the massive stone walls closing in around me.

She's too fast.

I'm losing her.

I reach out to touch her. Stop her.

She turns.

It's not Mia at all.

It's Chloe.

Go back, *she says.* Go back.

And then she pushes me. Hard.

I tumble down the mountain.

I'm falling, falling, falling.

Into the darkness.

CHAPTER THIRTY-SIX

BEEPING.

That's all I comprehend the first time I open my eyes.

Beeping. Steady and sure.

Mia's heartbeat.

I'd know it anywhere.

The next time, I stay a little longer.

Mom and Dad above me.

They tell me something. My brain doesn't hold it.

Warm palms on my arm. Gripping my hand.

They're gone again.

The third time, I'm alone.

The room is dark except for the light from the cracked door to the hallway.

I'm attached to machines and tubes. Little electrodes scattered across my chest.

A nurse's voice somewhere close.

You gave us quite a scare, young lady.

Her face above me. She's smiling.

Why?

Chloe's gone.

Isn't she?

And I'm going, too.

Aren't I?

After all the pain. All the waiting.

This is how it ends.

What's there to smile about?

CHAPTER THIRTY-SEVEN

WHEN I WAKE UP FOR GOOD, MOM'S HERE.

Because of course she is. Even after I lied, after I snuck away. She was probably terrified.

And still, she's here.

"I'm sorry," I whisper.

She looks up from her book with a start.

"You're awake!" she says. "Oh, honey, honey, how do you feel?"

"For everything, Mom. I'm sorry."

She shakes her head. "Let's not even think about it right now. All that matters is you're here and you're safe and you're going to be okay."

"I am?"

Tubes and wires and beeping machines surround me. I'm in the ICU. Mom nods and wipes a tear from the corner of her eye.

"You are." Mom sits on the edge of my bed and strokes my arm. "You know I wouldn't let anything happen to you."

And even though I know no one can make that promise, I choose to believe her.

I swallow hard. "And Chloe?"

Mom's fingers pause. She closes her eyes and shakes her head slightly. "She got an infection in her chest tube. It progressed so fast they couldn't fight it. And she was already weak from the surgery and—"

"It's okay," I say. "She's gone. I guess that's all I need to know."

"Yeah," Mom says. "I guess it is."

No one uses the term *rejection*, at least not right away. Dr. Russell says phrases like *bump in the road* and *setback*. But when we get right down to it, my body is attacking my heart.

"We've got it under control," she says. "Seems like a combination of factors. The virus you were fighting off. Overexertion." She gives me a little scolding eyebrow raise. "And then there's the traces in your blood of cold medicine, which you know is off-limits for you."

I shrink back into my bed.

"Also, I missed a pill," I say. "About a week ago. My tacrolimus."

"One wouldn't have caused this. But miss a whole bunch and you'll be right back here in a lot worse condition," Dr. Russell says. "Bottom line, Sydney, you have to work *with* your new heart, not against it. That includes running over state lines in the middle of the night."

I feel about two inches tall. I risked everything. And we failed—I failed.

We didn't get Mia to the ocean.

I didn't even get to see Chloe.

Chloe.

I didn't say goodbye.

I didn't make things right with her. And now it's too late.

Dr. Russell asks my parents for a moment alone and then sits on the edge of my bed, which is something she never does.

"I heard about Chloe," she says.

I wait for her to tell me how her death should be a lesson for me. How fragile and precious this life is. How lucky I am to be alive when she's not.

But she just puts her hand on my arm and softly says, "I'm so, so sorry. This disease—it's unfair. Sometimes after all we can do, it still wins. I hate that."

"Me too." I fight the little lump of emotion at the back of my throat that's working hard to keep me from breaking into sobs. "Did you know seventeen years is six hundred and twenty million heartbeats?"

Dr. Russell seems surprised.

"I did the math," I say, as if I'm talking about a homework assignment and not my best friend's life. Six hundred and twenty million beats. How can it sound like so many? And feel like so few? I put my hand over my chest, feeling my heart, the one that's given me more beats, more years. "She should have gotten this heart."

Dr. Russell nods calmly.

"That wasn't your choice, though, was it? Wasn't mine, either," she says. She pauses a minute. "Want to know what I love most about my job?"

"The money?"

She laughs. "Doesn't hurt, but no. I get to touch people's hearts. I get to hold them in my hand. And that's not something I take lightly, because the human heart is a miracle, an engineering marvel. Soft when it needs to be. Tough when it needs to be. And above all else, persistent. Relentless. Did you know, when I took your heart out, it kept beating? Even though it was sick and tired, when we put it on the specimen tray, it did its job, what it's always done—it kept going."

"For how long?"

"Just a few beats. And when I put in your donor heart, it started beating, too, without me even shocking it. I barely had the stitches done and it took off." She stands up and looks out my window, which has this impressive view of the Wasatch Mountain Range. "I took that heart out of your donor's chest that same morning. I officially ended her life. And then I gave it to you. I was there, at the precipice of the human experience, and what I've learned from doing this hundreds of times is that the only thing more persistent than the heart itself is the love it creates."

I scoff. "You're way too smart to believe love comes from the heart."

Dr. Russell turns back to me, her eyes glistening, which is so shocking I look away, like I've seen something I shouldn't. "Love comes from every part of us." She puts her hand on my arm, right above where the IV goes into my vein, full of all the drugs and fluids that she's ordered to keep my heart going. "And of all

the ORs I've been in, all the hearts I've held, that's the one constant: Life isn't measured in the number of beats. It's measured
in love."

The rest of the day, I'm a test subject. A body to be poked and
prodded like a pincushion. Someone measures my ins and outs,
making sure the pee I'm producing matches the liquids I'm
drinking. Someone else snakes a wire into my neck for a biopsy.
In between, there's bloodwork and a steroid blitz via IV and
EKGs galore.

By the early evening, I'm ready to go back to sleep. But my
parents have other plans. Dad sits in a chair, his chin resting on
his steepled fingers, a serious expression on his face. Mom sits
on the edge of my bed.

"We need to talk," Mom says.

"It was my idea," I say quickly. "California . . . the whole thing.
I was going to see Chloe."

Mom and Dad look at each other for a second, some understanding passing between them.

"Clayton told us everything," Mom says.

Everything. It's just one word, but it says it all. They know
about *everything*, every lie, every risk I've taken this summer.
And even though that's slightly mortifying, it almost feels like a
relief.

Mom turns her phone screen toward me. She's on TheMia-
Project, on my recent post: a photo of an open highway. The
caption reads: *Follow your heart.*

"This girl, this Mia," Mom starts. "She's the one you think was your donor, right?"

"She *was* my donor," I say. "And Clayton's best friend."

"Oh, Sydney . . ." Her voice is filled with so much disappointment it makes me want to yank the IVs from my arm and end it all. "Why didn't you tell us?"

"Because you would have told me to stop. You and Dr. Russell would have said I *need to move on,* except that's what I was trying to do. That was the whole point. Don't you see? I owe her."

Mom puts her hand on my arm.

"I don't know if this girl was your donor or not, but it's natural that you would feel like you owe her something—"

"Not something. Everything. Every breath. Every borrowed beat," I say. "I mean, don't you ever think about that? Don't you ever think about the person who we wished would die? The death we *wanted*?"

Mom's eyes meet mine.

"Every damn day," she says. Her eyes are filling up with tears now, and there's a wobble in her throat that makes me want to cry, too. "I think about that other mother, the one whose child didn't get to live. It haunts me. But the worst part is, deep down, I'm *happy* about it. Happy that *you* get to be the one who's here. And sometimes I think, well, I worry, that makes me a monster."

Dad comes up behind her, puts his arms on her shoulders.

"I think that just makes you a mother," he says. "And what your mother and I need you to know, Syd, is that this thing with Mia, it can't go on. You understand that, right?"

I look at Mom's phone again, all the adventures I've been on with Clayton this summer. All the things we were trying to do for Mia. All the risks I took with this heart.

I look around me at all the tubes and IVs, all the evidence of my fragile human state.

I'm not invincible.

Neither was Chloe.

"Yeah," I say. "I get it. It's over."

Dad smooths down my hair.

"That boy should never have taken you in the middle of the night—" He closes his eyes as Mom lays her hand on his arm. He takes a deep breath like he's centering his chi. "What I mean is, he made a mistake. A big one. But . . . Clayton also saved you."

They tell me how Clayton called 911 after I collapsed. How he helped the medical helicopter find us in the middle of nowhere, Nevada. How he drove like hell all the way to the hospital and set up camp in the waiting room, existing off Cheetos from the vending machine.

"I told him to go home," Dad says. "But he wouldn't budge."

I sit up, all the tubes and wires rattling.

"Did he—did he see me?"

"Family only in the ICU," Mom says. I lie back, relieved. Clayton isn't used to all this, to seeing me as the sick girl. I'm not sure I'd want him to.

"Did he seem okay?" I ask. The memory of his face pops into my head, like it was right before the world went dark—the fear in his eyes.

Mom nods. "Yes, and he finally did leave. This morning, when he heard you were awake. He asked me to give you this."

She hands me a note, written on the Primary Children's Hospital notepaper. It's creased up into a little square.

Mom gives me this little frown that makes me wonder if she's already read the note, but if she did, she doesn't say before ushering Dad out of the room with her.

I unfold the paper, slowly.

Sydney,

I love you.

It's unfair of me to start with that but there it is. I love you. I think I've loved you since I first saw you in that grave. Or maybe it was when you flashed me climbing into the tree house in that ridiculous dress. Or when I kissed you and the world stopped, just for us.

Or maybe I've fallen in love with you a million times in a million different ways over these last few months. Maybe when you love someone, you just keep falling, finding new reasons why.

But here's the thing.

Something changed inside of me on the side of that road. I thought you were dying, Syd.

And it broke me.

I should never have tried to take you to California. I should never have taken you out in the rain. I should never have let you push yourself that way. I was stupid and selfish. I guess I've been stupid and selfish this whole time, so focused on erasing my own guilt with this vision board.

So blind to how much you were giving up to finish it, how it was hurting you.

Do you remember at the slot canyon, when I asked you how we live with that guilt? With ourselves?

I don't know the answer, but I know this: I couldn't live with myself if you got sick because of me. I won't be the reason you die.

Because now I know the incredible weight, the responsibility of carrying someone else's heart. You let me carry yours, Sydney. But I was careless with it—I was careless with you.

I'll never forgive myself for that, and you shouldn't, either. Except, I know you will.

And I know if I don't leave, right now, I never will. Because if I see you, I won't be strong enough to go. I'll see that little crease in your forehead when you're overthinking, or the way you see right through me, and I'll stay.

But I'm not going to be stupid and selfish anymore.

I love you, Grave Girl. So I'm leaving.

> Here's looking at you, kid,
> Clayton

I read it three times, each time hoping the ending will change.

But it always ends the same way, with the same sign-off from *Casablanca*. And I guess this love story ends the same way as that old movie: we go our separate ways.

My tears well up at the pain, right in my chest, right where my scar crosses my ribs. And it's so quick and so sharp that it feels like I break open all over again.

Because Chloe's gone.

Because Clayton is, too.

Because I couldn't even finish the dreams of the girl who gave me her heart—this heart that does exactly what it's supposed to do: it feels. Every damn emotion, the good and the bad. Except right now, they seem to be the same thing, pain and love. Stupid, reckless love that feels like I'm wearing this heart outside my body—a small, fragile, unprotected thing.

The heart may be tough, but here's what they don't tell you: when it breaks, it doesn't break even. Because it's made of muscle, not bone. It twists and tears and rips at the seams.

And even the best surgeon in the world can't put it back together.

CHAPTER THIRTY-EIGHT

I CAN'T GO TO CHLOE'S FUNERAL.

I'm still in the hospital until all my labs come back with the levels Dr. Russell wants. Plus, she says no travel for a while. Too soon to be far away from the hospital, and now that I'm pumped full of steroids again, too soon to be around all those people and their sniffling noses.

Just too soon.

So Mom and Dad and I huddle together on my hospital bed to watch Chloe's final farewell on Zoom. Judging by the little chat icon at the bottom of the feed, there are a lot of us, all the transplant friends and online buddies Chloe collected over the years. I can see them logging on, signing in, joining this macabre broadcast from around the world.

You did it, Chlo, I think. *You left your legacy.*

The triumph and the tragedy of that makes me want to cry.

But I hold it together, mostly for my parents, who are sitting next to me, each holding one of my hands.

I wonder if Mom is feeling some measure of gratitude today, mixed in with her grief, like she said about Mia's heart.

She gives me a weak smile because I'm staring at her. Dad squeezes my hand.

"You okay, kiddo?" he asks.

"Yeah," I say. But the truth is, their grief is making me feel a little penned in. I want to pull my hands out of theirs, but I can't. I know they need it, to touch me, to reassure themselves that I'm here, I'm real. I'm not the one who died.

I wish Clayton were here. But it's probably best he's not. Then I might yell at him, ask him what kind of person breaks up with someone in a *note*. I might tell him he's being an idiot. That Mia was right—he *is* chickenshit. Because I can make my own choices, and if I want to almost die on the side of a highway on an ill-advised midnight trip to Cali, that's my own prerogative.

There's a small part of me, too, that wonders if Clayton *wants* this to be over. He had to call 911. He watched me collapse. Maybe it finally set in for him: This girl is sick. She'll *always* be sick. He's already lost so many people in his life. Maybe he's tired of losing.

So I didn't text or call or try to change his mind, but still, I wish he were here.

The funeral is 100 percent Chloe. She's only been planning it for years:

* No wailing or loud crying of any kind. The occasional modest, heartfelt tear is okay.

* No scripture passages or poems about death.

* Absolutely NO use of the following words: *battle, heroic, warrior.*

The church chapel looks like Chloe decorated it herself. Her demotivational posters are displayed on easels throughout the room, along with her artwork. Her favorite piece, the one of the heart on the ocean, is front and center, next to two poster-sized pictures of Chloe. One is of her in real life, standing on the beach, a wheeled oxygen tank behind her in the sand. The wind whips her curly brown hair as she faces the ocean, but her face is turned toward the camera with this big Chloe smile.

The second is a screenshot from one of her videos. Chloe's face is up close to the camera and she's laughing. It's not a great picture, but it's her, through and through, and it's how most of us knew her—through a screen, the internet incapable of containing her Chloeness.

I love her mom for picking these two pictures instead of "healthy" ones. Those air cannulas up her nose, that air tank behind her? That was Chloe. That was real.

Chloe's dad says a few words up at the pulpit, and so does her little sister. She makes a joke about how Chloe always had the biggest heart in the room.

After the speakers, a long white screen unfurls from the ceiling in the front of the chapel.

Then, Chloe's there.

Her face appears on the screen, exactly as she always was.

"Well, I coded, again. My lovely nurses and doctors brought me back from the brink, again.

So even though I've avoided making this video for seventeen years, it's time."

Her lips are slightly blue, meaning she filmed this when she was in decline, before the artificial heart. Before I let her down.

My heart stings, and I know it's not because of missing any pills or overexertion this time. It just hurts.

"You see, I've basically been dying since I was born. I mean, none of us are getting out of here alive—I just happen to know it.

When I was little, I used to do this thing before an operation where I'd pretend like this was it. I'd watch my parents sign all those horrific forms saying there was a chance I wouldn't wake up, and then I'd lie there on the table as the anesthesia set in and pretend I was a goner.

Anyway, you pretend to die twenty or thirty times before puberty and you think, hey, I got this. Death's not sneaking up on me. I'm prepared.

Spoiler alert: I wasn't.

I'm not.

Death is still death. And I'm still human. And I don't want to die.

Death sucks. No way around it.

So at some point, I decided my life couldn't be about dying.

Or about not dying. Sure, I take my pills, I go to the doctor's appointments, and I'm on the waiting list with all my fingers and toes crossed for a new heart, but my goal has never been more time—it's been making the most of the time I have.

I lived a full life. Short, yes. But full.

Full of people. Full of love. Full of moments. Full of life.

I mean, hey, I wasn't expected to survive that first heart cath in the NICU. Then I wasn't supposed to hit puberty, but I did, and I even kissed boys! Lots of them—sorry, Mom. I did lots of things the doctors said I'd never do. I've already beat the odds. I've already won!

And I've made friends from around the world. Thousands of you watch my silly videos every day, which I'll never fully understand, but I love you for it! You've given me something to look forward to. Something to connect to. Something to leave behind.

And no one and no disease can take that from me. So don't let your pity take it, either.

I wanted to film this at the beach, but my IVs won't go that far and my party-pooper nurses vetoed a field trip. So you'll just have to imagine some ocean sounds in the background while I tell you why the beach is my happy place.

The ocean has a rhythm, you see. The steady in and out. The crest and fall of the water. The push and pull of its power. It's alive—breathing, beating, being.

Each wave washes up on the shore, has its little moment of life and then fades back into the sea.

And another gets its turn.

We don't mourn the waves. They're not meant to last forever.

We just marvel at the ocean.

So today, do me a favor—do a little less mourning and a little more marveling. Because every life, short or long or in-between, is pretty damn marvelous.

Now, I hope no one out there is lactose intolerant, because that was CHEESY.

But for real, my peeps, go ahead and grieve my death. Cry, by all means. I'm dead, for goodness' sakes! I guarantee no one will ever fill the hole in your heart that I'm leaving behind.

But don't grieve my life. It was a good one. It made me who I am, and let's face it, I'm pretty freakin' awesome."

Through the Zoom feed I can hear a few laughs and a few sniffles. The chat icon is lighting up.

Yes, you are!

The most awesome!

Chloe snaps the oxygen mask back over her face and gives a big old grin.

"This is Chloe Munoz, signing off for the last time. As always, let the beat go on."

It's excruciating. Every last second.

My hands are white from Mom and Dad squeezing them so

tight. When it's done and we've turned off the laptop, Mom says she needs some water and leaves the room, as if we don't know she's going to bawl in a janitor's closet.

Dad and I sit there on my bed, kind of shell-shocked by the whole thing.

Finally, Dad says, "Do you remember what you first said when you woke up from your transplant?"

I shake my head. "I was pretty high."

"Well, I remember," he continues. "You looked up at me and you said, 'It hurts.' And then, immediately, you said, 'Guess that means I made it.'"

"That was probably the drugs talking."

Dad gives a little half laugh. "Well, *I* remember thinking my daughter was pretty profound. Here she is, fresh out of surgery, and she's already philosophizing about pain and life—how you can't have one without the other."

He lets the words hang between us for a while. The only other sound in the room is the rhythm of my heartbeat, blaring out loud and steady from the monitor, the background noise to my life.

"We had a fight," I say quietly. "Before she died."

Dad lifts his arm around me and pulls me into him, and somehow, that small act of comfort is the final straw, and I sob into his shoulder, like a dam's broken, like all the tears I've been trying not to cry in front of my parents come out at once.

"I just wish I could have talked to her one more time, you know? I never even got to touch her. She was my best friend, Dad, and I never even hugged her. It's not fair."

Dad holds me. And even though I'm seventeen, being all smooshed up in his shoulder, breathing in his aftershave, feels good, like nothing bad in the world can get me.

"It's not," he says. "It's not fair at all."

That's all he says, my dad, who knows a thousand poems about life and death but also knows that sometimes, just like hearts, words fail.

CHAPTER THIRTY-NINE

I SHOULD GET AN HONORARY DEGREE IN MOPING.

After a week at home, I've just about perfected the art. My parents haven't specifically told me I'm grounded for life, but it doesn't even matter—I'm medically grounded.

Dr. Russell says I can't drive until we're sure my heart isn't going to go berserk and make me pass out behind the wheel.

So my days go something like this:

8 a.m.—Get up to take tacrolimus. Wonder if Chloe hated me when she died.

8:30 a.m.—Bury myself under my comforter.

10 a.m.—Actually get up. Eat some sort of bran concoction.

11 a.m.—Mope.

12 p.m.—Go for a walk with Mom and Dad. Try not to think about Clayton when they hold hands.

2 p.m.—Stare at my blank walls. Check TheMiaProject. Hate myself for not being able to finish her dreams.

3 p.m.—Afternoon pills.

5 p.m.—Listen to the summer rainstorms pelt my window. Wonder if Clayton is out there somewhere, driving the hills again, going way too fast. Try not to think about wind in my hair and Clayton on my lips. Fail.

7 p.m.—Heart-healthy dinner. Parents try to sneakily find out how I'm doing.

8 p.m.—Tacrolimus.

10 p.m.—Lie in bed. Think of Chloe's seventeen years. Feel guilty for wanting more.

12 a.m. (Or after)—Fall into a fitful sleep. Dream about running after the girl with the purple hair. Fall down the canyon.

Fall

fall

fall.

There are a few variations, of course. Like when the Broken Hearts Club gets together for a Chloe memorial. I share a picture of Chloe to the Zoom call.

I talk about what a good friend she was (I leave out what a terrible friend I was). Sariah and Brody ask how I'm doing.

I say fine.

They nod earnestly.

The whole thing is grim. Without Chloe, nothing feels right. She was the heart behind the Broken Hearts.

Sariah asks about TheMiaProject.

"That's over," I say.

"What about the boy?"

"It's *all* over." I try to act unfazed. "It's good, though—better. For everyone."

We all promise to keep up the group. I think we all know it's a load of crap. But we say it anyway because that's what you do when someone dies.

"It's what she'd want," Sariah says.

"For Chloe," I say.

"For Chloe," they say like they're reciting an oath.

I want to text Clayton after. Tell him how terrible it was. After all, he knows what it's like to lose a best friend. To have your last horrible conversation haunt you. But that's exactly why I don't. We're both carrying too much grief and guilt already. He's right: we're better off without each other.

Chloe's the one I want to talk to, anyway. So I stare at my blank screen, wishing her face would appear. Wishing I could talk to her one last time. Because Chloe didn't get this heart, but she got *me*. She'd been where I've been—on the razor's edge of mortality.

She was the only one who understood.

And now she's gone.

I pull up TheWaitingList. Underneath Chloe's video of her artificial heart are all the latest comments—and there are thousands.

> We'll miss you, Chloe! You were such a bright spark in my life . . . in so many lives.

> Thank you for all your videos and the hope you gave my daughter. She always believed your heart would come.

> You fought a good fight my friend. RIP.

I imagine Chloe reading them with me, poking fun at the most earnest ones, making jokes about how she's got a thousand best friends she didn't know about, all it took was kicking the bucket.

> His Grace will make you whole, Chloe. You are
> now perfect, just the way He intended you to be.

That one burns. As if she weren't perfect before. She was—perfect and whole and amazing, even with her broken heart.

But these comments aren't for Chloe, I remind myself. They're for the people who write them. A place for comfort. A place to convince themselves that what happened to Chloe won't, couldn't, happen to them. She was a sick girl, after all. She was different.

Right?

I force myself to read each one, as if it's my own weird penance. As if I can unravel time and make it so she left this life knowing how much I loved her, that I was trying to get to California to be with her, to make things right.

That I would have given her this heart if I could have.

It takes me two hours to read every single one. I wish she could, too, and see how she touched people's lives. But I guess that's the cruel irony. People only say things like this once you're gone. They wait too long.

Just like me.

Eight days after getting home from the hospital, I get a call from her mom.

We say all the obligatory stuff. I tell her how sorry I am. She tells me it's good to hear my voice.

"She loves you so much, you know," she says. "I guess that's why I called. Wanted to talk to someone she loved. I guess that's kind of silly."

She laughs this hollow laugh that makes me feel hollow, too.

"How—how are you?" I ask, and she knows that I mean more than just a casual nicety because she inhales this big breath and takes a beat to answer.

"I'm here," she finally decides, which I guess is as good an answer as any. "It's funny. You know it's coming. And still, when it actually comes, you're not ready. Maybe you never are."

There's silence on the line, the kind that I know better than to interrupt.

"They said she was gone, but I had to be the one to say it was enough," she finally continues. "And it was. It was finally enough." She emits a little cry. "And you know what? Once they unplugged everything and the room was quiet, guess how long it took?"

"I—"

"Sixty seconds. Sixty damn seconds. After all these years, all this time we've begged and borrowed. All the times she fought. And she *fought*. But after all that, it only took one minute. And my baby was gone." She takes another big inhale. Then, like she's realized that she's talking to *me*, she exclaims, "Oh, goodness! You don't want to hear all this."

"No, it's fine," I say. "I don't mind."

And I don't. Because talking about Chloe almost makes her feel more real, like all my memories of her aren't gone just because she is.

"Well, I'm done now," she says with another little forced laugh. "Thank you for listening, Sydney. Chloe always said how good you were at that. Even when things were, well, you know, kind of rough between you girls there at the end."

I swallow hard.

"She told you about that?"

"Of course. Who do you think filmed that video for you?"

"What video?"

"You know, the one to you. A few days before—"

She cuts herself off, and I know I shouldn't make this about me, but I can't help myself. A video? From Chloe?

"This video," I say. "Do you still have it?"

She blows her nose.

"Can you send it to me?" I push.

"Oh, honey, you know I'm not good at any of that techie stuff. But I'm pretty sure she sent it or posted it or whatever it is you girls do with your videos."

"But if you could just—"

There's a scuffling on the line, and she says someone's at her door with another *blasted* casserole, and she's saying goodbye, and I'm saying goodbye, and then she's gone.

I stare at the phone for a good long minute, trying to process.

Chloe left a video.

For me.

I search my phone first. No videos from Chloe.

Then my email.

Nothing.

I slump back in my desk chair, a new kind of sadness sprouting. After all the time I've spent searching for signs from Mia—messages from beyond the grave—it's Chloe who leaves me one. And I can't find it.

I suddenly wish I'd spent half as much time with Chloe this summer as I did looking for a girl I don't even know, some paper-thin version of a person made up of photos and imagination. But Chloe? Chloe was real. And she was here—my best friend.

And I'm not giving up on her that easy.

I check our YouTube channel again, even though I just read all the comments yesterday. I scroll all the way to the bottom. There's nothing new here. Nothing for me.

In a last-ditch effort, I log into our account. It's a mess from the backside. I was always the tech-savvy one, keeping all our drafts organized and labeled so we knew what to post next and when. Chloe's got a bunch of stuff in there, all hodgepodge with no rhyme or reason.

Each draft title is progressively more ridiculous: *NextPost* and then *NextPostFinal* and *NextPostFinalForReal* and *NextPostFinalForRealIMeanItThisTime!*

Among the chaos, I see it: *ToSydneyFinal.*

I click on it, and the file image fills the screen. It shows Chloe in her hospital bed. Her lips are pink again. She must have filmed this after she got her artificial heart. I check the date on the recording.

July 24.

The day after she called me. The day after our fight.

My cursor hovers over the file, a weird mix of fear and excitement churning through me. What is she going to say? Do I want to hear it? Did *she* want me to hear it?

I can't wait any longer.

I click play.

"My best friend and I are pissed at each other. It sucks balls. And I know I'm probably going to apologize at some point for kind of overreacting, and I know she's going to, too, because she royally messed up. I mean, BIG-TIME.

But until then, I gotta get a few things off my heartless chest.

Because this friend, who shall remain nameless, is blowing her second chance. BLOWING IT. So here's what I want to say to her. What I will *say to her once we kiss and make up:*

You got the heart.

I didn't.

But I don't want your pity—I want you not to waste it.

I want you to stop chasing ghosts. Someone else died. You lived. No matter how hard you try, you can't make that *right. You're not supposed to.*

Because this life is still *going to kill you—one way or another. You don't get a say in the number of days.*

But you do get to decide how you spend them. Are you going to use them up fighting the past? Completing bucket lists that—I'm sorry—are kind of stupid? Or are you going to look forward? Find the things that make you feel alive?

People ask us sick kids all the time about our life expectancy, as if that's a totally appropriate question. FYI, it's not. We hate that. But I'm going to ask the question to you, my nameless bestie: What's your life expectancy?

And I don't mean the years you have left. I mean, what do you expect from your life?

This disease, this life, it takes. It takes and it takes. So take something back. Because whatever else your donor may have wanted, we know this for sure: she chose to give you that heart when she was done with it.

And she's done.

So what are you gonna do with it?

I know you want to honor her. So . . . honor her! Some of the plans she made are never going to happen, but one of them still can: she wanted you to live. I wish I could shake you right now and make you hear me: SHE WANTED YOU TO LIVE!

So live.

Because life doesn't wait.

And when it's gone, it's for good."

Chloe reaches toward the screen to turn off the camera but then pauses.

"Oh, and also, I love you. I'm too mad at you to tell you that right now, but I do. From the bottom of my counterfeit heart. Now and forever."

By the time the video stops, my face is covered in tears.

Freaking Chloe. Telling me what to do, even in death.

Outside my window, a summer afternoon rain has started, the drops hitting my window as I chew on Chloe's words, the ones she left just for me. Because she knew I'd need them . . . because she knew *me*.

I scroll back and listen to the whole thing over again.

She wanted you to live.

I don't know how to do that, exactly, but I know if Chloe saw me shuffling around like a geriatric heart patient, she'd tell me to get off my self-pitying ass. She'd tell me to stop making excuses, stop letting people choose for me, stop wasting this heart.

So live.

I dry my face and head into the family room. Dad's in his poetry-reading chair. Mom's watching something black and white on the TV.

"Guys?" I say.

Mom jumps up instantly when she sees my red, puffy eyes.

"I'm fine," I say, heading her off. "But I have a question."

Dad puts his book down.

I keep going. "I know I'm supposed to be taking it easy, and I know I'm probably grounded until I'm dead, so I wouldn't ask if it wasn't important. A matter of life and life, you might say." I inhale deep, relishing the feeling of air filling my lungs, a feeling I'll never take for granted. "I need a ride."

CHAPTER FORTY

BY THE TIME WE GET OVER TO RAWLINS, THE RAIN'S COM-
ing down in sheets. Out the window, I can barely make out Stoddard Hardware as we inch down Main Street, Dad going slowly,
his windshield wipers swishing like mad. Even with their whip-
whip-whip, it's hard to see the road.

Once we get off the pavement, it's even worse. Dad's Chevy
Malibu is definitely more poetry professor than backroads cowboy.

The creek is overflowing, washing out part of the road leading to Clayton's house. Dad has to navigate around it, but his
back tires spin out. As he pulls out, the car fishtails in the mud.
Dad slams on the brakes.

"What do you want to do, Sydney?" he asks.

Even though it's dark and wet and Mom's gripping her side-
door pocket like her life depends on it, we can't turn back. That's

what Chloe would say. Her message replays in my head: *Life doesn't wait.*

"Keep going," I say.

"Honey," Mom says. "We can do this another time."

"I'm done waiting!" I say, and I don't mean to yell but it comes out that way. Because seeing the rain, the rushing creek, the water rising so fast, it's all flooding me with fear, just like the night Clayton drove me down the mountain at warp speed. Like the night Mia died.

"Please," I say, lowering my voice. "We're close."

Mom looks like she's going to say no, like she's going to say what she always says—this isn't safe for me. I have to be careful. But to my surprise, she gives Dad a little nod. He eases off the brakes and starts moving again.

"Can't see a thing," he says, leaning forward to try to peer through the onslaught.

"Mike!" Mom yells, grabbing his arm. He hits the brakes again, barely missing the person in the road.

Nana.

She's got an umbrella and a raincoat on and is standing in the middle of the street, her hands cupped around her mouth. She's yelling.

I jump out.

"Nana. What are you doing? You shouldn't be out here."

She turns to me, her face drawn tight. She puts her hand on my arm. It's shaking.

"Oh, Syd, dear. Have you seen Clayton?"

I shake my head. Her face turns toward the mountains in the

distance, which are a slightly darker silhouette against an already dark sky.

"He's been out driving those hills all week, but he *always* comes home at night. I don't like him out in the dark, and in this weather. He *knows* better."

I slip my hand in hers, trying to lead her back to her house, out of the rain. Her hand is soft, the skin thin and pliable, almost as fragile as she looks in this storm.

"I'm sure he'll come back," I say. "He's probably already on his way. We'll wait with you."

Nana shakes her head and pulls loose of my hand.

"No. Something's wrong. I can feel it."

Mom and Dad have joined us. Mom slips her raincoat over my shoulders. She says I need to get inside, that I'm going to get sick again. Dad offers to call the police.

Mom pulls up the hood of my raincoat.

"Syd, you shouldn't be out here. . . ."

I pull my phone out from my pocket.

"I'll just text him. Tell him to come home."

Nana frowns. She holds up Clayton's phone.

"He was in such a hurry when he left," she says. "That was hours ago."

I look toward the mountains, too, the hills stretching north and south as far as I can see. He could be anywhere up there.

"What was he doing before he left?" I ask.

"Oh, I don't know," Nana says, worry creasing her brow.

"It's important," I say. "If we're gonna find him, we need to retrace his steps."

"Let me think," she says. "He was . . . he was doing some gardening and then he was, yes, he was out in the tree house."

Through the rain, the tree house is barely visible, but its bright purple hue pops against the night. I tell my parents to stay with Nana.

And I start running.

Mom yells my name, but I don't stop until I reach the wooden slats. One by one, I climb up.

Inside, the collage is gone. Well, not gone, exactly, but each picture has been torn off the wall and ripped into shreds, like someone was intent on destroying it.

Is that why Clayton took off? Because he was angry? About not finishing the board? Or about trying to do it at all?

I study the scattered remains of Mia's collage, trying to find some clue as to what Clayton was feeling and where he might have gone. The rain has made the colors bleed together, a mush of people and places and moments. On my knees, I gather up the pieces of Mia's dreams.

A flash of purple catches my eye. On the back of one of the remnants, there's a word written in purple ink: *adventure.*

I turn it around but can't tell which photo it's from. I lay it on the ground and search for the pieces that complete it. Piece by piece, I put the photo back together: Mr. Johnson's pond.

I do the next photo. The existential pancakes come into shape. And on the back, another word: *laughter.*

The third photo is the cornfield.

Tanner

As I move to the next, my mind is piecing together something, too. Something that has felt unsettled since Mia's former friend told me they already swam in Johnson's pond together. Why would it be on her bucket list if she'd already done it? And the cornfield: she hid there as a child with Tanner. She made pancakes with her family, too—on a day that even her mother remembers as being remarkable in its ordinariness, in its happiness.

On the back of the ukulele, another word: *music.*

On the ATV photo: *freedom.*

The back of the tree house reads, *refuge.*

I'm missing a picture.

I search the tree house. In the corner, I find it, wet but with Clayton's ten-thousand-watt smile fully intact. I flip it over, but this time it's more than one word, and they're not *about* him, they're *to* him.

Clayton. Find me in the stars.

The truth hits me like a shock to the heart. These photos, these words, aren't a bucket list at all. They're the pieces of Mia's life.

And you only make a list like that if you're leaving.

"It's a goodbye list," I say out loud, unable to keep the realization to myself.

I gather all the pieces of Mia's photos, hold them to my chest, right in the spot where Clayton held me to his weeks ago. He probably sat right here again tonight, holding the pieces, too, reading these words.

And then what? I close my eyes and try to picture him.

What did he do next? Where did he go? Did he come to the same conclusion? That Mia was leaving. Not for a road trip, but for good.

I think about everything he told me about that final night with Mia. She'd had a fight with her dad—a bad one. She'd shown up at Clayton's, panicked and needing to go on the ATV *right now.* I look at the pieces of Mia in my hands as the whole picture comes together.

She was leaving *that* night. And she needed to take her final picture in the perfect spot.

Which is *exactly* where Clayton would go.

I stuff the pictures into my raincoat pockets, clamber down the ladder and run back to my parents and Nana, who have huddled together under the carport.

I have to pause a moment and dip my head down to stop the little flecks of light that are starting to circle in front of my eyes. My head is woozy from running and from the adrenaline pumping through me.

"He's at the slot canyon," I say.

"In this rain?" Nana says. "He knows bett—"

"He's trying to make things right."

In the dark, I can barely make out the tip of the mountain, where I'd bet my life Clayton is racing, far faster than he should, risking his life as penance—chasing ghosts.

"I'll take the truck," Nana says, resolute. "You all stay here in case he comes back."

"You'll never make it in that," I say. "You need something off-road."

Nana's face falls. "We've only got the one ATV. And Clayton's on it."

It's hard to see through the rain, but down the road, a ways in the distance, I see a light.

"I know someone who may be able to help."

CHAPTER FORTY-ONE

"THIS BOY, MIA'S BROTHER, HE'S A FRIEND OF YOURS?" Mom asks as Dad parks in front of Mia's house.

"Not exactly," I say. "Actually, he hates me. Not a big Clayton fan, either."

Dad stares at me.

"Then why in the world are we here, Syd?"

"Because he has an ATV," I say, acting more confident than I feel, because Dad has a point: there's no reason in the world to believe Tanner will help me find Clayton. Unless . . .

"I'm going to have to tell them who I am," I say. "About Mia's heart."

"Syd—" Dad starts.

"He gave a speech once at her memorial—" I start.

"You went to her *memorial*?" Mom says, and then closes her eyes like she's silently praying for serenity. "Never mind. Not important now. Go on."

"He talked about the people who got Mia's organs. How her last act was to give of herself to others. Maybe if I tell him I have Mia's heart and how grateful I am, how all of this was to pay her back, I don't know . . . maybe he'll help me."

If I can appeal to the tiny flicker of humanity I saw in his face in the cornfield when he talked about Mia, I might have a chance.

"I don't know about this," Mom says.

"Me neither," I say. "But it's all I've got."

Mom shakes her head.

"No, I mean *any* of this. It's all too much. Just look at you, you're already all wet, and . . ." Mom's twisting her fingers in her lap so hard her fingertips are white. "I'm going with you."

She opens the door before I can talk her out of it. I hop out behind her.

"Mom, Mia's mother will be in there. I know you don't want to—"

Mom pulls my raincoat hood up over my head again.

"I know that. But I'm *your* mother. And I'm not letting you face this alone."

We walk up together, and I knock on the door. Relief washes over me when Mrs. S opens it instead of Mia's dad.

"Sydney!" she exclaims. "What in the world are you doing out on a night like this? Come in, come in."

She ushers us through the door, clucking at us.

"You're practically soaked."

"Is Tanner here?" I ask.

"Oh, well, yes, somewhere, let me see." She bustles to the

hallway and yells for him. Mom's eyes land on the photos on the wall, the family of four that no longer exists. She reaches out and grabs my hand.

Tanner appears, disheveled like he was sleeping. He groans when he sees me.

"What do *you* want," he says with zero traces of that hoped-for humanity.

"I need a favor."

"Well, then you're at the wrong house." Tanner sits down on the sofa.

"Just hear me out. I need to tell you something," I say as Mom squeezes my hand. Mrs. S is listening, all wide eyes and concern. I wonder how she'll feel after I've said what I'm about to say. "It's about Mia's heart."

"Oh, of course!" Mrs. S exclaims. "You're here about her heart."

"Yes, but—"

Before I can finish, she's bustled off again, leaving Mom and me and Tanner staring at each other, confused and awkward.

Mrs. S comes back, waving an envelope in the air.

"I texted Clayton about it just tonight."

"Mom, what are you texting *him* about?" Tanner says.

She waves him off.

"Never you mind. And your father doesn't need to know that, either, you understand?" She turns back to us. "He never responded, but I'm so glad he told you about it. And I'm glad you've changed your mind about reading it. It's the dearest letter. A girl, only ten. Can you even imagine? She used to play soccer—" She pauses. "Well, I better not give it all away. You can read it for yourself!"

She hands me the envelope. I open it slowly and pull out the paper inside. It's pink with little flowers in the corners. The words are written in a loopy cursive.

Hello,

I am 10 and I live in Idaho. My mom says you probably want to know more about me. I like to play soccer. I haven't been able to play in a long time. I have a dog named Cassie and a little brother named Owen. He's kind of a pain but fun to play checkers with.

Thank you for this heart. I am so happy I can play soccer again. And throw sticks to Cassie in the park.

I'm sorry you lost someone you loved. But Mom says because I have their heart, they're not really gone.

Emma

Mom's reading it, too, over my shoulder.

"I don't understand. How did you get this?" I ask.

"The transplant coordinator sent it to me. They like to screen them first, make sure they're appropriate and whatnot. But isn't that just the sweetest? Mia would be so happy to know that her heart got such a good home."

My brain feels like it's swimming. The words on the page in front of me are swimming, too, all the letters rearranging until they don't make sense anymore. Mom is saying something to me, but I don't understand a single word. The only thing I understand is one thought, the one that's screaming above all the rest:

I don't have Mia's heart.

I never did.

CHAPTER FORTY-TWO

I'M BACK OUTSIDE.

I don't remember how I got here. I remember Mom apologizing for me. Me saying I shouldn't have come. Handing Mrs. S back the letter.

And now I'm walking to the car as fast as I can as the truth hits me again, square in the chest: *I don't have Mia's heart.*

How could I be so completely, totally, ridiculously wrong?

"Syd," Mom says behind me. "Honey. Wait."

She catches my arm and spins me around.

"I'm sorry," I say.

She says nothing, just holds me by the shoulders.

"I shouldn't be here," I say. "This was all a big mistake. Mia. This summer. Clayton. All of it."

I wasn't supposed to go to that memorial. Should never have agreed to help Clayton. Should never have thought I could make anything right, make anything better.

"I've been such a fool," I say.

"You're not a fool."

I put my hand on my chest. "It's not Mia's, Mom. I don't know *whose* it is!"

Mom looks at me through the rain.

"Yes, you do. It's yours, Sydney. It belongs to you."

I can't tell if it's raindrops or tears making it hard to see. I wipe them with the back of my sleeve. Dad starts to get out of the car, but Mom shakes her head and he stops.

"Syd, look at me," she says. "Do you know why I quit my job? Why I spend so much time thinking about doctors and medicines and hearts? It's because I would do anything—anything—to get you more. More days. More memories. More life."

"Mom—"

"Let me finish. I'm not saying that to make you feel guilty. I'm saying it because I do it—and I *want* to do it—so you can live *your* life. Not Mia's. Or Chloe's. Or your donor's." Mom takes my hands in hers. "*Yours.* So what do *you* want to do?"

I can feel my lip start to quiver.

I don't have Mia's heart.

"I don't know. That's the whole point. I. Don't. Know. Those college brochures you gave me? They're still in my drawer. Because I have no idea—I don't know what to do with this future I wasn't supposed to have. And I thought Mia could help me figure it out. Send me some sort of a sign of what I should do with my life."

Except, how am I supposed to find my own life when I'm not even sure where Mia's ends and mine begins anymore?

Chloe was right—I've been chasing ghosts. The *wrong* ghosts.

And now she's gone, my best friend's gone, and I spent my

last months with her searching for a stranger whose heart I don't even have.

Mom touches her palm to my cheek, cradling my chin.

"I don't mean in the future, Syd. I mean right now, tonight. What do you want to do?"

The intensity in her eyes makes me remember why I'm here. Because Clayton's out *there*. Alone. Maybe hurt.

"Maybe he wasn't even going to the slot canyon," I say. "I've been wrong about pretty much everything so far. I'm probably wrong about this."

"Sydney—"

"I just need a minute, okay?" I say, walking out toward the road before she can argue with me. "I need to think."

The rain has slowed; a few straggler raindrops hit my head. Nana's walking toward me now from her front yard, worry etched on her face, probably wondering if I got the ATV or not. If I'm going to bring Clayton home to her.

Except I should never have even met him. I had no business in that cemetery, or in his life. I tricked him—and myself—into believing we had some kind of cosmic connection when, at the heart of it all, it was just a cosmic joke.

I don't have Mia's heart!

My fingertips hit the jagged edge of one of the photos in my pocket. I hold it out—the strings of a ukulele. I take out another, and then another—the corner of a pancake, the edge of a pond, the front tire of an ATV, Clayton's smile.

All the moments that meant something to Mia.

All the things I shouldn't have done this summer.

Except—I look at the photos again—I *did* do them.

I remember each day, each mission. How Clayton's smile lit up the night by the pond. How nervous I was before getting on that stage. The taste of syrup and carbs in Nana's kitchen.

These aren't just Mia's moments anymore—they're mine.

And if it weren't for her—for these photos—I'd still be in my house, living my life through the pages of books. Instead I met Clayton. I learned to play a ridiculous instrument. I got chased off by a shotgun. I know what it feels like to fly through the hills with a blue sky above and my arms around a boy I love.

I lived.

I don't have Mia's heart.

But she saved me.

The thought steals my breath.

I tilt my head back toward the sky. A break in the storm clouds reveals the stars, glittering like a thousand pieces of broken glass.

All the pieces of the universe.

The pieces of us.

Of Mia.

And Chloe.

And Clayton.

"We're all just borrowed stardust," I whisper.

"What?" Mom asks.

"Nothing, it's just . . . I found it," I say, putting the photo remnants back in my pockets.

"Found what, exactly?" Mom asks.

I smile, taking one more glance at the stars before I start walking back to the house.

"A sign."

CHAPTER FORTY-THREE

WHEN MRS. S OPENS THE DOOR, SHE LOOKS SURPRISED.

"Sydney, I'm so sorry if that letter upset you."

I step into the living room. Tanner's standing by the doorway to the kitchen. My mom is waiting outside.

"It wasn't the letter," I say. "Well, it wasn't *just* the letter. It's that I need to tell you something. Something I should have told you a long time ago."

Mrs. S sits on the couch, her hands folded in her lap, watching me expectantly.

I take a deep breath, hold it, then let it out all at once. "Six months ago, I almost died," I start. "But I didn't because I got a new heart." I tug down the top of my shirt, just enough to show the tip of my scar. "Just like that girl in the letter. Someone else died, and I lived."

Mrs. S's hand goes to her own chest. I keep talking before she can interrupt me with a *you poor dear.*

"I thought—I thought maybe it was Mia's heart."

Tanner steps forward into the room. "Wait, you *thought* you got your friend's heart?"

I shake my head.

"She wasn't my friend." I force myself to keep eye contact with him, even though I want to look anywhere but at his face, which is growing more confused by the second. "I never knew her."

"No, no, because you said she talked to you, about me," he says. "You said—"

"I lied," I say.

The silence in the room weighs on me.

Those two simple words hang in the air, make me feel like I'm coming undone. Tanner's face falls, the truth sinking in. Mia never told me about how she cared about her brother, never told me anything.

"But I *wanted* to know her," I add quickly. "I wanted to know who this heart came from. What it loved. What it wanted. And tonight, when I read that letter, I realized I never had Mia's heart. But I still need your help. Actually, Clayton does."

Tanner scoffs.

"Do you even hear yourself? You've been *lying* to us. You're sick. You know that, right?" He looks from me to his mother in disbelief. "In what life would we help you or *him*?"

I step toward him.

"In this one, Tanner. In this one. In this unfair, arbitrary life. Do you even know where he is right now?" I point out the front window. "He's out there, trying to finish something *she* started, trying to make things right, probably wishing he was the one who died that night."

"Maybe he should have," Tanner says under his breath.

"Oh, Tanner," Mrs. S says. I hadn't noticed, but she's crying, quiet tears falling down her cheeks. "You don't mean that."

"He stole her ashes, Mom!" Tanner says. "Put them back in her room like he didn't, but I know it was him."

"Because he wanted to get her out of this place!" My voice is rising now, too. "Like Mia wanted."

Tanner takes a step toward me.

"You didn't even know her!"

I don't move.

"You're right. I didn't." I pull the pieces of Mia's photos out of my pocket, arranging them on the coffee table. "But I think these photos are things Mia loved. Things that mattered."

I put in the final piece of the pancakes. I flip over a corner to show Mrs. S the word on the back: *laughter.*

She pulls it close to her chest.

"She remembered," she says.

I start putting together another photo—piece by piece.

"The cornfield," Tanner says quietly as the image takes shape.

I turn over the piece with the word on the back and hand it to him.

" 'Tanner,' " he reads, and his voice catches a little bit on the *r.*

I put together the pieces of Clayton's smile.

"There's something else you should know," I say. "Mia was the one who wanted to go to the slot canyon that night. She took the ATV on her own."

Tanner's eyebrows push together.

"No, no, he took her up there. He's the reason—"

I shake my head.

"No, he's not. Clayton was only up there because he went after her. He was trying to save her. And he's up there again, trying to figure out what Mia wanted. He thought—we both thought—that if we could figure that out, her death would make sense. But none of this"—I gesture to the photos on the table, the realization that I know so little about what Mia truly wanted out of her life suddenly sinking in—"even matters. She's gone. And we'll never know for sure what these photos mean, but I know *this:* she'd want you to help Clayton. Because he was one of the pieces that mattered, too."

Tanner's still holding out the little corner of the cornfield, studying it.

"You sure you didn't know her?" he says, an almost smile inching up the corner of his mouth. "'Cause that's exactly the kind of bull she would say."

Mrs. S turns to Tanner.

"Do this for her," she says softly, still clutching the ripped photo piece in her hand. "For Mia."

Before he can answer, a screen door slams somewhere in the back of the house.

"Margaret?" a loud male voice yells.

Tanner turns to me, fear suddenly painted on his face.

"How do I know you're not lying now?" he says, gesturing to the pictures. "About all of this? About what happened that night?"

"You don't," I say.

Tanner considers me a second and then looks down at the corner of the cornfield—the small piece of Mia in his hand.

Without another word, he walks to the front door. He turns to me.

"Well, you coming or what?"

CHAPTER FORTY-FOUR

I DON'T KNOW WHAT CHANGED HIS MIND. BUT I'M NOT stupid enough to ask. I follow Tanner outside.

"He's in," I tell Mom, who jumps back when Tanner opens the door. Dad's joined her on the front step. We follow Tanner to the garage, where he backs his ATV out into the driveway.

As I start to climb on behind him, Dad puts a hand on my arm.

"No way," he says. "Not in this weather. Not at night."

I put my hand out.

"It's barely raining anymore," I say.

"But *you* are still recovering," Mom counters.

"You told me to live *my* life, right?"

Mom nods. "Yes, but—"

"So let me." I look at Dad, pulling out the big guns. " 'I have no choice of living or dying . . . but I do have a choice of how I do it.' "

"Steinbeck," Dad says, and I can tell I've got him by the way he's trying not to smile. "Well, now you're just playing dirty."

Mom's not so easily swayed.

"But Dr. Russell said—"

"Mom!" My voice is loud because there's an urgency flowing through me. "My whole life can't be about *not dying.*"

This seems to hit Mom hard, because she kind of recoils. Fear etches her face, just like when I woke up in the hospital, like all the times I've almost died.

I look up at the mountain again, ominous in the dark. She's right—this is dangerous. And I'm *not* invincible.

"No more lies," I say. "No more unnecessary risks. But this one—*this* risk—is necessary."

I run to the car and grab the emergency blanket and flashlight from the back. I sling the blanket over my shoulders.

"We'll go slow. I won't go in the canyon. I'll be smart," I say. Mom still looks nervous. "Whoever gave me this heart wanted me to live, Mom. They trusted me with it. Can you?"

She looks to Dad, and they exchange one of those whole-conversations-in-a-glance because Mom nods and Dad takes a helmet off a hook in the garage and hands it to me.

"Does that mean I'm going?" I ask.

Mom puts her hand on my arm.

"It means you're right—this is your heart, your life," she says. "I trust you."

Dad helps me buckle the helmet on, giving it a good shake to make sure it's tight.

"It means, what are you waiting for?"

*　　*　　*

Dad steps back from the ATV, and I swing my leg over. I hold on to Tanner's waist, but not as tight as I usually cling to Clayton.

The clouds have lifted a bit, and the moon is shining down bright, silhouetting the peaks as we make our way up the mountain. I just hope he hasn't started climbing that slot canyon. Even though it's not raining here anymore, the water on the ground is flowing in wide channels down the mud.

No one knows better than Clayton how fast a flood can fill those narrow passageways. I wonder if this is what it was like the night Mia died, if it happened fast for her. If one minute she was in the slot canyon, thinking about leaving, starting her new life away from this tiny town and her angry father, and then the next minute, the waters were on her.

I think about what Chloe's mother said—sixty seconds and she was gone.

Tanner jerks the ATV to the right, and we head up the mountain, the back wheels sliding.

"Can we slow down?" I half yell over the hum of the engine, my promise to be careful humming equally loud in my head.

Tanner yells back, "Thought you were in a hurry to help your boy."

"Can't help him if we're dead," I say.

Tanner slows a little, and, somehow, we get there, almost all the way to the bottom of the slot canyon, where the upper creek is sloshing far beyond its banks.

There, through the dark, I can make out a shape—an ATV, tilted almost sideways in a ditch, with no rider in sight.

CHAPTER FORTY-FIVE

TANNER SKIDS TO A STOP IN THE MUD. I HOP OFF THE back while the ATV is still sliding.

I yell Clayton's name almost the same second I find him, pinned between the body of his four-wheeler and a muddy ditch.

"Sydney. What—" His face turns from surprise to anger. "You shouldn't be here. It's not safe for you."

"It's not safe for *you*," I say, pushing on the machine like an idiot, as if I can move it myself. It doesn't budge.

"Seriously, Sydney. Didn't you read my letter?"

"I read it," I say. I try to see where his leg ends beneath the ATV. "How bad are you hurt?"

"Nothing I can't walk off." The grimace on his face tells me this is a lie. "But you need to go. I'm not going to be the reason you get hurt. Not again."

Tanner comes around the side of the machine. Clayton visibly bristles.

"What's *he* doing here?"

"Saving your sorry ass," Tanner says. He stands back and surveys the situation. The rain has picked up again, the few errant drops quickly turning back into a steady downpour.

He pushes on the ATV, which is wedged so deep in the muddy ditch that two of the tires are barely visible.

"We're gonna have to drive it off," he decides.

"What? *Over* him?" I ask.

Tanner nods.

"You drive. I'll push." He points to Clayton. "But you got to help, too. As soon as Sydney here clears the ditch, you swing that leg out from under. But do it quick. I may not be able to stop that back tire in time."

Clayton scoffs.

"Like I'm gonna trust *you.*"

Tanner shrugs and steps back. "Your funeral."

They glare at each other silently. The rain is pooling on the ground already, rushing through the mud at our feet, streaming into the ditch that Clayton is half-inside. But he doesn't seem to notice or care.

"He's trying to help," I say.

"Right." Clayton folds his arms. "Even if I believed that for one second, I don't need *his* help."

His leg is half-hidden under the ATV, but even from the little I can see, it's bad. His jeans are marred with blood, and his face is getting paler as we talk.

Maybe Tanner can see it, too, because his tone softens. He squats down, almost in the ditch himself.

"You got a death wish, Cooper?" he says, moving Clayton's jeans to get a better look at his leg.

Clayton slaps his hand away. "What do you care?"

"I don't," Tanner says. "But Mia did. So here's what's gonna happen. Instead of you dying out here like the martyr no one asked for, you're gonna trust me. And I'm going to get you out from under this machine and back home, where you've got a mess of people worried about you."

The rain is falling so hard now that Tanner's kind of yelling over the sound of it hitting the mud and the ATVs, the metallic thwap-thwap-thwap filling the night.

"I'm not going back." Clayton catches my eyes for a second and then jerks his away. "Not until I figure it out."

"Figure *what* out?" I yell down at him over the sound of the rain.

His eyes drift up to the rock walls towering behind us.

"I think she was leaving, Syd. *That* night. And this was the last photo, don't you see?" He points to the canyon. "The answer we've been looking for is right there. For some reason, she needed to get to the top."

"I know! And she died doing it!" I want to shake him, tell him he's being an idiot not to let Tanner help him. But I force my voice back down to a regular volume, trying to stay calm, even though the water is beginning to fill the ditch. "You were right, Clayton. Death is unfair. Not because it takes everyone, but because it takes every*thing*. All the possibilities. All the cer-

tainty. It takes it all. And our theories on Mia's photo
guesses about her life, are just that—guesses. We'll ne
know."

My voice wobbles as the truth of my words hits me, t
"But what I *do* know is that Mia wanted to start a new .
say. "She didn't want to die here. And she sure as hell didn't v
you to."

Clayton stares down at his trapped leg.

"I have to do *something*," he says. "You, of all people, should
understand that. You know how it feels, Sydney. Every time her
heart beats in *your* chest."

"It's not even Mia's!" I say.

Clayton's eyebrows bunch together. "What?"

I heave myself down to where he is and sit in the mud.

"This heart," I say. "It's not Mia's. Her mom got a letter. I was
wrong."

I can see the shock on his face as the realization sinks in.

"So what are you saying?" he says. "That this was all point-
less?"

"I'm saying I *can't* make things right with Mia, and neither
can you." I look up at the sheer stone cliffs rising above us in
the slot canyon. "Getting yourself killed up there won't bring her
back, Clayton. Just like me dying wouldn't have saved my donor.
Or Chloe."

I turn to him, to make sure he's listening.

"Some things won't *ever* be right," I say.

"She's got ya there," Tanner says, still crouching with us in
the ditch.

"And what do *you* know about it?" Clayton says, an angry edge lingering in his voice.

"What do I know about it? About my *own* sister?" Tanner stands up and towers over Clayton with fire in his eyes. "I know more than you do, Cooper. I know she came to me first that night. Asked me to drive her up here, but I said no."

"Well, good for you!" Clayton's voice oozes sarcasm. "What a hero! You didn't drive her to her death like I did."

The flash of anger has gone out of Tanner's eyes. He squats back down.

"No, no, you didn't. Sydney told us." He shakes his head like he's having some internal battle with himself. "And I wasn't a hero. I was just scared. And when my dad blamed you, I went along with it. Even though I knew Mia would have hated me for siding with *him*."

He kind of half laughs.

"So yeah, I think I know something about guilt. At least *you* were there, at least you—"

He cuts himself off, tilting his head back, his eyes closed like he's praying.

The rain beats between us, the weight of a shared guilt pulling us together. Below us, Rawlins Ridge spreads out in the darkness. The hardware store. Mia's house. The bright purple tree house. Off to the left, Johnson's pond sparkles in the moonlight. The cornfield stretches into the night.

All the pieces of Mia's life.

And right then, all the pieces coalesce. What Dr. Russell's been trying to tell me about the delicate balance of the heart, the persistence of love, Chloe urging me to live, Mia's stars.

"You asked me once about how we live with ourselves, how we move on," I say. "I think the answer is, we don't. We move *forward*." I put my hand on his, our fingers intertwining. "Mia was right: we're made up of pieces of the past. But our hearts aren't meant to hold it all. We have to choose which pieces we carry with us, and which ones to let go."

Clayton's staring at our fingers, and then he looks up at me, his wet hair hanging in his eyes, the pain from his leg written on his wincing face.

"How do we do that?" he asks.

The rain is really starting to come down, falling in sheets between us.

"I don't have it all figured out yet," I say, "but it starts with getting off this mountain."

Clayton stares at the canyon one more time. I follow his eyes. It's probably Tanner's headlights mixing with the rain, but for a split second, I think I see her, the girl from my dreams, with Chloe's face and Mia's purple hair. And the raindrops chant, *Go back.*

"What's it gonna be, Cooper?" Tanner asks.

Clayton gives a slight nod, barely perceptible, but it's all Tanner needs. He jumps into action, showing me how he's going to push behind the ATV while I drive it out of the ditch.

He locks eyes with Clayton. "I won't lie: this is gonna hurt like hell. But it's the only way out."

Clayton grabs his thigh. "Let's go."

Without another word, Tanner leans his shoulder into the back of the bumper, which is barely above the mud.

"On three," he says, nodding to both of us. "One, two—"

I gas the ATV all the way. The wheels spin, flicking up mud. Tanner's yelling, "More, more!" And then, the wheels catch, not much, but just enough for the ATV to pull itself out. I drive forward until the wheels are totally out, hoping I didn't pulverize Clayton's leg.

When I turn around, Clayton's up. Tanner's got him by the waist, helping him stand. From the thigh down, Clayton's blood-soaked jeans are ripped open, revealing a deep gash down his shin.

We hoist him onto the back of my ATV. He throws his good leg over the seat and lets the other one hang kind of limp into the footwell.

"You ready?" I ask.

"If you are," he says.

I put the gearstick into drive. "I'm ready."

"I'm ready, too, if anyone cares," Tanner calls from his four-wheeler.

Clayton wraps his arms around my waist as we inch down the mountain, slow and steady, the rain hitting our faces and the headlights shining in front of us only a few feet at a time, just enough to get us home.

CHAPTER FORTY-SIX

THE CLOSEST HOSPITAL IS IN CHERRY HILL.

Dad drives like a maniac, with me and Nana in the back seat, Clayton stretched out between us, his head on my lap. Since we got off the mountain, he's gotten paler by the minute. Dad tied a belt around his leg to stop the bleeding, but it's still soaking through his jeans.

I brush his wet hair from his eyes.

"You still with me?"

"I'm not going anywhere," he says with a weak smile.

I wonder if it's true.

I don't have Mia's heart. Whatever her list meant, it's over. The thought makes my stomach dip, my heart squeeze in a painful pinch. Why would he stay?

The light from the streetlamps dances on his face as we barrel toward the hospital. We're getting off the highway now, passing Randy's Burger Joint, the junior high, my street.

"You know what I said out there, about Mia's heart?" I say.

Clayton's eyelids are heavy with pain, but he nods. "You don't have it."

I smooth down his wet hair. "So I know we don't have the connection we thought we had, but it doesn't change things for me."

In the front seats, Mom and Dad are doing a truly terrible job of pretending like they're not hanging on every word I'm saying, and Nana is staring so hard out the window, trying to give us privacy, that I'm afraid she might break the glass. I don't even care that they're listening. If this is the last time I talk to him, I want him to know everything, for there to be nothing left between us—no lies, no Mia, no guilt—just us.

"And I know that you're scared that I'm sick. But *I* get to choose who hurts me. I get to choose what I'm willing to risk for *this*, for *us*. I get to decide what's worth dying for—what's worth living for." I take his hand and press it to my chest, just below my collarbone, where my scar starts. "Whoever's heart I have, it's mine now, and I'm still me, and *I* love you, and I just—I just need you to know that."

The red EMERGENCY sign comes into view as Dad takes a corner like he's in the Indy 500. Clayton groans and grabs for his leg. A man with a stretcher opens the door and helps Clayton out and onto the gurney. They start to roll him away.

"Wait, wait!" he says, reaching out his hand to me. I grab it, and Clayton smiles, in pain but still that same brilliant way he did the first time at the swimming pond, the kind of smile that lights up my whole world. He takes my hand and places it palm down on his chest. The rhythm of his heartbeat pulses through me.

"I don't care whose heart you have, Grave Girl," he says. "Because mine? It's already yours."

CHAPTER FORTY-SEVEN

MY WALLS HAVE COME TO LIFE.

It's taken two weeks, but Mom and I and a stack of magazines have transformed my room from hospital-grade sterile to a menagerie of pictures and words and colors. My walls are covered in all the clippings we've found.

Clayton's on an ATV ban—doctor's orders—at least until his cast comes off, so our days of flying through the hills are on pause. But he comes over a few times to help with the decorating.

"So where'd we land on that big portrait of me?" he says, taping a picture of a red chrysanthemum to the wall. He backs up and makes a little square with both his thumbs and pointer fingers and looks through it, one eye squinting. "Oh yeah, some Clayton would definitely make this whole bucket list pop."

I shove him with my elbow.

"I'll consider a small photo, perhaps in a corner somewhere," I joke. "And again, it's not a bucket list. It's a *vision board.*"

"Consider me corrected," he says. "Mia would approve."

He points to a little section I put up last night—Mia's photos. I've left a space, too, for the final picture we never figured out, the piece we'll never know.

"Found Chloe!" Mom says, coming in, waving a four-by-six photo from back in the days when she'd print out her digital images. "I knew I had one somewhere."

She hands me the photo. It's the Chloe I remember from when we first met. She's beaming from my computer screen, and I'm giving this cheesy smile. We're both pretty pink and strong.

I stick the photo smack in the middle of the wall, right next to Chloe's painting of the heart hanging over the ocean. Her mom sent it—told me she was under strict Chloe orders that it should come to me.

"What's it mean?" Clayton asks, pointing to the words below Chloe's heart.

"*Dum spiro, spero,*" I say. "*While I breathe, I hope.*"

Clayton slips his arm around my waist and pulls me closer to him.

"What are you gonna do with the website?" he asks.

"Which one?" I ask. I haven't even looked at either TheWaitingList or TheMiaProject since the night of Clayton's accident.

"Both."

I shrug. "Haven't really thought about it."

Mom picks up the magazines littering my floor.

"Seems like a shame to let it go," she says. "All those people at the funeral. It really meant something to 'em."

"*She* meant something," I say, and even I'm not certain whether I mean Chloe or Mia.

"That's what I'm saying. Seems like a waste," Mom says. "Since both girls meant something to you, too."

Clayton juts his hip into mine.

"She's got you there."

Later that night, Clayton and Mom are gone, and I'm alone in my room, surrounded by a lifetime's worth of dreams, some of them mine, some Mom's and Clayton's, some belonging to Mia and Chloe. Dad even tore the E. E. Cummings poem right out of his *Poets of the 20th Century* book. The words look down at me:

i carry your heart with me(i carry it in my heart)

It's a hodgepodge, really. Things we love. Things we want. Things we've done.

All the pieces of us.

On my bed, I pull up both pages on my laptop: TheWaitingList and TheMiaProject. What *should* I do with them?

I open up my drafts folder with all the videos I've made since my transplant but was too scared to post. The first one starts with this:

"*I should have died.*

"*I was* supposed *to die.*"

I pause the screen.

I let the words sink in deep. *Supposed to die.* Did I really think that? Did I *want* that?

For a long time, I just stare at it all. Chloe's videos. My drafts. Mia's photos. The longer I stare at them, the more they blur together into one big mess of hospitals and ponds and air cannulas and ATVs on hilltops—a big mess of life, just like my walls.

What if . . . my brain starts churning . . . *what if they* were *one?* Not a site about waiting *or* living, but about both, about all of it?

It doesn't take me long to fill out a blank template, a brand-spanking-new channel that isn't just Chloe's or Mia's or mine, but a combination—the best parts of all of us.

I give it a name—TheLivingList.

And then I open the camera on my computer, settle into my chair, and start talking.

"Here's my deep, dark, dirty secret—I felt safe being sick.

No one expected much of me. I didn't expect much of me. I was waiting, I told myself. I'd do something with my life when I got a new heart—when I got better.

The problem was, even after I got the heart, I was still waiting for better. I was waiting to be happy. Waiting for my life to start.

I couldn't see that it already had.

So I'm taking a note from my best friend. Her name is Chloe Munoz, and she died.

But more importantly, she lived.

And she was about the bravest person I know. She marveled at this life, even in the face of death. And really, that's about the bravest thing we can do.

So, I'm trying to be brave, too. My first step? This channel—

TheLivingList. It's a place where you don't have to wait to be better. A place where kids who are sick or dying or waiting can tell their stories, share the lives they're creating, celebrate the joy they find in the moments in between. The big ones, the small ones, the ones you carry with you. That's something I learned from another friend, Mia.

TheLivingList will be a combination of Mia and Chloe and me. Because what is life but waiting and living, beauty and tragedy, sickness and health, all swirled together into a beautiful mess? And our job isn't to sort it all out. It's to be part of it. To feel it all.

I mean, isn't that what hearts are for?

People often tell me that this transplant is a gift. But it's more than that. I think maybe knowing just how fragile it all is, how precious and beautiful and fleeting—that's the real gift of life.

Because I may have a hand-me-down heart, but this life is mine, and I plan to live every single borrowed beat.

I hope you'll join me, even if you're not better *yet. Even if you may never be."*

I play the video back one more time before posting it, then I post a link on the other two sites.

As I click out of my browsers, something in my drafts folder catches my eye: *Donor letter.* The document I open is blank.

I've written and erased this sucker more times than I can count. And yet, I still don't have a word. One more thing I was waiting to do.

From my wall, fifteen-year-old Chloe smiles.

"No time like the present, right?" I say.

I dig into my desk drawer to find some stationery. It's buried deep, so I have to move the college brochures onto my desk to get to it. It's a stationery pack I picked out when we had this GoFundMe fundraiser for the transplant. Mom made me write thank-you notes to every single person who donated. But this letter, this thank-you, has to be more than an obligatory one-liner.

I smooth out a piece of the hideous pink-and-blue-paisley stationery and start writing.

"What's that?"

Dad startles me. I hold up the letter, which still feels woefully inadequate, even though it's almost a full page long.

"It's to my donor's family," I say, folding the letter into thirds and sticking it into a hot-pink envelope.

"You say everything you want to say?" Dad says.

I lick the envelope shut.

"No. But enough."

Mom's in here, too. She's sitting on my bed, staring at my new walls.

"Think they'll write back?" she asks.

I shrug. "Guess we'll find out."

"You gonna try to find them again?" Dad asks.

"Nah," I say, leaning back in my chair, scanning all the pictures on my wall—a whole lifetime of places and people and things to do. "I'm gonna be pretty busy."

I spin around in my chair to face them.

"Oh, and I just started a new channel. It's for kids like me, kids who are sick. And I'd really like to maybe do some fundraising, for transplant research or something. Or maybe to give kids experiences while they're on the waitlist. Or maybe for donor families to honor their loved ones—"

"That's . . . a lot of ideas," Dad says with a chuckle.

"But if I'm really going to do it right, I need to learn more about marketing, and maybe build a more legit website."

I flip open the top college brochure and start thumbing through, searching for a program that might help get me started.

"They've got a pretty good business program down at the community college, you know," Dad says. "You could meet your old man for lunch at the student center."

"And your mom," Mom says.

I turn to her. Mom and Dad beam at each other.

"What?" she says, a big old smile on her face. "It's just one film class a week. An adjunct position. Nothing big."

"Where did this come from?" I ask.

Mom shrugs. "Let's just say your new wall inspired me."

I look back up at the wall, my eyes drifting over all the possibilities ahead of me. I land on the photo on my desk, still in its frame, of me and Bree backstage before my final play. I take the picture out and stick it to the wall, too.

"I guess if I'm already on campus, I could check out the theater program," I say. "Maybe I'll message Bree. See if there are any local shows going on. I mean, it's been three years, and I don't even—" I cut myself off before I can launch into all my excuses. "Anyway, couldn't hurt to try."

"Couldn't hurt at all," Mom says with a smile. She stands by the collage. "I also couldn't help but notice you have a *lot* of pictures of the ocean on here."

"Yeah. I'd still like to get there, someday," I say, looking at Chloe's painting of the heart above the ocean. "See what she and Mia loved so much about it."

Mom taps her finger to her chin.

"Someday," she says. "That's pretty vague."

"*Very* vague," Dad reiterates. "And someday seems, I don't know, so far away."

"Good point," Mom says. She smiles at my dad, and he smiles back, and they're both being super weird.

"What are you guys talking about?" I ask.

"Oh, nothing," Mom says, throwing up her hands. "If you've got your heart set on going to the ocean *someday*, we'll keep waiting."

"Mom!"

Mom laughs, and I laugh, too.

"Fine, fine, forget someday!" she says. My parents look at each other and then back at me, big, goofy grins on their faces.

Dad shrugs. "Why not now?"

CHAPTER FORTY-EIGHT

THE OCEAN TAKES MY BREATH AWAY.

And for once, it feels good not to breathe. Like it's all too much to take in at once, like my body, my heart, my lungs just need a minute.

I give it to them.

I inhale again as I run toward the waves, laughing, feeling the sunshine on my face. Clayton runs next to me, hand in mine, as we gallop toward the water.

My parents lag behind, walking slowly, Mom carrying an enormous bag of just-in-case supplies of sunscreen and water and egregiously enormous sun hats.

"No wonder Chloe loved it here," I say, walking into the water up to my ankles. "It's so . . . so . . ."

I try to think of a word to describe the way the water stretches away from us, vast and enormous and endless. But also how it laps toward us in waves, inviting us to feel endless, too.

"Breathtaking."

Clayton gathers me to him.

"Couldn't agree more," he says, his arms around my back, his lips centimeters from mine.

"Your cast!" I say, and jump back. "It can't get wet!"

Clayton groans and hobbles back to the sand and plunks down. I take off my cover-up, revealing the new swimsuit Mom bought me. It's bright purple, Mia's favorite color, and dips down so low in the front that you can see a good chunk of my scar.

"Quit leering, perv." I toss my cover-up so it smacks Clayton in the face.

He flushes red.

"It's just, I've never seen quite so much of you."

"Well, here I am," I say, opening my arms wide and doing an extra dramatic spin in the water. I venture out until it's up to my thighs.

Chloe was right, there's a rhythm to it. It tugs me toward it, then pushes me back—the give and take all happening at once. New waves forming, dying waves crashing, others rolling back out to the sea.

I hold my phone out to take a video for TheLivingList.

"Well, I finally made it, Chlo. And I can feel you here. And I'm not going to say something cheesy like *live, laugh, love,* because you'd come back just to haunt me for it, but I do love you, from the bottom of *my* heart." I do a 360-degree spin and lean into the camera. "And I'm taking your advice. I'm letting it go wild."

Back on the beach, Mom and Dad have joined us now. Mom makes Clayton and me pose for a picture.

"You know what today is?" she asks.

Dad and I smile at each other and answer in unison.

"A big day!"

Mom laughs. "Well, it's true!"

I give her a hug and tell her she's absolutely right. She starts setting up a sun umbrella and asks me if I have on sunscreen.

"Already slathered," I answer. "And before you ask, yes, I took my morning pills."

"Sorry, old habits," she's says with a shrug.

It's going to take some time for her to fully trust that I'm serious about taking care of this heart the way it deserves. But I am—this heart *and* this second chance.

"They're here!" I yell, looking past Mom. I wave up the beach, where Tanner and Mrs. S are making their way toward the water. Mom invited them, and Mrs. S didn't hesitate. Said if it's a place Mia wanted to go, she couldn't say no.

On the beach, Mrs. S hugs me. Tanner gives a half nod to me and Clayton.

"Isn't this something," Mrs. S says, taking in the view. "Heaven knows I needed a break from all the boxing up I've been doing."

"Boxing?" I ask.

"Yes," she says, taking my arm. "I realized I had a lot of stuff I didn't need anymore. I took the important pieces. Got rid of the rest." She snaps her fingers. "Oh, that reminds me. I found this at our house. Not sure how it got back there."

She rummages through an enormous beach bag at her feet and then holds out Mia's ukulele toward me.

"Oh, I don't"—I wave my hand in the air—"she didn't even know me."

Mrs. S pushes it toward me again.

"But we do," she says. "Mia would want someone to play it. And you're the only one who can."

Clayton slings his arm around my shoulders.

"*That* is questionable," he says, giving me a little bump with his hip. I bump him back.

Mrs. S digs into her bag again.

"And, I brought this!" The sun glints off the silver urn, setting it aglow. "We couldn't come to the ocean without her."

Tanner decides we should scatter the ashes from a cliff, so we follow him through the sand, over a bunch of shallow tide pools and then up a craggy overhang. Below us, the waves crash onto the rocks. The wind whips my hair, whistles in my ears.

Mrs. S offers the urn to each of us. Tanner makes a grossed-out face but grabs a handful anyway. It's so fine, some of it sifts through my fingers. The wind carries it off.

We all kind of wait on each other.

"Should someone say something?" Tanner asks, a gust blowing away some of the ashes from his fist.

Nobody speaks up. I hesitate, too, afraid empty platitudes will only cheapen who Mia actually was, the *real* Mia, the one I'll never know—a girl with flaws and fears and dreams who left pieces of herself for strangers, so they could have her tomorrows.

"'And this is the wonder that's keeping the stars apart,'" I say instead.

Dad has his eyes closed, nodding along to the poem. I say the final line quickly before the wind can steal all my ashes.

"'I carry your heart. I carry it in my heart.'"

Mrs. S smiles, and I think she's going to say something, but then she abruptly turns and, without a word, extends her arm and opens her fist.

The wind carries Mia away.

One by one, everyone does the same, watching as the gray dust swirls away from us, into the air, over the water.

I hold my fist out and open it. I let her go.

Clayton wraps his arms around me because I'm shivering in the wind. He rests his chin on my shoulder.

"So what's next, Grave Girl?"

"We keep moving forward, I guess."

Clayton squeezes me tight. "As my embarrassingly hip grandmother would say, you only live once."

"I disagree."

Clayton pulls me tighter. "Of course you do."

"Well, as much as I love Nana, she's wrong on that one," I say. "You only *die* once. But living? You get to do that every single day."

Dad's next to me now, listening. He has his arm around Mom, who has tears in her eyes.

"My daughter, the poet," Dad says.

"Not quite sure what I am, yet, Dad," I say.

Dad hugs me to his side. "You've got time," he says.

We stand there like that, Clayton, me and my parents, our arms around each other's shoulders, sheltering each other from the wind, for a good long while.

Out in the water, Mia's ashes drift away. I can't see them, but I know they're there, part of the give and take now.

And I think of all the people—all the pieces—that are part of me, too, as the ebb and flow of the ocean rolls in and out against the rocks, like the sure, steady beating of my heart.

ACKNOWLEDGMENTS

My heart has scars.

Lucky for me, my heart also is filled with people and love. This book—and my life—wouldn't be what it is without them.

First, thank you to the other heart warriors, doctors and nurses who helped me tell Sydney's story. Megan Hand, who is one tough heart transplant survivor, let me into her darkest moments, as well as the beautiful ones. Megan, the world is a better place with you in it. Thank you also to Roger Allred, a rock-star transplant survivor who reminded me that there is so much hope even in hardship. Grace and Deanna Gourley, thank you for opening your hearts to me by sharing your stories. To transplant coordinator Sharon Ugolini, MSN, RN, thank you for the technical guidance to give Sydney's story the accuracy it deserved.

To groups like Donor Connect, thank you for sharing your guidance and survivor stories, and most importantly, for giving people—and hearts—a second chance.

To all the medical professionals that helped me when my own heart was failing fifteen years ago, thank you, thank you. I'll never forget the doctors at the University of Utah who first diagnosed my cardiomyopathy just days after my first child was born, or Dr. Stuart Russell at Johns Hopkins Hospital, who helped me have my second child despite my weak heart. Dr. Russell, thank you for that gift, and for also telling me when it was time to stop pushing my cardiac luck and start trying to be around long enough to see my babies grow up. Sorry I didn't take your advice to name my daughter Stuartina, but I'm hoping naming the cardiologist in this book after you can be a consolation prize of sorts. Fortunately for Sydney, fictional Dr. Russell has all the same kindness and brilliance as the real one.

There would be no book without my team at Delacorte Press, with Wendy Loggia and Ali Romig at the helm. Thank you both for always believing in me and what I want to say. Thank you also to my agent, Rebecca Sherman, who is a constant in my corner, turning my rough ideas into stories people actually want to read. Copy editors Kerianne Okie Steinberg and Colleen Fellingham, thank you for making this story shine. To artist Beatriz Ramo and designer Casey Moses, thank you for bringing Sydney and Clayton to life on this beautiful cover.

To my critique partners Jaime, Cheryl, Kim, Libby, Lorianne, Michelle, and Matt, thank you for giving me encouragement and hard truth, and always knowing when I need which one. Matt, an extra special thank-you for being my personal editor and cheerleader on this project. You can make any scene sing! And to RuthAnne, Sarah, and Amalie, you are the best beta readers around.

This book also wouldn't have happened without my supportive friends and family, who cheer me on every step of the way. My mom was at my doorstep within minutes of me saying *something doesn't feel right* on the night I came home from the labor and delivery unit. Mom, thank you for always being a phone call away, even when I didn't think I needed your help. I guess sometimes it takes becoming a mother to realize just how much you need your own.

To my dad, thank you for teaching me about poetry and stars, and the reasons why we desperately need both.

To my proxy parents, Don and Kathie, thank you for loving me like your own. I've never doubted my place in your hearts. To my sisters, Jenny and Katie, I'm so glad we get to go through the ups and downs of this life together. And a big hug to my found sister, Meredith Iorg, who makes me laugh, talks me through anything and everything, and takes me on old-lady walks around the neighborhood.

Of course, the biggest pieces of my heart belong to my own little family. Getting each of my children here was not easy, but it has always been worth it. To Ellie, my heart baby, I'm so lucky to have stuck around to see you become the amazing person you are. To Avery, who has one of the biggest hearts of all, thanks for being my ultimate fan and unofficial publicist. And to Cayden, my caboose, you were exactly the final piece our family needed.

Kyle, you have my heart. You always have. Sorry I almost died on you.

And finally, my sincerest gratitude goes to a God who gave me not only a second chance but also people to fill my heart with enough love for a lifetime's worth of beats.

ABOUT THE AUTHOR

ERIN STEWART is a heart failure survivor who believes in second chances, first loves, and staring at the stars as often as possible. A Virginian at heart, Erin now makes her home in the shadow of the Rocky Mountains with her husband, three children, and one goldendoodle. She is the author of the Schneider Family Book Award–winning novel *The Words We Keep* as well as *Scars Like Wings.*

erinstewartbooks.com

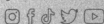